FLAT-OUT LOVE

FLAT-OUT LOVE

─ JESSICA PARK ─

SKYSCAPE

SKYSCAPE

Amazon Children's Publishing first edition, July 2012.

ISBN-13: 9781477810255
ISBN-10: 1477810250

For Lori, who makes her own hinges.

It's not what you know—or when you see—that matters.
It's about the journey.

PART ONE

PART ONE

CHAPTER 1

Julie Seagle stared straight ahead and promised herself one thing: she would never again rent an apartment via Craigslist. The strap of her overstuffed suitcase dug into her shoulder, and she let it drop onto the two suitcases that sat on the sidewalk. It wasn't as if she had anywhere to carry them now. Julie squinted in disbelief at the flashing neon sign that touted the best burritos in Boston. Rereading the printout of the e-mail again did nothing to change things. Yup, this was the correct address. While she did love a good burrito, and the small restaurant had a certain charm, it seemed pretty clear that the one-story building did not include a three-bedroom apartment that could house college students. She sighed and pulled her cell phone from her purse.

"Hi, Mom."

"Honey! I gather you made it to Boston? Ohio is missing you already. I can't believe you're already off at college. How is the apartment? Have you met your roommates yet?"

Julie cleared her throat and looked at the flat roof of the restaurant. "The apartment is...airy. It has a very open floor plan."

"How is your room? Is it tiny?" Her mother sounded concerned. "Well, even if it is, it's probably better than some concrete dorm room, right?"

"My room? Oh, it's, uh, rather sparse, I'd say." Julie sat down on one of her bags. A city bus squealed to a halt just behind her, and she flinched at the high-pitched noise.

"What was that? Is your room right on the street? Oh God, are you on the first floor? That's dangerous, Julie. It's much easier for some criminal to break in. Are there locks on the windows? Let me ask your uncle about that. Maybe there is something you could do to make it more secure."

"I'm not seeing any windows at the moment, Mom." Julie felt her eyes begin to tear up. This was a nightmare. She had been in Boston, or more specifically Jamaica Plain, for a mere hour, and already her hopes for a glamorous college life were beginning to smell a lot more like South American specialties than she'd envisioned. "I don't seem to actually have a room."

Her mother paused. "What do you mean you don't have a room? I sent first, last, and a security deposit, just like the land-lord asked. A cashier's check, for God's sake! He gave away your room?" The rising panic in her mother's voice was not helping.

"I'm at the correct address. The taxi driver assured me I was in the right place. But my supposed apartment building is a burrito restaurant."

"Burritos! Holy mother of God!"

"I know. Burritos are always alarming." Julie looked around, totally unsure what she should do next. "Mom, what am I going to do?" Although she didn't want to freak out her mother more than she had to, Julie couldn't control the waver in her voice. She was alone in an unfamiliar city, knew no one here, and was sitting on a mountain of luggage.

At least the advantage of being stranded on a crowded street was that no one seemed to think she looked at all out of place. Plenty of people had walked by without giving her a sec-ond glance. It was the first week of September, and she was in a college town; more than one U-Haul truck could be spotted weaving through traffic, delivering students and their possessions to actual apartments that did not double as restaurants. Julie quickly wiped her eyes and pulled her sunglasses down from her head. She'd give anything to be riding in one of those moving trucks, crammed in with a pile of friends.

"I don't have anywhere to live. And all that money you spent…This was supposed to be cheaper than the dorms. And it wasn't supposed to smell like burritos." Leaving home for the first time, getting scammed into paying for a nonexistent apartment, and finding oneself homeless in Boston was proving to be agitating.

"Julie, don't worry about the money right now. This isn't your fault. I thought the ad looked perfectly normal too. You sit tight for a few minutes, and I'm going to call the college and see if they can help you, OK? Just hold on. You all right?"

Julie sniffed. "Yeah, I'm fine."

"Don't move. I'll call you right back, and we'll fix this."

Julie put in her earphones and passed the next excruciating twenty minutes by listening to morose music, chipping off the deep purple nail polish she'd applied the night before, and updating her Facebook status.

Julie Seagle *Boston, Day 1: Refuse to refer to city as Beantown as would sound too touristy. Still, am full resident now despite not having actual residence.*

The pavement radiated heat, and so far this sauna of a city was not winning her over. A little self-pity seemed in order. All she wanted was a normal college experience and the chance to enjoy school without worrying that her friends would think it was ridiculous that she actually liked learning. She didn't need to go to the most expensive university in the country or to the top-rated, be-all-end-all of schools. She just wanted to be free from feeling like she had to hide who she was. It would be nice to finally be comfortable admitting that she was crazy about literature, that she thought curling up with a textbook was soothing, and that she wanted nothing more than to delve into lively classroom discussions. So wanting a place to live while she started her college career seemed reasonable enough.

Surely Whitney College wouldn't let a progressively more anxious southern Ohio transplant fend for herself on the streets of Boston? She could always spend the night in a hotel, obviously, but it would certainly be preferable to find a more permanent solution. There must be a few students who had changed plans at the last minute, freeing up a dorm room, right? Maybe. Well, the burrito restaurant was hiring, so perhaps this was a sign that she should brush up on her Spanish, cultivate an interest in ethnic cooking...

Julie's phone barely got out a full ring before she answered. "Mom?"

"That damn college was no help whatsoever. Apparently every school within a thirty-mile radius is in the same awful housing crunch, and Whitney is stuck putting up students in hotels themselves. I had another idea. Do you remember Erin Watkins?"

"Your roommate from college? The big-deal lawyer? I didn't know you were still friends."

"Well, we're not really. I haven't talked to her in years, but I remember reading in the alumni magazine that she lives in Cambridge. Her note said she was teaching at Harvard now, and by a stroke of luck, I caught her in her office."

"God, this is embarrassing, but does she know of an apartment?" Julie asked hopefully.

"Well, no. But she insisted that you come and stay with her until you can find a suitable alternative. Her son Matt is on his way to pick you up. I gave her the address. She says you are not in a good part of town, and it's a good thing it's only four o'clock and not getting dark. He'll be driving a blue Volvo and should be there any minute."

"OK. Matt. Dangerous town. Blue Volvo. If I get into the wrong car and get myself murdered and dumped in an alley, I want you to know how much I love you. And don't look in the third drawer of my desk."

"That's not funny. Anyway, Matthew goes to MIT. Some sort of physics major. Or was it math? Can you believe that? With Erin's genes, I shouldn't be surprised she'd have a genius son."

"I'm sure he's incredibly cool. Just the word *physics* already has me hot and bothered."

"I'm not running an escort service here, Julie. I'm trying to get you somewhere safe where I will not worry myself silly about you."

"Yes, Mother. I will find another Boston-based dating service online." Julie stood up and smoothed the front of her top. She faced the street, relieved to at least be able to stand expectantly waiting for a ride rather than attempting to look anything but misplaced. "When was the last time you even talked to Erin?"

"Years ago. We've only spoken a handful of times since graduation. Every now and then I hear something about her. The friends you make in college are friends you'll have for life, even if you don't talk for years at a time. You'll see."

A dark car slowed and pulled to a stop, double-parking in front of Julie. "Mom, I have to go. I think this Matt character is here."

"Are you sure it's him?"

Julie peered into the car as the window lowered. "I see a maniacal-looking guy with brightly colored candy in one hand, and he's waving a bloody sickle with the other. Oh! He's beckoning me to the car. This must be my ride."

"Julie, stop it!" her mother ordered. "You have no idea how I feel, knowing that my only child is stranded in Boston. I wish I were there with you. Make sure it's Matthew. Ask to see his license."

"I'll be sure to do that. I'll call if I make it to the house. I love you, Mom."

"I love you too, honey. I'm so sorry about this mess. Thank Erin for me, and I'll talk to you both later."

Julie hung up and looked hopefully at the guy rounding the car and walking toward her. "Matt?"

"I'm guessing by the suitcases that you must be Julie? Or else I'm about to kidnap the wrong girl." He smiled softly and reached out to shake her hand.

He was tall, at least six feet, with dirty blond hair that hung over his eyes. His pale skin told Julie that he hadn't seen much sun this past summer, and a peek at his T-shirt gave a clue why. The shirt, tucked into his ill-fitting jeans, read, *Nietzsche Is My Homeboy.* Clearly he was not a run-with-the-in-crowd kind of guy, and she suspected that he'd been holed up in the library all summer. But he was kind enough to drop whatever he'd been doing to come and get her. Besides, Julie had her geeky moments herself—though she wasn't dumb enough to announce them on a T-shirt. She hid them. The way any socially skilled person would.

"Thank you so much for picking me up. I really didn't know what I was going to do. I hope I'm not putting you too much out of your way?" Julie helped Matt load her bags into the trunk of the Volvo and then slid into the front seat. The September sun had heated up the car, and Julie automatically fanned her shirt, trying to get some air flowing across her skin.

"No problem. Sorry it's so hot. The AC doesn't work in this car, and no one's bothered to get it fixed. It's not a long drive, though." Matt turned the key to start the car, and a blast of sputtering noises had Julie fearing a longer stay on this now-hated street. "Don't worry. It always does this when I try to start it so soon after turning it off. Just a little more gas…There we go!"

Julie glimpsed herself in the passenger-side mirror. She looked undeniably haggard. And sweaty. And not sweaty in a way that could be construed as *glistening*. She ran a finger under each eye, wiping away the brown eyeliner that had started to smear, and quickly tried to smooth out her bangs, which were beginning to curl. Her highlighted brown hair was not faring well in this humidity. She wasn't about to whip out a compact and pat powder over the dusting of freckles that ran across her nose, but she would have preferred to make a better first impression when she showed up to crash at the Watkinses'.

Matt yanked the wheel to the right, narrowly avoiding a speeding car that cut him off. "Welcome to Boston, known primarily for its vehicular aggression."

"I'm loving it already. Between being ripped off, now broke, without permanent housing, and about to start college, I'm really off to a good start here, huh?" Julie smiled weakly, leaned her head against the window frame, and took in the breeze.

"It could be worse. You could be living at home, like I do. And you *will* love Boston. Any major city has its drawbacks, but Boston is a great place to go to school, so once you get everything straightened out, you will be fine. You're starting at Whitney?"

"Yeah. It's not exactly MIT, though," she said with a teasing smile. "I'm sure Literature 101 can't compete with, what? Adoration of Differential Equations?"

Matt laughed. "Close. That was last year. This year it's Obsessive Devotion to Fourier Analysis Theory and Applications. And my personal favorite, Quantum Physics II: Romantic Entanglements of Energy and Matter."

Julie turned her head to Matt. "You're a double major? Physics *and* math? Jesus…"

"I know. Nerdy." He shrugged.

"No, I'm impressed. I'm just surprised your brains fit in your head."

"I was fitted with a specially designed compression filter that allows excessive information to lie dormant until I need to access it. It's only the beta version, so excuse any kinks that may appear. I really can't be held responsible."

"Thanks for the warning." Julie nodded seriously. "I don't know what I'll major in. Maybe psychology? Or English? Not sure. So, are we still in Jamaica Plain?"

"Nope. Now we're in Cambridge. And that," he started, as they turned a corner and went over a bridge, "is the Charles River. This is Memorial Drive, and Harvard Square is right there. We can cut through if you want to see." Julie nodded eagerly. "There's a T stop right here, and it's only a few minutes' walk from my parents' house."

For the first time since the plane had landed, Julie felt excited to be there. The river was gorgeous and dotted with people canoeing and kayaking, their bright vests smattering the water with color. They drove past archways and iron gates, crowded sidewalks, cobbled pathways between buildings, and plenty of shops and restaurants. She liked the busy atmosphere.

"How far is Whitney? Maybe I could find an apartment around here?"

"Not far on the T. Whitney is in Back Bay, which is Boston, not Cambridge, so you'd get off at Hynes. It's right near Berklee College of Music."

"Nice. So if I get hit by an impulse to belt out some Lady Gaga, I'll be able to find some backup singers without any trouble." Julie frowned at Matt's blank look. "Lady Gaga? Atrocious headpieces? Shoulder pads galore? Took the music world by storm a few years ago? Skintight outfights with feathers and leather and buckles, oh my? Nothin'?"

"You lost me," he said. "Well, here we are." Matt pulled the car into the driveway of a large blue-gray house with white trim and black shutters. This side street was lusciously green with trees and flowing gardens, each gorgeous old house nestled behind a fence or an evergreen hedge. It was hard to believe that they were just off a main road, so close to the bustle of Harvard Square. It didn't take an MIT student to see that this was an extremely wealthy neighborhood.

"My mother should be home by now. I know she wanted to be here when you arrived. And my father and Celeste are probably on their way home. He had a meeting at her school."

"Your sister?" Julie guessed.

Matt got out of the car. "Yup. She just turned thirteen. Hope you like takeout for dinner. Nobody here has cooked a real meal in years."

"As long as it's not burritos, I'll be thrilled."

Matt opened the trunk and then stopped. "Julie? I should probably…" His voice trailed off.

"Yeah?" She looked at Matt. "What is it? Is something wrong? I'm mortified. We're having burritos, aren't we?" He shook his head. "Oh. I knew it. Your parents are totally annoyed that I'm getting pushed on them, right? Nobody wants some stranger staying in their house."

"No. Not at all. It's just that Celeste is…" He seemed to struggle to figure out how to say what he wanted. "Well, she's an interesting kid."

"I like interesting," Julie said, pulling a suitcase from the trunk. "I like interesting a lot."

CHAPTER 2

Julie considered the possibility that she might have walked into a library rather than a residence. The front hall was lined with white shelves that were absolutely packed with books. And not paperback thrillers. This was obviously not a house of casual readers. A small room opened off to the right, where a piano took up most of the sunlit space. She followed Matt to the left, into the living room, and immediately loved the feeling evoked by the décor. Tribal masks and paintings covered the walls, and a globe and a large world map sat on two end tables that encased a comfortable-looking beige sectional.

Julie couldn't help but notice the stark contrast between this house and her own. She liked her mother's affinity for country plaid, yellow walls, and yard sale findings, and the way the house was always orderly and clean. Simple but homey. But as she looked around this room, Julie had to admit that there was something terribly enticing about the cluttered mass of unique statues and bold patterned pillows, as well as the general aura of academia.

"Matt? Is that you? Did you find her?" A voice rang out from another room and was followed by the sound of quick footsteps. Julie looked up at the relieved face of the woman who entered the room. "Julie Seagle! Are you the spitting image of your mother or what? I'm Erin Watkins. Welcome. Thank goodness your mother was able to reach me." She crossed the floor and shook Julie's hand.

"Thank you so much for helping me out. It's really nice of you to let me stay here tonight. I'm going to look for an apartment first thing in the morning."

Erin was nearly as tall as Matt, and Julie could feel the bones in Erin's cool hand. Good Lord, the woman was thin. Not unhealthy-looking, but certainly delicate.

Erin waved her hand and then brushed back a stray hair from her thick, tightly pinned bun. "I'd do anything for Kate, so you're more than welcome to stay until you find a place. Speaking of your mother, you should let her know that you're safe. Let me take you upstairs and show you your room, and then you can call her."

"I'll show her." Matt walked briskly over to Julie's bags.

"Nonsense. I know you have schoolwork to do. I'll tell you when your father and Celeste get home with dinner. Julie, follow me." Erin moved smoothly through the living room and picked up one of Julie's suitcases. "I hope you'll be comfortable here. I know you were expecting to move into your apartment today, but at least you're not at a hotel."

"Mom, I really need to talk to you."

"Yes, yes, Matt. Relax," Erin said.

Julie grabbed her other bags and trailed after Erin, while Matt stood seemingly frozen in place. She turned her head back. "Thanks again for picking me up."

Matt nodded and rocked back on his heels, his hands in his pockets. "Sure thing."

Matt seemed nice enough. He was easy to talk to, if not terribly easy on the eyes, and he was certainly smart and had a sense of humor. He was a bit quirky, she supposed, but Julie guessed that she could be pretty good at handling quirky—she enjoyed a challenge. Besides, she liked that he was different from the boring crew of classmates whom she'd left behind in Ohio.

Julie made her way up the airy staircase to the second floor. The landing was a roomy open square with four doors that presumably led to bedrooms, and a short hallway off to one side. More bright-white walls and expensive-looking artwork.

"You're right here," Erin said as she pushed open a door with her shoulder. The bedroom had a definite masculine feel to it, with dark bedding and wooden shelves and a few books, pictures, stereo equipment, and DVDs. A small flat-screen TV hung across from the bed, and an empty spot on the desk had just enough room for a laptop.

"Make yourself comfortable. The bathroom is right down the hall. I'll put some fresh towels out for you, and…Oh, this must be Roger calling." Erin turned her head toward a phone ringing from another room. "Do you like Thai?"

"That's great. Thank you."

"Take your time getting settled. There are empty drawers if you want to unpack," Erin said, backing out of the room to take the call.

Julie sat down on the bed and scanned the room. Yup, this had *boy* written all over it. Not that she minded. She liked boys, after all. But she was looking forward to making a run to Target and picking out her own girlie room accessories with some of the money she had left over from the summer. Thank God she'd won that essay contest the school district had run, or she would have had to use all her savings on a computer. It'd taken her weeks to write her piece on the United States' responses to natural disasters, but it was not a bad trade for a new Mac laptop.

It was a good thing that her friends didn't follow high school news—unless it had to do with sports, dances, or a battle of the bands—because she would have been teased mercilessly for having participated in such a socially warped endeavor.

The truth was that her friends didn't entirely *get* her. Her mom didn't *get* her either, although she was certainly proud of how well Julie did in her classes. In fact, her mom had kept secret the fact that Julie had stayed after school to do extra-credit work for her English class. Her friends would have snorted with laughter. And while Julie had been happy to sacrifice time after school to hear her teacher's thoughts on Graham Greene, she hadn't been willing to try to explain to her less academic friends why she had done so. They just didn't care about school the way she did and half the time didn't seem to understand what she was talking about. Jared, her ex, would have rolled his eyes at the notion of volunteering to spend more time studying.

Speaking of Jared, Julie wondered what he was doing right now. Probably sporting a toga and doing keg stands at the miserable state university he was attending. She hoped he was lost in a crowd of dumb jocks and getting rejected by every busty, tank-top-wearing, fake-tanned airhead he hit on. Arizona could have him. And yet Julie couldn't resist seeing if he'd commented on her Facebook status.

She set her laptop on the desk and turned it on. Yes, she had her fancy phone; she just wasn't a big fan of typing on the miniature keyboard if she didn't have to. She liked capital letters and some semblance of punctuation, and the margin for error on the handheld device was too great. Julie was a traditional typist.

She realized that she needed a password to access the Watkinses' network. Great. She'd intruded on their house and now needed to ask for this. Internet access came before pride. Julie caught Erin as she was getting off the phone.

"Mrs. Watkins? I hate to bother you, but I was wondering if I could get the password to go online?"

"Call me Erin. Please. And of course you can. Let me get it from Matthew. He generated a random, meaningless code so that none of the neighbors would be able to pilfer our service. He is our own private security expert. Hold on." Erin disappeared for a moment and returned holding a scrap of paper.

"Thank you." Julie took the paper and looked at the fifteen-digit password. Paranoid much? No one could remember this. Except, it seems, Matthew.

"I'll let you know when dinner is here." Erin shut the door.

Julie opened her Facebook profile page and frowned. Already eight comments under her status from concerned friends who actually gave a damn about her ("What happened????" "What R U going to do?" "Ack! Call me!"), but nothing from Jared.

Jared had up and announced that they shouldn't even attempt to maintain a long-distance relationship, and so he was preemptively breaking up with her. Not that it really mattered. He wasn't the guy for her, and Julie should have dumped him herself months ago. It was her own fault for letting that mundane relationship go on too long. Granted, she shouldn't have expected any polite concern from her ex, but a friendly check-in wouldn't have hurt. It would be nice if they could at least be civil to each other, but perhaps Julie was too angry at herself to allow that to happen even if Jared made an attempt.

Now she was out of small-town Ohio, out of that below-average high school, and out of a social circle dominated by girls blindly cheering on their sports-playing boyfriends.

Boston could be different. It *would* be different. She could be who she was without worrying about dumbing down her vocabulary or hiding her interest in school.

Julie took a last peek at Jared and his new college wrestling buddies, silently wished him well (or mostly well), and promptly removed him from her list of friends. Her new status update?

Julie Seagle *Have survived streets of Boston with no permanent injury (save for crushing ego blow regarding stupidity of renting unseen room via nefarious internet site) and am currently in safe haven.*

Julie leaned back in the desk chair. She hesitated for a moment, then checked the Gmail account that she'd set up. Her father was the only person who had that e-mail address, and her inbox was empty. He'd write when he had time. She closed the laptop.

She sighed, blew her bangs out of her eyes, and picked up a framed picture from the desk. The photo was of someone bundled up in winter gear on a snowy hillside, snowboard in hand. It didn't look like Matt, although it was hard to make out who it might be in the blurry picture.

Julie unpacked a few things from her suitcase, folding her clothes neatly and setting them into the dresser and hanging a few casual dresses in the closet. As much as she hated to keep all her clothes stuffed into suitcases, where they were getting permanently wrinkled, it didn't seem right to unpack everything she had as though she were moving in for the long haul.

After dinner she would go online and start trying to find somewhere to live. Whitney's freshman orientation was on Thursday, so that gave her all day tomorrow to come up with something. She'd really love to take care of this quickly, and in a city this big, there simply had to be something decent available.

She glared at her reflection in the mirror and quickly rifled through her luggage until she located her makeup bag and flat iron. A few minutes later, she practically resembled a normal human being again. Maybe not by cheerleader standards, but she'd get through dinner without frightening anyone and then take a good long shower before bed.

"Julie? Do you need anything?" Matt knocked as he opened the door.

"I thought you were supposed to be studying," she teased. "Thanks, I'm all set. Whose room am I in, by the way?"

"Finn's." He stared over her shoulder, looking vacantly into the room. "He's away. Traveling."

"Finn is your brother?"

"Yup. He's my brother."

Julie smiled. God, Matt was so…odd. "Older or younger?" she prompted.

"Older. By two years."

"Making him…?"

He dropped his head, his hair falling over his eye, and laughed softly. "Twenty-three."

"So you're twenty-one. And a junior? When is your birthday? Did you take a year off from school after high school?"

"I did. You know, you seem to have your own interest in math. This flagrant fascination with numbers might mean you're headed for a new major."

Julie crossed her arms. "Unlikely. I haven't been fitted with your newfangled compression filter."

"I could put in a good word with the developer. Maybe get you on the list for the next model?"

"I'll pass, but thanks."

"Yeah. This beta version still needs some tweaking."

Julie smiled. "No kidding. But it's all right."

CHAPTER 3

"Dinner will be here in a few minutes. You must be ravenous." Erin reached into a kitchen cabinet and retrieved a stack of ceramic plates. She had changed into a linen vest and dark jeans and retightened her long hair into a neat twist at the nape of her neck.

The air conditioning relieved the heavy air Julie had been suffering through all day, and she knew she should enjoy it while she could; the odds of renting an apartment with central AC were extremely unlikely. Julie took the plates from Erin. "I'll do this."

"Thanks. Matthew has the placemats and silverware." She nodded toward the dining room. "Oh, Julie? Did you reach your mother?"

"I did. And she asked me to thank you again."

"No more thanks necessary. It's a good thing she hadn't shipped out the rest of your things yet. They would be sitting on a street corner. I told her to just send everything here, and Matthew can help you move them when you find a place."

Julie moved to the dining room as Matt set down the last fork. She set the plates on the table and frowned as she recounted the settings. "There'll be five of us, right? You, me,

Erin, your dad, and Celeste? We've got an extra place set." Julie went to remove the plate.

"No. Just…um…" Matt cleared his throat. "Just leave that one. I should probably tell you," he started, while busying himself with the napkins, "that Celeste has this thing she does. She has this…I guess it would be considered…"

Julie waited while he started and stopped a few times, and finally she leaned in to whisper, "I'll need to hear more actual words in order to understand you."

"I don't know how to explain it to you." He sighed. "Celeste—" The front door opened and Matt mumbled something.

Julie looked questioningly at him. "What?"

He shook his head. "Just try to go with it."

✳✳✳

Well, the food was good. Cambridge Thai restaurants had a clear win over the single Thai restaurant back home that served generous portions of distinctly unappetizing dishes. And the company was entertaining, if not alternately overwhelming and altogether intelligible.

Erin had kept up a stream of information regarding Massachusetts politics ("A tangled web of corruption, nepotism, and general discombobulation"), the hierarchy of Harvard professors and chances for tenure ("Dominated by a goddamn miserable social infrastructure!"), and the history of Boston's public transportation system ("A toxic blend of poor planning and archaic engineering"). Just when she feared Erin might absolutely run out of breath and collapse face-first into her meal, Julie managed to ask Roger, Erin's husband, what he did for work, prompting the quieter man to let loose a slew of information.

"I'm particularly drawn to the study of nutrient dynamics and interdisciplinary investigations of coastal habitats." Roger was now in the middle of a complex explanation about his most recent research paper. He was a researcher at the Laboratory for Microbial Oceanography and had received a grant to travel to Southeast Asia. "But my trip will focus primarily on shrimp defense mechanisms and immunomodulation to enhance sustainability and reduce antibiotic usage in shrimp culture."

Julie poked at her curry. "Shrimp culture. Yes." She essentially had no idea what Roger was talking about, but she enjoyed his enthusiasm. He had a real *Dad* look about him: button-down shirt, khaki pants, loafers with no socks, thinning gray hair, soft blue eyes, and charming wrinkles that appeared when he even hinted at a smile.

Roger adjusted his wire glasses and leaned his thin frame into the table, gesticulating with a forkful of chicken satay. Despite his flailing hand motions, his voice was soft, soothing. "Refining techniques to determine the activity of shrimp defense mechanisms is important. Pagocytic activity, phenoloxidase activity, and of course, bacterial clearance ability. There will be a lot to explore on this trip." He spilled some peanut sauce onto the cuff of his wrinkled button-down shirt and smudged it dry with a napkin. "Which reminds me that I have to go back to the office tonight. I've got more paperwork that needs to be filled out for the grant commission."

Erin reached for the container of ginger noodles. "I have to go to the office tonight too. I've got mountains of work ahead of me, and I still have to finalize the syllabus for the classes I'm teaching this semester. My apologies, Julie. And Matt, classes start next week for you too, so you should get a jump-start gathering materials for your independent study. I'm sure you could find something more challenging than the last set of articles I saw you reading." She frowned at him.

Matt remained expressionless, as he had through most of the meal. "Sure. I'd love to." There was an edge to his voice that momentarily silenced the table.

Erin set her fork down. "Matthew, don't sulk. One of those articles you were fussing over had been published in some unheard-of journal, and it was beneath you."

"Maybe Julie can help Matt?" Celeste suggested.

Julie looked across the table and smiled at Celeste. The thirteen-year-old was breathtaking, and Julie found it impossible not to be drawn in by her appearance alone. She looked like one of those pitiable children forced to don ridiculous wings and pose for angel-themed calendars. But with that long blond hair that fell in wild waves and those penetrating blue eyes, Celeste was positively...Well, *ethereal*, appropriately enough.

"Celeste, I'm sure Julie has zero interest in helping me root through online article databases," Matt said. "Not everyone finds the American Institute of Physics as titillating as I do."

"Oh!" Celeste clapped her hand to her mouth, stifling laughter. "Matt said a bad word!"

"I said *titillating*, not *tit*."

"*Now* you said a bad word!" Celeste squealed.

Erin sighed loudly. "Matthew, is that necessary?"

"It's just a little dinnertime social intercourse, Mom. Nothing to get upset about. Besides, you're the one who's prone to flinging around terms like *penal system*, *rectify*, and *annals of law*."

"Matthew! That is enough!" Erin spoke loudly in order to be heard over Celeste's stream of giggling. Erin wrinkled her forehead in disapproval, but Julie detected the beginning of a smile. "Celeste, get control of yourself."

Julie had to bite her cheek to stop Celeste's laughter from rubbing off on her. "Anyway, I'm sure I would be more of a hindrance to Matt than a help. Maybe after I get a semester of college under my belt."

Celeste, who had managed to compose herself, studied Julie's face. "You look too smart to be going to Whitney."

"Good God, Celeste!" Erin said sharply. "Julie, I apologize. I don't know what is going on with this dinner."

Julie laughed. "It's OK. I'll take it as a compliment. I know that Whitney isn't the most prestigious school."

"How *did* you choose Whitney?" Roger asked. "You're pretty far from home. Is there a program there that you're very interested in?"

Julie didn't know how to answer this. She was aware that studying at Whitney probably wasn't looked at with high regard by the Harvard/MIT/Laboratory for Microbial Oceanography crowd at the table. "I guess I just wanted to try something new. Move to a big city. And to be honest, I didn't get in to some of the other places I applied," Julie admitted. "Even though my grades and test scores were good, my high school's reputation probably didn't carry much weight with admissions offices. I did get into a few other schools that would have been great, but I didn't get the financial aid I would need. I'm going to have big loans to pay off as it is."

"Whitney is a good school," Erin reassured her. "The college admission process is nearly impossible to navigate. And you can always transfer to another school if you do well at Whitney."

"Did you pick your classes yet? I could help you," Celeste offered. "I read through the entire online course catalog when Finn was at Brandeis. He majored in creative writing and minored in journalism."

Julie smiled. "I have to register on Friday, and I would love your help."

Celeste was petite, with more her father's build than Matthew, and her round face hadn't yet slimmed down with age. And despite being obviously bright and overly articulate, there was something very immature about her. The light green pinafore-style dress that she had on looked more appropriate for a second-grader than a teenager. Julie would never have been caught dead in something like that, and she could only imagine how well it went over with Celeste's fellow students.

But what struck Julie the most about Celeste had to do with what—or who?—was in the chair next to her.

"Oh, Julie! I didn't introduce you properly, did I?" Celeste chirped happily and then turned to the seat next to her. "Flat Finn, this is Julie. Julie, this is Flat Finn."

Erin poured herself some sparkling water, and Roger continued daydreaming about brine, but Julie was sure she heard Matt catch his breath. She eyed the seat again.

Frankly, she'd been hoping to get through dinner without addressing this issue.

No one else had mentioned anything so far, but this must be what Matt had started to tell her about: A life-size cardboard cutout of their brother Finn leaned stiffly angled against the chair, his gaze fixed rigidly on the ceiling's light fixture.

The funny thing was that—even with the fixed stare—Flat Finn was undeniably cute. Hot, actually, which Julie knew was inappropriate to think considering that, except for the flat cardboard form, he had a lot in common with a deflated blow-up doll. She hadn't gotten a good look at the real Finn in the snowboarding picture, but in this large picture version she saw perfectly mussed-up blond hair, an athletic, ruddy complexion, and a lean but muscular build.

Finn was decidedly adorable. Even in pancake form.

Julie looked across the table and tried not to pause too long before speaking. "It's very nice to meet you, Flat Finn. I thought you were traveling."

Celeste wrinkled her nose. "*Finn* is the one who is traveling. Right now he is volunteering at a game reserve for rescued animals. This is *Flat Finn*. He is a symbolic representation of my brother."

OK, this was obviously not normal. In fact, it was downright weird. But Julie was a guest in their home, and she would be as polite to this Flat Finn thing as she was to the rest of the family. "In that case, Flat Finn, would you like some basil and lemongrass duck?"

Celeste quickly shook her head. "He already had dinner. He is experimenting with not eating after five o'clock because he suspects that he can improve his metabolism and get more *cut*. His word, not mine. He is *quite* interested in women, though, and he thinks he would have better luck if he could just get rid of his tiny love handles." She rolled her eyes, whispering, "I know, it is beyond outlandish. He looks good just the way he is."

"I admire his self-control," Julie said. "See if I can pass up hot fudge sundaes at midnight."

Celeste glanced at Flat Finn. "He does not approve. But I think that he is just jealous because you have such a naturally svelte figure."

"If Flat Finn loses what he perceives to be love handles, I'll reward him with a one-time double sundae."

"Deal. But Mom better not sneak him any Oreos. Those are his favorite treat."

"I promise." Erin held up her hand, palm outward, pledging not to serve cookies to her son's unresponsive twin.

Julie shrugged to herself. She didn't particularly care about Flat Finn's presence. If everyone wanted to act as though it was perfectly ordinary to hang out with a flat, replicated family member, it was fine by her. After all, he was polite, not at all bad to look at, and didn't hog more than his fair share of the Thai dumplings. Granted, his conversational skills were lacking, but he was probably just shy around new people…

Look, everyone has a few psychological idiosyncrasies, right? Julie reasoned. She probably had a few, and this was Celeste's. Hell, there were worse things than this. Maybe not more bizarre, but there were worse. Probably.

"Julie, guess where Finn is right now?" Celeste asked excitedly.

"Antarctica?"

"No."

"Syria? Mongolia? New Zealand? Tallahassee? No? Must be Boise then."

"There are no game reserves in Boise. At least, not that I know of. He is in South Africa. The Eastern Cape, right by the Indian Ocean. He sent me pictures of antelopes yesterday and said that next time he will send a picture of a serval. It looks much like a regular cat, but it is not."

"Very cool," Julie agreed. "How long is he gone for?"

"That is unclear," Celeste said. "He has been going all over the world for months now, and he still has a long list of places he wants to see. He finds jobs and charity work wherever he goes, so he is *not* just some spoiled brat on a permanent vacation. He might even climb Kilimanjaro."

"That sounds terrifying," Erin said. "I'm not one for heights myself, but Finn is certainly qualified. He climbed Denali and Rainier."

"Really?" Julie said. "That's impressive."

Matt coughed and made a show of reaching across the table for another carton of food.

"He did. I will show you those pictures later too," Celeste said.

Erin smiled. "Finn is our adventurous child. When he was eight years old, I came home from work one day to find him at the top of the telephone pole outside our house. The babysitter was talking on the phone and failed to notice that her charge had scaled up forty feet. I fired her, obviously, and when I asked Finn what had possessed him to do that, he told me that he'd been hoping to see into Ellie Livingston's bedroom window."

"Trying to peek at a girl in his class?" Julie guessed.

Erin laughed. "Her mother, actually. Mrs. Livingston heard about this and was flattered. She sent a tray of cookies over with a thank-you note. Finn was such an interesting child." Erin dabbed her mouth with her napkin, her fingers clenched tightly around the cloth, and stood up. "I hate to run, but I really should get going."

"I'll walk with you," Roger said. "It's a beautiful night. I should be done around eleven. Will you be ready then?"

"Perfect. Julie, you're welcome to use the car tomorrow to look at apartments. The keys are hanging in the kitchen. We both leave early for work, so we'll see you at dinner? And I'd love to hear more about how your mother is." Erin pushed her chair in. "OK, good night, everyone."

Erin and Roger vanished faster than you could say *Type A personality*, leaving Julie and Matt alone with Celeste and Flat Finn.

Matt backed his chair up and looked wryly at Julie. "Interesting enough for you?"

CHAPTER 4

Julie studied Celeste's face, watching her peruse the Whitney course catalog. They'd been on the couch together for the past half hour, weighing the pros and cons of the classes that Julie had to choose from. It was odd the way this thirteen-year-old was glued to the course listings. But the truth was that she'd been surprisingly helpful in figuring out a schedule. Julie was even starting to get used to her rather formal style of speech.

The house was chilly now, with the central air on full blast, and Celeste pulled a light blanket over her lap. Julie adjusted her computer, which sat on her lap, and rested her fingers on the keys. She peered at Celeste's scrawling in the book. "So which English class am I taking? The eight thirty one?"

"No. English is at ten on Tuesday and Thursday, and Introduction to Psychology is at noon Monday, Wednesday, and Friday. Write down these course numbers." Celeste pointed to the page and waited as Julie typed. "See, you have to be totally prepared on Friday morning, or you will *not* get the schedule you want. At least you get to register online and avoid waiting in a line with lots of annoying people."

"So you think all my fellow students will be annoying? I *was* hoping to make friends, but now I don't know..."

Celeste snapped the book shut. "Normal people can become very annoying if put in annoying situations."

"That's true. Then you're right. I'm glad I'm registering from home."

Celeste leaned her head back against the couch. "Did you have lots of friends at home? What about a boyfriend? I bet you have a boyfriend. Is he very handsome?"

"I still have lots of friends at home. They didn't evaporate when I left. I just won't be seeing them as much now that I'm in Boston. I used to have a boyfriend, and yes, he was cute, but he was also a brainless pain in the neck."

"Do you have pictures of everyone?" Celeste asked.

"Of course." Julie opened her photo program and scrolled through albums until she found a set of pictures from August. "These are from my going-away party. My mom threw a barbecue in our backyard."

"You had a big party? It looks wonderful," Celeste said breathlessly.

"Yeah. Hot dogs, congealed macaroni salad, a cake with my name misspelled, the whole works. OK, there I am with Kristen and Mariam. And here's one of Amy and my mom." Julie scrolled through countless pictures while Celeste demanded details on nearly everything.

"Do you have a picture of your father?"

Julie continued pulling up photos. "Nope. He was away on business. But he did send me the most technologically advanced phone there is as a gift. And he called during the party."

"That was a kind thing for him to do. Sometimes my own father is unable to be present for events, but I do not get a phone call."

"Oh."

"One time my father opted to have Matt leave paper dolls under my pillow. Mini Flat Finns. I found that a clever and unusual way to express that he missed me."

"That is a very cool idea. I like it."

"He does not do that very often, though. I wish he would."

This is something that Julie understood. It was hard to have an absent parent, even when that parent adored you.

Celeste pointed to the screen. "Is that your cake?"

"Cute, huh?"

"Who's that? You had a band playing? Is that your boyfriend? Your dress is very pretty." Celeste wanted every detail. "Where did you buy that? How did you get in and out of it? Your boobs look huge! No wonder you had a boyfriend!"

"First of all, the dress is not that tight. It's *fitted*. And my boobs look regular sized. And we're not talking about my boobs. But, yes, the party was really fun. I didn't want anything too fancy, so it was perfect. So what kind of birthday parties do you have?" Julie asked.

Celeste looked straight ahead, seemingly transfixed by something on a shelf. "I do not really do parties anymore. They never work out terribly well for me," she said simply. "We have to show Flat Finn that red dress. He is going to love it! And the one of you at graduation. You look so happy getting your diploma."

Celeste pushed the blanket aside and retrieved the cardboard cutout of her brother, which she'd left by the piano in the small room off of the main hall. According to Celeste, Flat Finn loathed practicing scales, but he knew that Erin would never forgive him if he slacked off. Even cardboard brothers felt obligated to please their parents. Celeste entered the room carrying the cutout in front of her, eerily giving the impression that Flat Finn was able to glide around by himself. She stood him next to the coffee table near Julie and adjusted the panels by his feet that kept him standing, struggling to make him balance on the thick rug.

"Come on, Flat Finn!" she muttered, the wavering figure looming over her. She looked up to his head, her blond curls falling off her face and revealing the determination in her eyes. "Please!" she said with agitation. "You have to help out."

She reached a hand up to his midsection, trying desperately to keep him vertical, but each time she seemed to find the perfect spot for the base flap, Flat Finn would lean precariously forward or backward, causing Celeste to tighten her free hand. Julie could see that the carpeting was not going to allow a successful outcome, and Celeste's cheeks flushed as she became increasingly frustrated. Panicked, even.

"You have done this before, Flat Finn! You can do this!" she pleaded.

Julie watched the scene before her and wondered what the hell she'd gotten herself into by setting foot in this house. Celeste was looking rather frazzled, and it was hard to watch this kid in such a state, so Julie stood up and took Flat Finn by the shoulders. If everyone else was going to normalize this, she might as well hop on the bandwagon.

"You know what? Guys always like to lie down and just sprawl out. They're lazy like that. I wonder if that's what he wants." Julie noticed Matt poised nervously at the far side of the room, clearly considering whether or not to intervene. He took a step forward. Julie shot him a look and he stepped back. "Besides," she continued to Celeste, "Flat Finn can't see the computer from up there. He should be on the couch with us."

Celeste looked at Julie for a moment, and then her face brightened. "I think he would like that very much."

Julie lifted Flat Finn from the nubby, unsuitable carpeting, swung him sideways into the air, and laid him on his side on the couch.

"Be careful," Celeste urged from her crouched position on the rug.

"He's fine. And there's still room for us." Julie took her seat again, leaving enough room behind her so that Flat Finn did not risk getting any flatter. "Just don't lean back, or we'll be in trouble. Come sit down and tell me which pictures he wants to see."

Celeste rounded the table and sat down gingerly. She leaned her head over Julie's lap, peeking at Flat Finn's face jutting out from behind Julie's back. "He definitely wants to see the red dress ones first. He could hear me talking about them and suspects that you look hot and sultry. Again, his words, not mine."

Julie laughed. "Well, *I* suspect Flat Finn is a pervert, and he's going to be disappointed, but he can see the pictures anyway." Julie opened the photo and waited for an assessment. She did look cute that day, she had to admit. While the dress was a little low-cut and fell a few inches above the knee, it was also soft and flowing. She liked how the straps crisscrossed over her back and tied in a bow.

Celeste paused for a moment. "He is not disappointed. He thinks that you are beautiful and that you should Facebook Finn." She paused again. "He doesn't mean that to sound as dirty as it does."

Julie swallowed. "Flat Finn is on Facebook?" She'd love to see *those* status updates. *Got strapped to the roof of the car today for a trip to Starbucks. Would have loved to taste caramel mocha, but can't move arms and so was forced to stare longingly at delicious, hot beverage. Will the taunting never end?*

Celeste sighed, clearly exasperated at Julie's stupidity. "Not Flat Finn. *Finn.* Go find him on Facebook. You are on Facebook, aren't you? Matty and Finn are, and Matty lets me sneak on with him so I can see Finn's page. Shhhh," she said, holding a finger to her lips. "Mom and Dad would not approve whatsoever. They hate any sort of social networking site and consider it indicative of lower intelligence."

"I suppose he's on Twitter too?"

"Absolutely not. Are you?"

Julie shook her head. "I have a strong aversion to Twitter, and yet there is a social obligation that forces me to pop in and spy on celebrities now and then. I don't get Twitter. It's impossible to follow conversation threads, and it's too easy to spend hours and hours clicking on random names, and the next thing you know, you've become infatuated with Tweet photos from the Kardashians."

Celeste stared at her. "So are you or are you not on Facebook?"

Man, this kid was a piece of work. "Yup, I am on Facebook. And if you don't tell your parents that, then I won't tell them about you and Matthew. And I would be honored to be Finn's friend." Julie logged into the site. "Finneas or Finn?" she asked Celeste.

"Always Finn. He hates Finneas. But he made his account under Finn Is God."

Julie laughed. "Why did he do that?"

"Because he has no interest in having undesirables from high school finding him. He gets to hide out a little more this way. Be selective. That's important to him. Being selective with your friends."

Julie tapped the keyboard, found the real Finn, and sent a friend request. With only thirty-two friends compared to Julie's four hundred-and-something, he was indeed selective.

She saw Matthew's name on Finn's friend list and added him too. Julie's philosophy was that you could never have too many friends. Virtual ones, at least. She had a few real ones she could do without.

"Update your status! Update your status!" Celeste demanded. "Something funny."

Julie thought for a moment. "How's this?"

Julie Seagle *Never moon a werewolf.*

Celeste leaned her head against Julie's shoulder. "I like it. It's practical and witty. Flat Finn likes it too. Do one for him."

This was new. Julie had never had to come up with a status update directed to someone's flat brother.

Julie Seagle *is unable to find any financially Finnish finches for Flat Finn, but will finagle finger-painting fingerling finery as a final finale. She finks.*

"You have made substantial use of alliteration." Celeste stared at the computer screen. "Flat Finn is *finking* about it," she said, glaring at Julie. "I, however, am not *fond* of this update."

Julie typed again.

Julie Seagle *You can never be too rich or too Finn.*

Celeste patted Julie's arm. "Better."

✳✳✳

Julie cracked the ice cube tray and dropped a few cubes into her water glass. "You want some?"

Matt nodded. "Thanks."

"Is Celeste asleep?" Julie took a glass from the cupboard.

"Out cold."

"Are you actually packing yourself a lunch for tomorrow?" She eyed the selection of healthy items that Matt was putting into a lunch bag: carrot sticks, grapes, whole grain crackers, and a yogurt drink.

"I'm *not* actually packing myself a lunch for tomorrow. It's for Celeste. That damn private school she's at makes the kids take a break and nourish themselves before the teachers continue indoctrinating them with foolish lessons about Predynastic Egypt and curtal sonnets." Matt picked up a wedge of cheese and began cutting uniform slices.

"What the hell is a curtal sonnet?" Julie lifted herself up so that she was sitting on the counter and stole a piece of cheese. "It makes me think of curds and whey."

"It was invented by this guy Hopkins, and the curtal sonnet has exactly three-quarters of the structure of a Petrarchan sonnet, shrunk proportionally. Interestingly enough, he has an equation for it, and some argue that a true interest in sonnets stems from their relationship to math. If the Petrarchan sonnet is described as eight plus six equals fourteen, then the curtal sonnet would be twelve over two plus nine over two..." Matt put the knife down. "Julie?"

"Sorry, I think I fell asleep for a minute." Julie yawned and patted her cheeks. "Kidding! I'm kidding! The unification of math and poetry is jaw-droppingly interesting. But you lost me at *equation*."

Matt smirked. "Well, it *is* interesting because lots of poems have mathematical imagery or structure. Concrete triangular poems and syllabic verse, for example. Did you know that we subconsciously track the sound properties in poetry?"

"No, *you* subconsciously track sound properties and then wreck perfectly nice poetry by breaking it down into mathematical elements. Some of us just enjoy plain old poetry."

Matt zipped up Celeste's lunch bag and moved to stand in front of Julie. "I enjoy it too. Just in a different way than you do. I can't help it. I'm a nerd."

"So you've said."

"I suspect that on some level, you respond to the mathematical components in writing."

"And I suspect that you're wrong." Julie hopped down from the counter and pointed to the lunch bag. "So will Flat Finn be needing a lunch too?"

"Nope. He has a large breakfast. A stack of pancakes, an egg white omelet with green peppers and Swiss, and a fruit smoothie. That usually tides him over until dinner."

Julie crossed her arms. "I'm serious. Flat Finn can't possibly go to school with her, right?"

"He already went to Brandeis so, no, he doesn't need to repeat seventh grade. Although they did make him take a bunch of tests in order to qualify out. He barely passed the oral exams, though, because the instructors found him 'withholding and tight-lipped.' It's a terribly biased system, but at least he passed and won't have to suffer through the school's annual reenactment of the first Thanksgiving. He has a pilgrim phobia."

"Funny. Really, what's the deal with Flat Finn?"

"After an unfortunate incident involving Wile E. Coyote and an anvil, Three Dimensional Finn had to change his name."

Julie laughed. "Matt, come on! I assume this has something to do with her brother being away?"

Matt groaned. "Something like that." He moved to the fridge, tucked the lunch bag on a shelf, and rearranged the left-over cartons.

"And nobody has suggested that she lose the accessory? I mean, she's kind of old for this sort of thing, don't you think? Not that I can think of a good age for it."

He shrugged. "I don't really know. I just follow orders and nod and smile."

"Well, when is the real Finn coming back? That would take care of this, right? Does she take Flat Finn out of the house? What do her friends think when she shows up at soccer practice and asks if Flat Finn can play fullback?"

"No idea when Finn is coming home. He's off on his adventures, being cool and carefree," he said brusquely and shut the fridge. "And unless she's at school, Celeste takes Flat Finn everywhere. But she doesn't…She doesn't go out much. Restaurants aren't really an option, hence the regular takeout. She doesn't play soccer, and she doesn't have friends. Anything else, or are you done making fun of her?"

"Hey," Julie softened her tone. "I am not making fun of her. I like her. Flat Finn too. And did you say *hence*?"

"Yes, I said *hence*." Matt busied himself cleaning off the kitchen counters. "I think it's making a comeback."

"But I don't get why Celeste—"

"Leave it alone," Matt said sharply. "I'm not saying anything else about it, OK? And please don't bring this up with my parents."

Julie froze. "I'm sorry," she stammered. "It's none of my business. I shouldn't pry."

"No, *I'm* sorry," Matt said apologetically. "Forget it. Listen, I have to take Celeste to school tomorrow morning, but after that I could help you find an apartment. I called a friend of mine who knows a realtor that I got in touch with, and he's got some places for you to see. I assumed you wouldn't mind a little help."

"Really? That's awesome. Thank you so much." She wasn't about to refuse any apartment leads. "You're not busy tomorrow?"

"I've got time. This realtor said we could meet him at ten, and we'll go from there. Sound OK?"

"Very OK."

CHAPTER 5

Julie pursed her lips. She didn't like this realtor. How could his pants be falling off when he had such a substantial belly willing to hold them up? But the real reason she didn't care for this jerk was because he'd just brought them to yet another dumpy, probably condemned apartment.

"Well, this is obviously the apartment I was meant to have. No wonder the one in Jamaica Plain didn't work out. It was a sign from God that I needed to find this gem. The cockroaches are a nice bonus. I've always wanted to live with animals. And I can make extra money working as a hooker. Those girls outside looked really friendly, and I'm sure they'd take me under their wing and teach me the tricks of the trade. Pardon the pun."

Matt stepped soundly on a particularly beefy cockroach. "Odds are their pimp would be highly interested in obtaining the services of a nice Midwestern girl. Boston men are forever complaining about the same old, same old with East Coast prostitutes."

The realtor growled and tugged on his sagging pants. "Look, you two, this is the eighth goddamn place I've showed you. This is what you get in your price range, missy. Take it or leave it."

"She'll need to see another goddamn place, then, because the roaches have unionized and put a stop to further negotiations regarding new tenants. Also, I think I smell a dead body."

The realtor threw his hands up in Julie's direction. "Sweetheart, with what you're willing to pay, you'd be better off squeezing in with five roommates in a one-bedroom. And I don't have those kinds of listings. Check Craigslist."

Julie squinted her eyes. "Sweetheart will not be using Craigslist. Sweetheart will not be living here. Sweetheart will likely collapse in despair and move back to Ohio, where she will wait tables at Dirk's Drink Dive and give up on her dream of attending at least one college class before the turn of the century."

She briefly considered calling her father to bail her out of this hell. That was, if she could even reach him. Forget it. Way too embarrassing. She was paying for college with money from her mother and student loans, and she could surely figure out this situation without humiliating herself in front of her father. She wiped her forehead. God, it was stuffy and rank in here, and she could feel the sweat practically streaming down her back. Who knew Boston was so humid? Well, Bostonians probably.

Julie knew that she had better get out of this building before she further insulted this jackass. She'd already been rude enough, but she couldn't be held responsible for what came out of her mouth right now. Poor Matt had trekked around various Boston neighborhoods with her to look at one uninhabitable place after another. After four hours of searching, she was no closer to finding a place to live than she was when they'd started. And now here she was mouthing off and acting like a total lunatic.

She took a deep breath. "Here's what I'm going to do. I'm going to," she started slowly, hoping that, if she spoke positively, a brilliant idea would come to her and let her complete the sentence. "I am going to consider the many simple solutions to my housing crisis and deduce what the best strategy will be." She paused. "And I choose to wander around and…and look for fliers from people seeking roommates. Yes. That is the plan."

Matt looked doubtful. "If that's what you want, sure. Let's go back into Harvard Square. It's probably your best bet. And less corpse-y."

"Corpse-y? Really? Is that an MIT word?"

"You bet. Let's get out of here."

Julie followed Matt out of the apartment and walked silently next to him for ten minutes as he led them to the nearest T stop. "Where are we again? I'm totally confused."

"Just outside Davis Square. It's mostly a nice area, but like anyplace, it has its not-so-good parts."

"I appreciate your help. I really do. This is all my fault, and you shouldn't have to give up your day to visit every hellhole in a ten-mile radius." Julie was exhausted and dejected. She was beginning to realize that with the amount of money she had for rent, finding reasonable accommodations was going to be next to impossible.

Matt held the door to the T station open for her. Julie thought that it seemed awfully crowded for a weekday afternoon, and the top landing by the stairs was mobbed with people talking on cell phones, bumping into her, and blocking her view. The heat from the swarm of commuters added to her increasing exhaustion and discomfort. She stepped closer to Matt so she wouldn't lose him and followed him onto the staircase. Or what she thought was the staircase.

And then her heart started to pound. "Wait, no! No! No escalators. Matt, I don't do escalators." Julie tried to step off, but she was too late, now feeling as though she were plunging straight down, unsecured and helpless. She glanced at the bottom of the landing, aware of the hideously steep incline and the slow pace of the escalator. Dizzy and overwhelmingly anxious, Julie could see shapes begin to blur and felt her knees tremble as the vertigo took over.

"Julie? Julie?" She was aware of Matt's voice, but it sounded foggy and unnatural. She could make out his green T-shirt as he turned toward her, slipping his arms around her waist and pulling her in as she started to drop. "I got you," he said. "I won't let you fall. Just hold on." He held her tightly against his chest, and she briefly wondered if he was wearing Axe body spray.

"Boooo," she murmured.

"What did you say? Are you OK? Just hold on for another minute."

And then suddenly they were off the horrible escalator, Julie still awkwardly slumped in his arms while people swarmed around them.

"Oh. Sorry." Alert enough to know that she didn't want to faint in a T station, she pulled back a bit, trying to steady herself against Matt as she forced her legs to work. He was surprisingly strong for someone who likely spent most of his day hunched over a scientific calculator. Slowly the world came into focus again, and she found herself staring at his shirt, which enthusiastically announced *FTW!*

For. The. Win, she mouthed and shut her eyes in dismay.

She felt drunk, the way she had after those three shots of putrid peppermint schnapps at the prom. She wasn't a big drinker (as evidenced that night, when she hurled up chicken divan in the ladies' room at the Hotel Carnegie), and she didn't care for the similar feeling she had now.

She poked her finger into his chest. "Matthew, my friend, you need some new clothes."

"Thank you."

She looked up at him dizzily. "Do you have one geeky shirt for every day of the week?"

"More than that. Don't worry."

"I am flooded with relief."

"Are you OK now?"

"Oh." Julie realized she was still slouched into him. "Yes. I'm…I'm perfectly OK. Brilliant." She dropped her hands from his chest and took a step back. There. She could see normally, and her knees were no longer comprised solely of gelatin. "Sorry about that. Let's go get our train."

Matt looked at her skeptically. "If you're sure."

"Yeah. I'm fine. See?" She jumped up and down. "All motor function has been restored. Physiological integrity is intact. I can now continue not finding an apartment."

"You're very goofy."

The underground platform area was cool and helped Julie feel human again. The downside of which was that she could now fully appreciate how embarrassing her near-fainting spell was. She was very good about avoiding situations that brought on an attack, but she hadn't been able to see that damn escalator through all the T riders.

They had to wait only a few minutes before the next train screeched to a halt. She and Matt stepped onto the train and sat down in seats that faced the center of the car. Julie crossed her legs and tried to appear as composed as one could after such an incident.

She tucked her hair behind her ears. "So now you know that I don't like escalators. Or elevators, I imagine, although I haven't been on one in years. Maybe I've improved. It makes me fall apart. I call it moving height freak-out syndrome."

"That doesn't make any sense," Matt informed her. "You're acrophobic, which is one of the space and motion phobias. You have an irrational fear of heights that results in severe discomfort. And you didn't exactly freak out. You probably experienced dizziness and some panic, right?"

"Thank you for ruining my attempt to bring levity to my traumatic event." Julie managed not to glower, although it took some effort.

"I'm not ruining your attempt at levity, but you should come up with a name that is factually accurate." Matt stood up and grabbed a metal bar that ran above his head, swaying with the movement of the train.

"I can come up with whatever the hell name I want to. It's my syndrome, so I get to name it."

"Well, it's not really *your* syndrome, considering that other people—"

"Oh my God!" Julie pleaded. "Can we not argue about what this mortifying thing is called?"

"We're not arguing. We're discussing. And you shouldn't be mortified. It's really not that uncommon."

"I don't care if it's common or not, I have the right to be mortified if I want to."

"Of course you have the *right*. I'm just telling you that if your feeling of mortification is based on the belief that this is an unusual pathology, then statistically speaking, you have no reason to." He was more animated now than Julie had seen him before, color coming into his cheeks and his murky gray eyes actually shining. "You can take comfort in being part of a community. If you look at the percentage of people with any phobia at all, then you've got substantial company."

"So now I'm pathological?" Julie clenched her hands. Good Lord, Matt was exasperating, particularly because he had an annoying grin plastered on his face and seemed to delight way too much in being difficult. Great. She finally had the annoying brother she'd never wanted.

"No, *you're* not pathological, but acrophobia is pathological in the sense that your reaction to heights deviates from the norm."

"Why do you have to correct everything I say?" Julie glanced at his *FTW!* shirt. "Out of the two of us, I don't think I'm the one who deviates from the norm." The train slammed to a stop. "You're the one who seems to get off arguing."

"You sound exactly like Finn. We're exchanging ideas. Debating." Matt looked down at his shorts. "And so far I haven't gotten off."

"Don't be rude. Then let's call it a draw, and we'll agree to disagree. Come on. I don't suppose I can get a Coolatta around here? I need caffeine if I'm going to regroup and find an apartment today." Julie stepped onto the platform with Matt close behind her.

"Watch it," he warned. "Make sure you get on the stairs here. This station also has a really steep escalator."

They took the stairs and emerged in the center of Harvard Square. Matt directed her to a community board where people had pinned information about everything from bands and jobs to lecture series and free film nights. Julie liked it here, where a diverse crowd could make anybody feel comfortable: students, professors, parents with toddlers, and punked-out teens skipping school all crowded the brick sidewalks. Groups of people were clustered on concrete steps; musicians were playing instruments and singing James Taylor songs; and a puppeteer across the street was making elaborate marionettes dance while little kids laughed. Even the man in a floral dress on roller blades who was shouting a profane version of the Declaration of Independence seemed to fit in. There was an energy here that she found enthralling.

"What about this one?" Matt pointed to a flier advertising a one-bedroom apartment.

"First of all, I can't afford that. Second of all, this ad looks really old. All the phone number tabs have been torn off."

"You never know. Maybe they had a slew of undesirables and lowered the price, hoping someone normal will call. I bet the last applicant was a wealthy but deranged middle-aged clown who tried to juggle the roommates."

Julie raised an eyebrow. "Or it was an unhinged MIT nerd who wanted to take over the apartment with his techie gear, leaving little room for necessary things like furniture."

Matt tapped the side of his head. "Now you're thinking."

There were a few ads that looked like possibilities, so Julie stored the numbers on her phone. Matt had to get home to get the car and pick up Celeste from school, so they grabbed sandwich wraps to go from a place on Mt. Auburn Street, and then Julie set her sights on locating her coveted coffee beverage as quickly as possible. "I need a Coolatta, Matt. Please tell me we can get one here? I may accidentally reenact the escalator scene if I don't find one soon." Julie tripped on the cobbled sidewalk. "See? I'm already beginning to derail."

"Yes. Right away."

Matt led them across the square to a quieter side street, then back down Mass Ave., then down a shorter one-way street, occasionally glancing at Julie.

Julie followed him obediently, wondering why he'd passed three Dunkin' Donuts without heading into any of them. She stopped him and dropped her head to the side. "Oh, you poor thing. You don't know what a Coolatta is, do you?"

Matt actually appeared to squirm a bit. "Well, no. I don't."

"Hold on, I have to mark this event." Julie whipped out her phone and updated her Facebook status, which she read aloud to Matt.

Julie Seagle *Have discovered noticeable gap in know-it-all's knowledge base. Will celebrate enchanting news with Coolatta.*

She was unable to stifle a grin.

Matt put his hands on his hips. "Hysterical. I never said that I knew everything. I'm just confident that I'm well-informed on many subjects."

"Apparently not important subjects." Julie marched ahead. "And, by the way, there's a difference between *confident* and *cocky*. Look, there's a Dunkin' at the top of this street. Do you know how far I have to drive at home to find one? And here you are, surrounded by one on every street corner! This is obviously the best city in the world. And the reason you've never heard of my favorite drink is because you're probably an uptight coffee-house, double-espresso, no-sugar kind of guy?"

"I'm miserably transparent, huh?"

"No. I'm a coffee psychic. You have that bitter double-espresso look about you. But today you're joining up with the masses and getting a Coolatta."

A few minutes later, Julie was happily inhaling her large frozen coffee drink while they headed out of the square.

Matt looked less than thrilled and made an exaggerated disgusted face after his first taste.

"This is a very popular drink, you know," Julie informed him. "There's no reason to be making such an expression."

"This must be why I'm not a social icon. You've finally pinpointed it. I don't blindly follow popular culture's love for overly sweet, pseudo-coffee, ice-crystal concoctions. It's a relief to finally understand why my social status is on a downward course."

"It's either that or the shirts," Julie muttered. "Hey, can we walk home by the river?" Julie could just glimpse the blue water and was aching to stroll back to the house along the picturesque path that ran through the grass.

Matt brushed his shaggy hair from his face. "Unfortunately, we don't really have time right now. It's faster to cut directly through the square, and I have to get Celeste."

"Sure. No problem." Julie took another sip of her drink. "Thank you for helping me out today. I'm sure this was a huge drag, but I really appreciate it. This was incredibly nice of you, and I'm sorry if I've been grouchy. I didn't expect to start off my freshman year in such flux. You've become a social icon to me," she teased.

"Yeah, right. You haven't been grouchy. You've been expressive and feisty. Both of which I like. Considering that your first days in Boston are far from what you were expecting, I think that you're doing great. I'm happy to help."

They walked quietly for a few minutes, and Julie noticed that despite the lull in conversation, there was nothing the least bit uncomfortable about being with Matt.

"So, do you pick up Celeste every day?" She hoped that he wouldn't bite her head off for this Celeste-related question.

He nodded.

"And do you stay with her after school too, until your parents get home?"

"I do."

"How do you get your schoolwork done? I imagine you've got more homework than the average student."

He shrugged. "It's not a big deal. I stay up late, which I like. Sometimes I go back to school at night if I need to use one of the labs. It works out fine."

"Is that why you don't live in the dorms? Or an apartment?"

"It would be rather silly to pay rent when my parents' house is so close to school."

"I guess so."

Matt took another sip of his drink. Aha! Julie smiled to herself and kept walking. He *did* like the Coolatta. Everyone did.

CHAPTER 6

Julie tapped her foot anxiously as she listened to the outgoing message. She had just called the last number from the group of potential apartment rentals and was hoping this would be it. A girl's chipper voice said, "Hi! You've reached Sally (that's me!) and Megan, Barb, and our newest roommate, Chelsea! Leave us a message, and if we're not too busy having fun, we'll call you back!" Julie growled and hung up. She didn't know if she was jealous of that fourth roommate or not. That Sally sounded an awful lot like the perky-yet-vacant crowd she'd left behind at home. On the other hand, there was something to be said for a core gaggle of girls who would love nothing more than to order pizza, do each others' hair, and watch tawdry reality shows.

Julie left her mom a falsely optimistic voice mail saying that she had some very strong housing possibilities and would likely be happily settled into a new place by the weekend. It could happen, right? Except that it was becoming apparent to Julie that she and her mom had been grossly naïve about what living in Boston would entail. Julie swore under her breath. Now she was another step closer to having to call her father for money. It was Wednesday night, so that gave her a few days to make good on her white lie. She had orientation tomorrow, and she'd just have to interrogate everyone she met for apartment leads.

Julie turned on her computer and checked the rental sites that she had bookmarked. Nothing new had come up. Even though her first few days in Boston had been a bit unsettled, she couldn't complain. At least she had a good place to stay, even if it was temporary. Finn's room was comfortable, and it somehow felt natural for her to be in here. Things would work out.

Plus, she was getting a kick-start to her undergraduate education just by eating dinner with the Watkins clan.

Dinner tonight had been Indian takeout complemented by a themed discussion about the religious diversity of India, arranged marriages, and the cash-for-votes scandal of 2008. Not that Julie had had much to contribute, since her knowledge of Indian culture and politics was embarrassingly limited, but she'd enjoyed the heated discussion. Erin had banged the table a number of times when making a point, Roger had thoughtfully tilted his head and delivered soft-spoken comments that sympathized with the people of India, and Matt had referenced several historic events, citing the year and exact date. Even though she had mostly just listened during the meal, Julie had found the conversation thoroughly enjoyable.

This was what she hoped her college classes would be like: dynamic, thought-provoking dialogue, piles of new information, and everything opposite from the dull, rote classroom teachings of her high school. Although presumably there would be no Flat characters in the college classrooms.

Right now Celeste was asleep with Flat Finn standing next to her headboard, Erin and Roger were back at work again, and Matt was holed up in his room. He'd applied and been accepted to be a research assistant for one of his professors, and so tonight he was pondering "effective decomposition strategies for certain nonconvex mixed-integer nonlinear optimization problems." Whatever the hell that meant. According to Matt, his work involved lots of coding and testing of some new algorithm and then doing numerical experiments on the performance of said scintillating algorithm. This was apparently about as exciting as it got for Matt. Maybe he had a nice mainstream hobby that she didn't know about?

Julie's e-mail notified her that she was now Facebook friends with both Matt and Finn. Oh, and that Finn had commented on her status about never being too rich or too Finn. *Best. Update. Ever,* he'd written. So he had a sense of humor. Although Julie wondered if he even knew who she was. Had anyone in his family let him know that she was a guest in their house? She sent him a quick private message:

Dear Finn–

Despite appearances, I am not in fact some weirdo who befriends strangers on Facebook and works their names into status updates. At least not on a regular basis. Our mothers went to college together, and I'm in Boston starting Whitney in a few days. My housing fell through, and your parents were nice enough to let me crash in your room while I figure things out. Not sure if anyone had told you about me…

Any booby traps in here that I should know about? I wouldn't want Flat Finn to have an accident should he stop by to chat.

–Julie

Julie clicked on Finn's profile page. He had a bunch of online albums, and she browsed through tons of photos of him in one picturesque spot after another: posing in the foreground of a mountain range; wading through a river; surrounded by tropical foliage; bundled up in ski gear during blizzard conditions;

and kayaking on a pristine lake. And then there were pictures documenting his volunteer work, showing him unloading boxes of food from the back of a rickety truck, huddling with a group of children in a bare-bones classroom, and balancing on a ladder as he hammered nails into the beam of a house under construction. And her personal favorite, a tan Finn emerging from the ocean with a surfboard and wearing only a pair of swim trunks. She couldn't help it. Finn was decidedly gorgeous, and anyone would have drooled a bit. Rugged, lean, perfect hair, adorable smile…

Her e-mail alert sounded. She had a message from Finn.

Hi, Julie–

Truthfully, I'm a little disappointed that you're not a stalker. I've been doing what I can to lure one in, and I thought I'd finally succeeded. Oh, well. I'll keep trying. Hope the monsters under my bed haven't been keeping you up at night. (They tend to enjoy late night keg parties and loud doo-wop music.) If they give you any trouble, I suggest singing anything from 2000–2006. They don't care for those years because it was during that time that the monster economy crashed, and they all had to cut back. Try a little Green Day (monsters don't respond well to any pop rock anthem). John Mayer used to work, but after he said something about "the Joshua Tree of vaginas," the monsters couldn't stop laughing. Noisily. If all else fails, there's a baseball bat in my closet. Don't be afraid to use it.

So Flat Finn hasn't freaked you out too much? He's a cool guy. Keep an eye on him, though. He likes to take the car out once in a while, and he never refills the tank.

–Finn

Julie laughed and wrote back.

Finn–

Thanks for the heads-up. I had a feeling FF might have a sneaky streak. He has that look about him. Something about the way he refuses to make eye contact.

I appreciate the tips. Ohio monsters can only be banished by showing reruns of "According to Jim," but I've never been able to make myself do that.

–Julie

She clicked on Facebook's news feed. Both Matt and Finn had recent updates. Oh, good Lord. These were some weird brothers.

Matthew Watkins *I like Facebook more than I like conversations with real people because here I don't have to wait until someone has finished talking before I say something else that's really inane and tangential.*

Finn Is God *They say if your ears are burning then someone is talking about you. Is that true? Because I have a question about what it means if it's a different body part.*

Julie could play weird too.

Julie Seagle *has a word in her status that doesn't really flugh anything.*

She checked her Gmail account. Finally there was a message from her father.

Dear Julie:

What do you think about a trip to California for your winter break? Three weeks up and down the coast. Send my secretary your vacation dates, and we'll spend Christmas together. Your mother said this would be acceptable to her, so I hope that you'll agree.

Dad

Julie reread the e-mail. This would be more time than she'd spent with her dad since she'd been a little kid. But what about her mother? She would be upset not to have Julie home for the holidays, although she'd obviously already talked this over with Julie's dad and agreed. *Of course* Kate had understood that this opportunity couldn't be passed up. She was that kind of mother. Julie wrote her father back.

Hi, Daddy! So happy to hear from you! Yes! The trip sounds perfect. I'm so excited to see you! Call me and tell me more. I love you. Julie

She sent her father her cell number in case he'd misplaced it, as well as the Watkinses' home phone number.

Julie closed the computer and picked out her outfit for tomorrow. Orientation started with coffee and bagels at eight thirty and ran until two fifteen. She stuck a notebook, a pen, a map of the school, and the directions Matt had given her into an oversized purse. As she fumbled to get everything into her bag, a paper slipped to the floor. Julie picked it up and laughed. Matt had slipped a map of the Boston T system into her things and had put gigantic skull and crossbones symbols next to T stations with escalators. Near the map's key, he had added an identifying description: *Horrifying threat awaits. Be on high alert.* Julie laughed. But see? She really had no business questioning Flat Finn when she couldn't even get on a damn escalator without having a total collapse. Of course, she'd rather faint in public than cart around a flat person.

She turned off the overhead light and crawled into bed, pulled the cool sheet over her, and easily fell asleep. For a few hours.

The noise from the two-fifteen train in Ohio used to wake her up. Even from across town, Julie could hear the horn and the rhythmic clacking as the train rolled by. It took months after the train schedule changed for her to get used to the sound and be able to sleep through it. She remembered when the sleep issues had started because it had been around the same time that her father moved out. Right now she missed that noise, and the silence woke her up.

Julie turned on the small lamp by the bed and took her book from the nightstand. Usually she could read until it was impossible to keep her eyes open any longer and falling asleep became inevitable. But tonight she was wide awake and unable to focus. It had less to do with being nervous about starting school and more about feeling antsy to get going. She dropped her book and picked up the picture by the lamp. She smiled at the image of Finn running across the backyard while carrying a young Celeste on his back. She had her hands over his eyes and her head thrown back as she screamed with delight. Julie guessed she'd been about five years old, and she was just as beautiful then as she was now.

Julie turned off the light and spent thirty minutes tossing and turning. She had to shut down her brain and get some sleep, but there was so much swirling through her head: college, where to live, strange and wonderful Celeste with her cardboard brother, Matt's nerdy shirts, her pathetic near-collapse on the escalator, Roger's shrimp, Erin's strong opinions on nearly everything...

She pulled a pillow over her head and tried picturing serene scenes. Then she tried to bore herself to sleep by thinking about things like yogurt and the structure of a gas pedal. It wasn't working. It must be those damn monsters under the bed. Julie rolled onto her back, wondering how to clear her head. She had one idea. It was stupid, but she was getting desperate.

She started quietly singing. God, this was moronic. At least Green Day was Finn's dumb idea and not hers. Julie ran her hands through her hair and took a deep breath. Who the hell could fall asleep to Green Day? Julie hummed for a moment and then kept singing.

It only took one verse for Julie to lull the monsters under the bed into peace. As she drifted to sleep, she knew that she'd have to thank Finn.

CHAPTER 7

Julie crossed her legs and tried to get comfortable in the hard auditorium seat. It just wasn't going to happen. The seats had obviously been designed to maximize physical discomfort and prevent students from falling asleep during lectures. Effective, if not cruel. She'd survived a rather tedious breakfast reception during which students had quietly stood around awkwardly nodding and smiling at each other while they waited for orientation to begin. This welcome lecture had to be better. The tiered seats faced a lectern where a few people were struggling to get a Whitney orientation video to work.

"Sorry," Julie apologized to the girl in the next seat as she accidently elbowed her while attempting to get her notepad from her bag.

"No problem. We're like goddamn anchovies in these chairs, huh?" The girl smiled at Julie. "I'm Dana. I don't know anybody here, and I'm hoping you're a normal person and will be nice to me. Unlike the man on the T this morning who humped my leg. Although he seemed to think he was being nice."

"I'm Julie from Ohio, and I promise not to hump your leg."

"Thank God!" Dana said, looking upward and clapping her hands. "I'm going to hold you to that."

The guy on Julie's left leaned in to Dana. "I, on the other hand, might hump your leg. Apologies in advance. I really can't control it. So sorry."

Julie laughed. "Since you've given fair warning, maybe she'll excuse you."

He held his hand out. "I'm Jamie. I grew up in Milford, west of Boston."

Julie and Dana each shook his hand. Dana's shiny, jet-black hair was cut in a perfectly sharp bob, and her hair barely moved as she nodded to Jamie. "Milford boy, you're much cuter than perverted T guy, so I just might let you hump my leg. For a small fee."

"I'll remember that," Jamie said, his dimples appearing as he grinned. He flopped back into his seat, adjusted his baseball hat, and rubbed the stubble on his cheek. He definitely looked as if he had rolled out of bed about five minutes ago. "What dorms are you in? I'm in Thompson."

"Actually, I'm living off campus in an apartment," Dana said. "Julie, where are you?"

"Nowhere, actually. Well, somewhere obviously. I'm staying with some family friends until I can find a place. Do you guys know of anything?"

"Ugh," Jamie groaned. "Family friends? Sounds awful."

Julie shook her head. "No, it's not so bad. They're really nice."

"I can ask around for you," Dana said. "The dorms are totally packed, I know that."

"Yeah, and the housing market around here is the pits. I'll check the campus for signs, though. See if there are any roommate ads for you," Jamie offered.

"That would be great. Thank you." Julie gave Jamie and Dana her cell number and programmed theirs into her phone.

"Look. They got the video working." She glanced down at her program. "A thirty-minute campus tour video, followed by a lecture from the head librarian on how to use the online catalogue system. Fun."

Jamie slumped down further in his seat. "Wake me when it's over."

Dana leaned over. "I'll hump your leg to signal the torture has ended."

Jamie shut his eyes and smiled. "Nice."

***

College orientation was about what Julie had expected it to be: boring, monotonous, and loaded with speeches that touted professors' accomplishments and promised fascinating classes. They were divided into smaller groups and given a more personal, non-video tour of the school, and that had been fun. Julie did her best to memorize where department buildings were so that she wouldn't have to walk around school with the embarrassing campus map in front of her face. One might as well carry a sign that said FRESHMAN.

Afterward, Julie took the T to Harvard Square and walked along the Charles River to get back to the Watkinses' house. It was a bit longer route, as Matt had said, but it was worth it to enjoy the scene. This would be a great place to study. She could take a blanket and sit on the grass, bring a snack, bury herself in a textbook. Who knew if she'd end up living anywhere near here, though?

She let herself into the house with the key Matt had given her. The lock on the front door was a nuisance, and it took a few minutes to get it open. She went into the kitchen to grab a drink. The fridge was positively packed with takeout cartons, and Julie had a suspicion that no one was ever going to eat the leftovers. Her phone rang, and she fumbled in her bag to find it.

She didn't recognize the number. "Hello?"

"Julie? Hey, it's Matthew. How was school?"

"Jam-packed with stimulating information. Where are you? How'd you get my number? Don't you have to get Celeste soon?"

"That's why I'm calling. Is there any chance you could pick her up? I'm really sorry. One of my professors is insisting on meeting with me about the research I'm helping him with. I'm sure I could get him to reschedule, but it would look better if I didn't."

Julie moved a container of Thai food and took out a bottle of sparkling water. "Sure, I guess so. Is it far from here?"

"Only ten minutes or so. This meeting is important, otherwise I wouldn't ask. You can take the car. The keys are hanging on the wall by the phone base. There should be paper there too. I'll give you directions. It's easy. I promise."

"You sure your parents won't mind if I drive their car?"

"Not at all. They rarely use it anyway."

Julie examined the large white pegboard on the wall. It screamed obsessive-compulsive. Hooks and small compartments held everything from pens and thumbtacks to business cards and the much-used takeout menus. She located the car keys and grabbed a sticky note and a pen. "OK, go."

Matt gave her directions. "If you leave in ten minutes, that should give you plenty of time. Just pull the car into the drive-thru pickup in front of the school, and Celeste will be out there." He paused. "And there's one more thing."

"I should bring Flat Finn?" she guessed.

Matt was silent for a moment. "Yes. The back seat is down, and there's a blanket in there so you can cover it up."

"You mean *him*."

"What?"

"I can cover *him* up. Be respectful. How'd you like it if Flat Finn referred to you as an *it*, huh?"

"If Flat Finn referred to me as anything, I'd have a whole new respect for *him*. So far *he's* refused to call me anything. It's a little rude, if you ask me."

"I'll talk to him about it. See if I can soften him up a bit."

"Excellent," Matt said. "Thanks for getting Celeste. I think she'll be OK with you being there. She seems to like you. Tell her that I'll call her after my meeting."

"She'll be fine."

"She's rather regimented. Changes in her schedule and unexpected people—"

"She'll be fine," Julie repeated. "I promise."

"You can't promise anything—"

"Good-bye, Matthew. Have fun at your meeting." Julie hung up before he could protest. For crying out loud, she was perfectly capable of picking up someone at school—with or without a cardboard boy in the back seat.

She ran upstairs and changed into a breezy knee-length tank dress and pinned her hair up. A quick touch-up to her makeup, which had begun to smear in the heat, and she headed out the front door to get Celeste. She stopped on the front steps and spun around.

Flat Finn stood poised expectantly in the living room. Julie approached the figure. God, this was messed up. "Come on, dude. We're off to get your pal. Now, normally people are not allowed to ride in the way-back, so keep your head down, and maybe we won't get arrested."

She lifted up the cutout boy and tucked his waist under her arm. Figuring out how to open the front door without smashing

Flat Finn was a bit of a challenge, and she had to set him on the front porch while she locked the door. She lifted the trunk open, got Flat Finn into the car, and covered him with the large blue blanket that was waiting there to conceal Celeste's secret.

The old Volvo was blistering hot, and Julie wondered why a family that clearly had money would not bother to maintain what could be a perfectly running car. Granted, it was a Volvo and would probably run forever no matter what. And they only had one car, too, which seemed odd, since two busy professionals and a student could certainly get use out of two vehicles. Apparently people with money did funny things sometimes.

She was pleased to note that Flat Finn had not left the gas tank empty. "Thank you, FF. I appreciate the consideration."

Julie found Celeste's school easily. She pulled into the arched driveway and idled behind a Lexus sedan. Students were just beginning to pour out of the front doors, and Julie scanned groups of girls, looking for Celeste. The middle-school students milled around in easily identifiable cliques, and Julie remembered exactly how it felt to be thirteen. It was such a strange age, that screwed-up, early-teen time when you vacillate between desperately wanting to be a full-fledged adult and still feeling like a little kid. The torture of trying to figure out how to dress and get your eyeliner exactly as they do in music videos, which singers were cool and which singers you shouldn't be caught dead listening to, what to do to get boys to like you, and what to do if they did. Ugh. Thank God Julie was done with that.

A girl in a miniskirt and a ponytail stepped aside, and Julie saw Celeste. Julie dropped her head to the steering wheel, hitting her head lightly a few times. Why was Celeste wearing a pastel plaid shirt and pale-blue pleated pants? Julie lifted her head and sighed, wanting nothing more than to leap from the car and yank the dorky backpack off the girl's shoulders. This kid stood out for all the wrong reasons. Like it or not, other kids cared about how you looked, and Celeste looked…*Wrong.* Gorgeous underneath the horrible clothing and totally unstyled hair, but still wrong.

But worse than how she looked was the undeniable fact that she was alone and quite obviously invisible to her peers. Julie cringed as a boy passed by Celeste, failing to notice or care that he bumped into her elbow as he joined up with a cluster of trendy, T-shirt-wearing guys.

Julie beeped the horn and waved, finally getting Celeste's attention. Celeste scanned the cars and then headed toward the Volvo. She stopped by the passenger door, her eyes wide and her face expressionless.

"Hey, kiddo. Hop in," Julie said warmly.

Celeste stood still, waiting a moment before she spoke. "Why are you here?" There was a noticeable shake in her voice that Julie couldn't miss.

"Matt asked me to pick you up today. He is really sorry. I guess he had something important to do at school. Celeste? It's OK. Flat Finn is with me. He helped get me here, because Matt's directions were dreadful."

Celeste opened the door and slipped into the seat. "Oh. This is fine." She turned to Julie. "This really *is* fine."

"Good." Julie pulled the car out to the main road. "So what should we do?"

"What do you mean *do*? We go home after school."

"Let's do something. Come on!"

"Like what?"

"I don't know." Julie turned up the radio and tapped her fingers on the wheel. "I don't even know what street I'm on right now. Maybe we'll get lost and spend the next few hours trying to navigate our way home. We'll listen to old-school Kelly Clarkson power songs and sing until we lose our voices."

"That is not a good plan." Celeste turned and peered into the back of the car. She inhaled deeply, then slowly let the air escape from her lips. "I always just go home."

Julie took a left turn onto another main road and drove for a few minutes. "Aha!" She pulled the car into the parking lot of a supermarket. "Let's make dinner tonight. I want to thank your parents for letting me stay at your house. Do you like Italian? I make a mean manicotti."

"Oh." Celeste thought for a moment. "That could be acceptable."

"Acceptable? It's going to be more than acceptable. Homemade tomato sauce with fresh basil? Ricotta and spinach stuffing? And my secret touch? Cheesy white sauce drizzled over the top. And we can all discuss Italian Gothic architecture or ancient Rome during dinner. I know how you guys like theme nights."

"Or the Italian Renaissance. Dad likes the Renaissance."

"You got it." Julie parked the car and started to get out. But Celeste didn't move. "Celeste? You coming?"

"Me? No. I should wait in the car. That's what I do."

"You don't go into stores?"

"No."

"Not ever?"

"No."

This was unbelievable. Julie tightened her fist around the car keys until they dug painfully into her hand. Somebody had to fix this. She walked to the back of the car and opened the trunk. "Well, that's too bad because FF and I want your help picking the best tomatoes." She flung the blanket off Flat Finn and eased him out of the back. "So I don't want to hear you complaining about the poor quality of the produce we select." She slammed the trunk shut, pulled a shopping cart out from the stack next to the car, and stuck the cutout brother into the cart, angled so that his entire top half jutted out.

Celeste flew out of the car. "What are you doing?"

"Shopping. What are you doing?"

"Beginning to have a type of anxiety attack that I would prefer to avoid."

"What else are you doing?"

Celeste pursed her lips together, hiding a smile. "Shopping."

"Good. Let's go."

"And do not call him FF. He doesn't care for abbreviations."

"Tell him to stop calling me JS and I'll consider it."

CHAPTER 8

Matt set his messenger bag on the stool next to him and sat down at the kitchen counter. He looked at the plate in front of him. "What is this?"

"It's a gastronomical representation of *Cat on a Hot Tin Roof*." Julie put her hands on her hips. "Don't you see it? The clear depiction of the struggle for sexual identity as evidenced by the two phallic shapes?"

Matt looked at her. "What are you talking about?"

"What are *you* talking about? It's manicotti, you nut. What do you think it is?"

"I know *that*. I was referencing the noticeable absence of takeout cartons. You made dinner?"

"Celeste and I made dinner," Julie corrected.

"And they did a wonderful job." Erin swooped into the kitchen and set her wine glass down on the counter. "Thank you again, Julie. It was wonderful. I don't remember the last time we've bothered to cook dinner ourselves. I'm surprised the stove is still working." She turned to Matt. "You're home late. How was school? Did your meeting go well?"

Matt nodded as he wiped his mouth with a napkin. Half his food was already gone. "Very good. Sorry I'm home late. And even sorrier that I've managed to double my workload by agreeing to be a research assistant."

"This is with Professor Saunders, correct? He has an excellent reputation, so this is an important opportunity for you." Erin took a sip of wine. "I do hear he's very demanding, Matthew, so you'll have to be incredibly diligent with your work."

"I realize that. In fact," Matt said as he stood up, "I should get upstairs and get to work. I'll finish dinner up there. Thanks, Julie." He picked up his plate and started out of the kitchen. "Hey, Julie?" He stopped in the doorway.

"Yeah?"

"So things went all right today?"

"Totally fine. I told you that when you called. Both times."

"OK. Thanks again."

Julie wiped down the counter and moved to the sink to start washing the pans that hadn't fit into the dishwasher. Erin took a towel and stood next to her.

"Julie, tell me how your mother is. Until she called me the other day, I hadn't heard her voice in years. She's doing well?"

Julie nodded. "Yeah. She still works for her parents' copier company as the office manager. She seems to like it." She rinsed a saucepan and handed it to Erin.

"She's still working for them?" Erin said with surprise. "Bless her, because I could never work for my family. Kate is a better woman than I am."

"Erin? This might sound weird, but you and my mom seem very different. I have a hard time seeing you two as friends." In fact, Julie found it impossible to see her mother and Erin hanging out and swapping approaches to socioeconomic policies in between classes and dorm parties.

"We were. We roomed together for three out of the four years. We may be different people now, but when we were in college, we were probably more alike. Your mother was an excellent student, and it came so naturally to her. Did you know that? She's very bright. We chose different paths after we graduated, though. You mother and father were already dating, and they got married a year after they graduated. I worked for a few years and then went to law school. I was simply more career-oriented than your mother. Kate chose a path that was comfortable for her. There's nothing wrong with that, of course. I'm glad she's so happy."

"Did you think she was going to go to law school or something, the way you did?"

"She could have. She certainly had the intellect. It just wasn't what she wanted. Kate wasn't interested in graduate school or a more prominent career. She wanted your father, and she wanted the life she got." Erin paused. "Until...I'm sorry. That was thoughtless."

"It's OK. The divorce is the divorce. It happens all the time, so it's not a big deal."

"They separated when you were about four or five, is that right?"

Julie nodded.

"Do you see him much?"

"Once or twice a year. After the divorce his career really took off, and he just hasn't been able to see me as much as he would like. He's really busy with his job. He comes into town for business sometimes, so I have dinner with him when he can. It's the nature of his work, I guess. I understand."

"He's still with that fancy hotel chain?"

Julie nodded. "Yup. He's the regional vice president for the West Coast. And he's taking me to California over winter break this year. My first Christmas without snow."

"That sounds wonderful," Erin said. "I'm glad you'll have some time with him."

"Yeah. I'm sure it will be great," Julie said. She turned off the water. "I'm glad my mom called you."

"I'm glad Kate called me too."

"I hope you know that I've been doing everything I can to find an apartment. I don't want you to think you'll have to put me up permanently."

"Well, why not?"

"What do you mean?"

Erin shrugged and refilled her wine glass. "Why don't you stay? Free room and board. That's a pretty good deal, don't you think? You shouldn't have to worry about rent and bills and all that nonsense when you should be focusing on school."

"I couldn't let you put me up all year. That doesn't seem right."

"If you have morning classes, then you could take care of Celeste in the afternoons. How about that? She enjoys you. I noticed her hair looked different tonight. Did you do something to it?"

"Oh, yeah," Julie said distractedly. "I did a quick French braid for her. She seemed to like it. So, seriously? You would really be OK with me staying here?"

"Absolutely. What's the big deal? Although I understand that you might prefer to live with friends and experience a more traditional undergraduate social life. You're an adult now, so you should certainly set your own schedule here. I have no interest in monitoring your every move. You're obviously smart and responsible."

Julie thought for a moment. Why not? She'd save her mom a ton of money, and if she found a good deal on an apartment in a few months, she could always move out then. "I'd love to stay, Erin. Really. That's incredibly generous of you. I assume you need to talk to Roger about this, though, and I understand if he doesn't want an unexpected boarder."

Erin waved her hand dismissively. "He won't mind in the least. Besides, he's going off on his trip soon, and we could use an extra hand. And this way Matthew can really apply himself to his studies."

Julie smiled. "OK, then. This sounds great. I like Celeste. A lot."

"Good. Not everyone is respectful of her choices," Erin said pointedly. "You are. Then it's settled." She raised her glass in a toast. "Welcome home."

"You're a lifesaver. Thank you so much," Julie said happily. "I'll go grab the rest of the things from the dinner table."

She started collecting the salt and pepper shakers and the placemats. God, what a relief! This was actually much better than being in a cramped apartment with a bunch of other girls. She'd still be on campus enough to make friends, and now she didn't have to stress out over money or even contemplate going to her father for help. Not that he'd offered, but she knew he would come through if she asked. Of course he would.

Even with four people in the Watkinses' house, it seemed like a wonderfully quiet place to get work done, so she wouldn't have to yell at roommates to turn down music at three in the morning or put a pillow over her head to block out the all-night rager in the building next door. It's not what every eighteen-year-old would want, but it's what Julie wanted.

"I don't know how to thank you." Julie set the placemats and plates on the counter. "I hope Finn won't mind my moving into his room. Will he be back soon? He didn't say when I e-mailed him."

"You've been in touch with Finn?" Erin didn't hide the surprise in her voice. "I didn't know you two...I didn't know. How...funny."

"Yeah. Just a quick message to introduce myself. I guess I felt strange about staying in his room without his knowing."

"The room is all yours." Erin smiled. "Now go run upstairs and unpack. We can't have you living out of suitcases, can we?"

"OK. Thank you so much for letting me stay." Julie headed up the stairs to settle in. No more worrying, no more looking at cockroach-infested slum apartments!

Tonight, Flat Finn stood outside Celeste's bedroom door, tirelessly guarding her while she finished her homework. "S'up, Flat Finn?" Julie leaned in and whispered to the cardboard head, "You and I will be spending more time together, so I expect continued model behavior. Deal? You're thinking about it? I understand. Let me know. Excuse me while I go to your namesake's room and unpack. We'll talk later."

Julie went into what was now her room and looked around. She could happily stay here. A large shelf that held travel guides, photo albums, a series of thick books on rocks and minerals, and a stack of old *Time* and *Newsweek* magazines still left plenty of room for her things. As a whole, the room was a little sparse in some places, which was good because she could easily fill up the empty space.

She unzipped her suitcase and began putting away her now very wrinkled clothes and the few pairs of shoes she'd crammed into the bags. The dresser was empty except for two things: a frayed navy-blue T-shirt with the outline of a skydiver that read, *Don't forget to pull,* and an old sweatshirt that read, *Skydivers like to do it in groups.* Clearly Julie had moved into the witty-shirt family's house.

She pulled her laptop onto the bed and messaged Finn again through Facebook.

Dear Finn–

Hope you don't mind if I hang in your room for a little longer. Your mom suggested I ditch the impossible idea of trying to find

a Boston apt. and stay here. Mornings at college, afternoons with
Celeste, and evenings defending your room against monsters.

    Being a girl and all, I'm resisting the urge to immediately
paint your bedroom pink and plaster the wall with pictures of
unicorns and rainbows. No promises on how long I can hold out.

    How is South Africa? Celeste is waiting for pictures...Hint,
hint.

–Julie

    She put on her robe, gathered what she needed to take into
the shower, and went into the hall. As she passed Matthew's
room, she could hear soft conversation behind his closed door.
He and Erin were talking, and even without being able about to
make out any words, Julie could tell that the tone of their talk
was less than jovial. In fact, they were having a muffled argument. She kept walking and shut the bathroom door.

    The hot shower felt wonderful, and she let the water steam
up the room while she decompressed. It was a relief to be done
worrying about unpleasant logistical issues. Hanging out with
Celeste would be cool. OK, maybe *cool* wasn't the right word.
Unique, unusual, interesting, and challenging. All of Julie's
favorites. Plus, it was impossible not to wonder what Flat Finn
was all about.

    When she got back to her bedroom, she threw on her usual
bedtime outfit, a pair of lightweight pajama bottoms and a tank,
and turned on the television. She found a good celebrity gossip
show and left it on in the background while she sat in bed with her
computer. A number of her friends had e-mailed her with stories
about their first days at college, rumors about her ex-boyfriend,
and early complaints about the miseries of campus dining. She
wrote her friends back and then read a message from Finn.

Julie–

OMG, I love pink! And unicorns! And rainbows! Really. So awesome! I've always wanted one of those super cute posters of a kitten dangling from a tree limb that says, "Hang in there!" Maybe you can find one? My room is gonna be, like, totally the best ever! Julie, you're a peach!

South Africa is definitely fantastic. Rehabilitating elephants this week. Did you know elephant rehab is very similar to human rehab? Well, it is. Except that we don't have hideous artwork hanging on the walls. But we do allow cell phones. Elephants get wicked pissed when they can't call their loved ones or order out for pizza. Canoeing tomorrow and then sleeping in the bush under the stars.

Good luck with the family. Here's a free tip: Matt is a geek.

Tell my girl that I'll send pictures very soon. I'm not the tech nerd that my brother is, but I'll do my best.

–Finn

For some reason, Julie found it reassuring that Finn was as quirky as the rest of the family.

Finn–

KNEW you'd like the new décor! Will search faithfully for coveted kitten poster.

Thanks for the help with the monsters. Worked like a charm. No other tips needed just yet. Your family is very nice. Took Flat Finn grocery shopping, and although I suspect he considered stealing a can of artichoke hearts, he restrained himself. He did, however, eat a handful of trail mix from the bulk bins, but everyone does that.

Yes, Matt is a bit geeky. He's rather proud of that, huh? I should get another free tip since that one was a no-brainer. And will there be a fee for others? I'm on a student budget. I could probably do with a Celeste tip. I'm rather unclear on the Flat Finn situation.

And I can't resist asking: What's up with your "Finn Is God" Facebook name?

–Julie

Finn must have still been online because he replied right away.

Julie–

No worries. House tips will come free of charge.

"Finn Is God" is my attempt to start a new religion. I'm working on a merchandise line now because all good religions come with fashionable accessories. And I wanna be rich.

–Finn

Finn–

I'll take a "Finn Is God" tote bag and a visor.

–Julie

CHAPTER 9

Matthew Watkins *"Sometimes it is useful to know how large your zero is." —Author Unknown.*

Finn Is God *In order for this status update to make any sense, I need you to assume I'm covered in some sort of spray-based cheese product.*

Julie Seagle *thinks that Twitter is like Facebook's slutty cousin. It does everything dumb and whore-ish you're too responsible to do.*

"What's in this one?" Celeste asked.

"I have no idea. Open it up." Julie handed Celeste the scissors and let her cut the tape off the cardboard box. Her room had quickly turned into a disaster area now that the rest of her things had arrived. She had her puffy comforter on the bed and one box of clothes put away.

Celeste opened the box flaps and peered in. "It appears that a beauty parlor has exploded in this box."

"Ooooh, nice!" Julie clapped her hands and turned up the music. "Now, if we can just find the box with the shirt I want to wear tonight, I'll be set."

Dana had texted her earlier and demanded that Julie meet her at a dorm party that night. Jamie had promised he would come too, and Dana was evidently unable to pick out an appropriate outfit without Julie's *divine* fashion sense.

"Celeste, will you pull out the black bag in there for me? Pick out a nail polish color." Julie walked across the bed and hopped to the floor, narrowly missing crashing into Flat Finn, and grabbed more hangers from the closet.

"You have too many colors in here to choose from," Celeste said as she pulled out nail polish bottles and set them in a row on the rug.

Julie held up a pale-blue silky top. "I'm wearing this tonight, so pick something that will look nice with it." She wondered briefly if it would be rude not to invite Matt to come with her, but the thought of showing up at her first—or any—Whitney party with him was not at the top of her list.

Celeste stared at the row of little bottles. "I'm not equipped to make this decision, Julie. I don't want to choose the wrong one. Let me ask Flat Finn."

"No, I want you to pick it out. There is no wrong one, silly." Julie took the deep purple and the bright red and held them up. "Seductive, vampire bad girl versus traditional, hot, all-around sexy gal. There are no losers in this color game. Unless you just buy some stupid color like metallic green. Never do that. So let the nail polish speak to you. You try one."

Celeste nodded seriously and then examined a light-pink bottle. "Whimsical, gentle, and tasteful. A classic?"

"Brilliant! Now give me your toes." Julie sat down in front of Celeste and began applying the polish.

Celeste sat quietly, occasionally peeking at Flat Finn, who stood monitoring the pedicure. "It was her idea, not mine!" she quipped. "He is a bit unsettled by this. I've never had my nails painted."

Julie turned around and glared at Flat Finn. "Every girl has a right to painted nails, so you better get settled quick, Flatty."

Celeste giggled. "Oh, he didn't like that name one bit."

"Tough. OK, give me your fingers now. Different color or the same?"

"I have no idea."

"Here, this one will be nice for you. It looks sort of orange in the bottle, but it's a nice muted red when it's on."

Celeste gave Julie her hand. "I trust you. Although Flat Finn has his doubts because he thinks the color resembles tangerines."

Julie grabbed a shirt from the nearest box and flung it at the figure, landing the shirt perfectly on the cardboard head. "There. Now grumpy boy doesn't have to watch. This is girl stuff anyway." Julie opened the bottle and started on Celeste's fingers before she could protest. "So, it's Saturday night. What are you doing?"

"Flat Finn and I are going to read *All Creatures Great and Small*."

"Sounds like an outrageous evening. Hey, whose piano is that off the front hall? I haven't heard anyone playing." Julie looked at Celeste. "I mean, besides Flat Finn."

"Oh. The piano. I used to play. Not anymore."

"Got bored?"

"Not bored so much as disenchanted. What is your party going to be like?"

Julie shrugged. "Drunk boys, crying girls, loud music." She smiled. "But it'll be fun anyway."

Celeste's eyes widened. "What are your plans for the drunk boys?"

"I'm going to sit them down and give them a long lecture on the unappealing nature of overindulging in beer and Jell-O shots. Then I'll ground them and send them to bed. Alone."

"That is not what I meant. How will you protect yourself?"

"I don't need a plan. They'll be harmless and mildly cute in a pathetically boozy way."

"What if one of them wants to be your boyfriend? What will you do then?"

"I wouldn't worry about it. I'm not looking for a boyfriend anyway." Julie blew across Celeste's nails. "Don't touch anything for at least fifteen minutes."

"Why don't you want a boyfriend?"

"I don't know. Maybe I do. I'd just have to meet the right guy. Someone who isn't ordinary. Someone who gets me. Someone I fit perfectly with. I want heat, chemistry, an undeniable connection. You know what I mean? I want it all. I'm done with ordinary and mediocre."

"You believe in true love," Celeste stated.

"Maybe. I don't know yet."

"So you think that you're going to find true love at this party tonight?"

"Doubtful."

"Why are you going then?"

"For fun. To meet people and make friends. To be eighteen and silly. To escape the existential dreariness of the real world," Julie added dramatically. She set her makeup in front of the floor-length mirror, knotted her hair on top of her head, and started putting on mascara. "Mostly to go flirt. I have to keep my skills honed because I might need them one day."

"I bet it's easy for you," Celeste said as she examined her fingers and toes.

"What? Flirting?"

"Yes."

"Depends. There's *flirting*," Julie said, jokingly pushing her chest out, "and then there's *flirting*." She tapped the side of her temple. "It's the second one that's hard because you're putting more of yourself out there."

Celeste moved to stand next to Julie and looked at herself in the mirror. She turned sideways and then forward again, holding her fingers splayed in front of her so she wouldn't smudge her polish.

"Here. Try this on." Julie handed her a sheer lip gloss.

Celeste took the gloss and examined it as if it were a specimen from the moon. "I really do not think that this is necessary. I do not think that Flat Finn will view this positively."

"It's not *necessary*. But it's what thirteen-year-old girls do. You've never worn makeup?"

Celeste shook her head emphatically. "I cannot begin to imagine what Finn would think."

By the time Julie had turned thirteen, she'd already experimented with numerous disastrous shades of shadow, framed her eyes with crooked streaks of black liner, and infuriated her mother with her embarrassingly large collection of lipstick.

"Here, I'll do it for you." Julie got up and put one hand under Celeste's chin, steadying her face as she dabbed some sheen onto her lips. "A little lip gloss on you won't kill Finn. He'll deal with it."

Celeste's already pale skin became nearly translucent, and her eyes glistened. Julie pulled back. "What's wrong? What did I do?" Great. First Erin and now Celeste. Either this family was insane, or Julie was causing some sort of panic reaction in everyone she came in contact with.

Celeste clamped her hand onto Julie's arm and looked at her. She turned to face the mirror and rubbed her lips together.

A single tear rolled down her cheek as she continued to clutch Julie's arm.

Julie, with the lip-gloss wand still held in front of her, felt her hand tremble slightly. Something was happening to Celeste, something she didn't understand. Julie closed her eyes for a moment. "See what Flat Finn thinks." She pulled off the shirt that she'd tossed at him. "Does he approve?"

Celeste cautiously moved to stand by Flat Finn. She held very still and stared directly into the photographed eyes. The color returned to her cheeks. "Yes. He likes it. He likes it very much." She inhaled and exhaled deeply, and slowly a cautious smile emerged. "Can I watch you put on the rest of your makeup?"

✳✳✳

Julie drove home from the campus party, parked in the driveway, and did her best to shut the car door quietly. She was home later than she'd expected, and although Erin had been quite clear about giving Julie the freedom to come and go as she pleased, it was still hard not to feel some obligation to come home before dawn. She started fiddling with the tricky old lock on the front door, but in the dark, it was tough. The party had been fun, just not fun enough to be worth spending the night on the Watkinses' front porch.

She'd met at least thirty other Whitney students. Although she'd been a bit hesitant about walking into a party alone, it had been a good crowd, and she'd had fun. Even with the beer flowing freely, there was a different feel from high school parties. Yes, there'd been the drunk boys and crying girls she'd predicted, and surprisingly more than enough sober(ish), non-hysterical people. She'd even been hit on a few times, which, while amusing and a little flattering, hadn't led to anything more than the mention of meeting up for coffee between classes. But she was tired and so had ducked out around twelve thirty after Jamie and Dana's public groping session had taken a breather and she'd been able to say good-bye to them.

Julie shut her eyes and focused on the key in the lock, listening for sounds that she was doing something right. After figuring out a combination of rotating the handle just a smidge while wriggling the key as it turned, she made it inside. The house was dark, and Julie tiptoed up the stairs to the second floor. In the quiet, she noticed that the fifth step from the bottom creaked loudly, the sound echoing up the stairwell. She'd have to remember that.

Matthew's door was ajar and his light on. Julie tapped lightly on the door, causing it to swing open. "Matt?"

"Hey, Julie." Matt was crouched over his computer, obviously wide awake.

She walked in and sat down on the bed. "What are you doing?"

"Working myself into a frenzy over an online debate about people who go around breaking into computer systems and claim their only reason for doing so is to expose security weaknesses."

"Oh. You didn't go out tonight?"

"Nope." He was still looking at the screen. "My father had a work party, so my parents were out until about an hour ago. Someone had to stay with Celeste."

Most thirteen-year-olds would have pitched a fit at having their brother stay home with them. For reasons Julie didn't understand yet, Celeste needed someone around all the time.

Julie leaned back on her hands and crossed her legs, bouncing one leg up and down. "Flat Finn couldn't do it?"

"His general incompetence reaches monumental and dangerous proportions," he said absently. "Totally untrustworthy."

"I feel bad that I had the car. You mom didn't mention they were going out when she said I should take it tonight."

"They prefer to walk."

Julie looked around. His bedroom looked more like an office than a college student's room. The only thing on the wall was a poster with a freaky glowing nebula thing and an incomprehensible equation. "What is that?" she asked.

"The poster? It's the dynamics of electromagnetic radiation shown through Maxwell equations."

"It's extremely decorative. Gives the room a warm touch."

Matt tapped the keyboard.

"I went to a party at school tonight. It was all right. Nothing thrilling."

She wondered again if she'd had some social obligation to invite him. They *were* living in the same house after all. She could have just introduced him as the son of the family she was staying with so that she wouldn't have scared off any potential dates. But maybe she wasn't that good a person. Plus, there was something about his tone tonight that was rather pissy and cold. He looked sort of pathetic here, slumped in his swivel chair, his evening's social activities confined to communicating with other loner boys. Not most people's idea of a raging Saturday night.

Matt was frowning at one of the forum messages. "Idiots. How anyone can justify hacking into the Chicago transit system? Yeah, *sure* we all think that guy was trying to prevent *someone else* from using access for malicious intent!" He turned back to Julie. "Sorry. What?"

"I said that the party was all right. I'm glad I went."

"Good."

"Listen, Matt," she started. Great. He was already back on his stupid forum. Maybe he didn't feel like talking, but something was bothering her. Especially with the way he could barely look at her. "Matt? Can I ask you something?"

"Yeah?"

"I didn't mean to, but I kind of heard you and your mom the other day. It sounded like a bit of an argument. I can't help wondering if it was about my staying here." Julie fidgeted with her watch strap. "Are you not OK with it? I mean, I would understand. Really. This strange girl moves into your house with no notice, takes over your brother's room, makes you eat metaphoric manicotti. I get it. Probably not what every boy dreams about."

Matt smirked as he typed. "I never said you were strange."

"That was an expression." Julie waited for him to say something else, but he didn't. She stood up and walked to the door. "Well, I'm sorry."

"Wait, what?" Matt looked up. "No, Julie. It's fine."

She stopped just outside the hall. "You don't mind that I'm here?"

"No. It makes sense. We've got an extra room."

Gee, thanks for the enthusiasm. "At least you won't have to come home to be with Celeste in the afternoons, since I'll be doing that. You'll get more work done, right?"

"That's true," he agreed. "I will. Just don't bother Celeste about Flat Finn, and everything will be fine."

"OK. Good. Well, good night."

"Good night, Julie."

She went to her room and shut the door. If Matt was cranky, it didn't seem to have anything to do with her. But there was still something bothering her. She yawned and opened her laptop. Maybe Finn could help.

Finn–

Hey. Are you online? I need that advice sooner than I expected. Wondering if you can help me with Celeste. I think I did something wrong and upset her. We had a little girl time today, which was great, and then...I don't know. I must have done something wrong, I can't think what. For a minute there, I thought she was going to cry. I feel terrible, and I'm worried she's mad at me. I hope she is all right with my being here because your brother seems less than thrilled. I know there is something going on with Celeste, and Matt won't talk about it. I'd like to help her out, but I'm at a loss.

Oh, and you could have told me about the tricky front lock and the creaky step! I'm lucky I didn't wake your parents up at this hour!

–Julie

Julie got into her pajamas and then took her laptop into bed. Two minutes ago, Finn had commented under Matt's post: *Mom used to make us take baths together. Believe me, your "zero" is nothing to brag about.* Julie laughed.

Yup, Finn was online. Her e-mail dinged.

Julie–

Celeste? Yeah. She's complicated. I'm sure you didn't do anything wrong. I can tell that you already care about her, and I'm glad. My parents consulted some highly respected shrink who thinks that Flat Finn is a creative response to nerves about starting a new school, missing me. Stuff like that. They were advised to just wait it out and support her. She freaks out if anyone hints Flat Finn might not be the most appropriate companion.

My parents went through a ton of babysitters who were less tolerant of Flat Finn than you are, so you're obviously doing something right. She wants you there. In fact, I got an e-mail from her tonight saying how great you were, that you did her hair up the other day, that you cooked dinner together, etc. She sounded really happy, so that makes me happy. (Oh, did she tell you that I sent her a few pictures?) Don't worry. It sounds like you're doing great. The best advice I can give you is to just let Celeste do her thing. Ignore Matt. He'll get over whatever problem he has.

Fifth step from the bottom? Sorry. I should have warned you. Slipped my mind. And the lock? You got the knob turn/key jiggle maneuver down already? Impressive. That one took me years to perfect. What were you doing out so late? Were you sneaking home late from a hot date already? In Boston only a few days, and you've already snagged a man. Celeste said you're a romantic. Hope he took you to dinner and the opera before returning you home so late. ☺

–Finn

Finn–

Yes, incredibly hot date tonight. I've only been in town a few days, and I've already snagged a native Bostonian, whom I plan on totally corrupting with my college girl wiles. I refused both the four-star restaurant and the boring opera tickets, and just dragged him to a cheap motel. I came home with smeared lipstick, my hair a mess, and my shirt inside out. How's that for romance, baby!

Or, I just went to a party on campus, chatted for a few hours, and came home alone. You decide.

OK, I'll try not to screw things up with Celeste. But Flat Finn can't just be about missing you. It's not just the flat you that's... well, different about her. I'm really confused. I'm missing an enormous puzzle piece here. How long have you been gone? Can you call home so Celeste could at least talk to you? And when are you coming back, BTW? Now that I've taken over your room, you might have to fight me for it.

I want to see pictures too! My travel experience is limited to a selection of boring cities in Ohio, one excruciating weekend in Jacksonville to visit some senile fourth cousin of my mother's, and a trip to Yosemite one summer where I stepped on a wasp's nest and was stung seven times.

–Julie

Julie–

Not sure when I'll be home. I'm really entrenched in all of this traveling business and have committed to volunteering for a number of different places. I'm going on a two-week scuba diving trip not far from here (just for fun), and then I'm off to coach kids' football in Ghana. I lost my phone in Palau and trying to replace it when moving around so much is a nightmare. I hop on computers at volunteer headquarters, etc. when I can, but phone service is usually sketchy where I am.

Here are the pics I sent Celeste. (I do have one picture of a senile Ohio wasp, but I don't want to make you feel nostalgic.)

I choose boring campus party.

–Finn

Julie checked out the three pictures he'd attached to his message. Any non-brain-dead girl would be impressed. The two photos of him standing next to an elephant were great, but the best one was a shot of Finn sitting on a boulder looking out at a sunset. Fine, it was a little corny. She didn't care. Even though his face was shadowed, she could still see how handsome he was. The way his cheekbones caught the light, the hint of a smile on his face, his arm muscles peeking through his shirt.

Then she did what any girl would do: she Googled him. Eight minutes of scrolling through search results and clicking on links got her nowhere, although she did learn that there was a Finn Watkins who played drums for a rather successful college band called Eggs Benedict and that a Finneas Watkins from New Jersey had won a 2006 award for his classical ballet performance. None of the results produced any information about her Finn. Well, not *her* Finn, but...whatever. This was annoying. Not that Googling herself yielded any information either, but it would have been nice to find something.

She looked at the pictures again. Yes, indeed. Finn was cute. Super cute. And funny, smart, and charming. And he adored his sister. And did amazing volunteer work in between adventurous travels. And...

Julie stopped herself. This was silly. She couldn't possibly have a crush on someone she'd only exchanged a few messages with, right? Because that would be abnormal. Insane. Completely not based in reality. She was not that desperate. Besides, Boston was likely teeming with smart, adorable boys. Not that having a boyfriend was really a priority, but it wouldn't be awful.

And while the pictures were attractive and distracting, she hadn't failed to notice that Finn had not answered her questions about Celeste.

CHAPTER 10

"What if the clip comes out?" Celeste squirmed as Julie fixed her hair.

"It won't."

"It might."

Julie walked from behind the kitchen chair and stood in front of Celeste. "It won't. On the off chance that it does, I can assure you that your hair will fall into gorgeous, billowing curls because of the anti-frizz serum I ran through your hair. And because you have naturally fantastic hair that most people can never achieve, even when they waste money buying celebrity-endorsed spiral curling irons on the off chance that three easy payments of nineteen-ninety-five will solve their hair woes. Just don't touch your hair. And here's the scarf I said would match the sweater I lent you perfectly."

Celeste eyed the pale blue scarf suspiciously. "This is not a scarf. A scarf is thick and warm and only needed in the winter."

"Oh my God. Relax, kid. This scarf is just an accessory. Like earrings or a belt. It's long and gorgeous with a little shimmer to it." Julie wrapped the scarf once around Celeste's neck and smiled. "The color brings out your eyes. Now here, take my iPod, listen to the playlist I made you, and completely ignore Matt when he drives you to school. Then when you get out of the car, glare at him with solid disgust and slam the door."

"Why would I do that? I do not consider that a fitting response to his driving me to school."

Julie sighed. "Fine, forget that last part. But at least listen to the playlist. I'm obsessed with this local band, In Like Lions. You'll love them. Support the indies, kid."

Celeste scrolled through the music Julie had picked out for her. "But usually Matty and I do reasoning games and logic questions in the car. I don't think he'll like this. And I don't know any of these songs."

"Big deal. I'll handle Matt, and you handle the Top Forty. OK, stand up and spin around. Let me check you out."

Celeste dutifully allowed Julie to assess her outfit. Matt entered the kitchen—a messenger bag across his chest and a stack of Internet printouts in his hand—as Julie was adjusting the sweater sleeves.

"Morning, Matt," Julie said. "Celeste looks nice today, doesn't she?"

"Morning. Celeste always looks nice." Matt hurried past them to grab a banana from the counter. "Why is she wearing a scarf?"

Julie practically snorted. "You two are definitely related."

Matt talked through a mouthful of fruit. "It's not winter. We have to get moving. You ready?"

Celeste nodded and took her backpack from the floor. "Julie, are you sure this scarf is a good choice for me?"

"You are a beautiful girl, and it doesn't really matter what you wear. I like the scarf on you, but take it off if you want. As long as you don't borrow your brother's T-shirts, you'll be stunning." Julie turned to Matt. "Don't think that bag strap is hiding your shirt from me. I can still read it." Today's T-shirt said: *ME: like you, only better.* "You're straight out of *GQ*, Matt."

"I do my best. Come on, Celeste. Julie, do you want a ride? I just have to run a few errands after I drop her off, and then I'll be back for a few hours before I have to be at school."

"No thanks. I have to leave in a few minutes for class, and I don't mind walking to the T."

"Bye, Julie. Thanks for the scarf. I guess. And my hair." Celeste followed Matt out of the room.

"And the music. Don't forget to listen to the music!" Julie called after her. "I'll see you after school!"

Julie sat down at the kitchen table and sipped her coffee while she went over her schedule for the week.

"Hello," Roger said as he came into the room. "Oh, you made coffee? Wonderful. I'll make a cup for Erin. We're both biking to work today, and we have these delightful cup holders that fit right on the handlebars."

"It's a beautiful day for a ride," Julie said. And it was. The humidity had vanished over the weekend, and the temperature had dropped to a comfortable seventy-five degrees.

"What do you have there?" Roger asked as he filled two stainless travel cups. "Is that your course schedule?"

Julie nodded. "Yeah. First day of classes today."

Erin breezed past her, clad in dark pants and a short-sleeve dress shirt, her outfit completed by a bike helmet and riding gloves. "What's on the educational agenda for today?"

"Applied Calculus and then Intro to Psych," Julie said. "Those are both Monday, Wednesday, and Friday classes. I'll be home with plenty of time to get Celeste, though, so don't worry."

"Applied Calculus, huh? Didn't you do that in high school?" Erin asked.

"I took an AP calc class, and this seems to be the next step. Tuesdays and Thursdays, I have Intro to Eighteenth-Century Literature and then Economics of Poverty in the US."

Erin adjusted her bike helmet and grabbed two water bottles from the fridge. "That's a good first-semester schedule you've chosen. Roger, are we set?"

"We are. Don't forget that I have my final pretrip meeting tonight, so I won't be home until late. Julie, hope your first day of classes goes well." He patted her shoulder as he walked past her. "I'll grab my gear and meet you out front, Erin."

"I don't know what time Matt will be back from school. If he isn't home by six, would you order dinner for us from the Bulgarian restaurant? The menu is by the phone, and they have our credit card on file." Erin tucked a strand of hair under her helmet. "Enjoy yourself, college girl." Erin turned to leave and then stopped. "I hope this isn't an awkward question, Julie, but do you have money for your textbooks? I know how overpriced they can be."

"I just got my financial-aid check, and since I'm not paying rent now, I should be fine."

"Don't be shy about letting me know if you need help with anything."

Julie could think of a number of nonfinancial things that she'd like help with. *Gee, would you like to tell me why the hell your teenage daughter is glued at the hip to a cardboard brother, has no friends, barely leaves the house, and is a complete social misfit? Huh?* But considering she didn't want to disrupt her happy housing arrangement and the fact that Matt had specifically told her not to bring this up with Erin and Roger, she kept her mouth shut. "I can't think of anything."

"I'm serious, Julie. I don't want you to go without whatever school materials you need. Ask if you need help." She turned to the front door and charged forward. "I'm coming, Roger! You might as well get a head start, since I'm going to beat you anyway!"

Julie laughed and reached for the *New York Times*. She was a bit surprised that she wasn't more nervous for her first day of classes. Eager, yes, but not the least bit nervous. She was finally where she wanted to be.

✳✳✳

Julie glared at the test in front of her. Fine, *now* she was nervous. She hadn't taken a test since last spring, and she hadn't even thought about anything calculus-related in months, but within three seconds of stepping into her class, the professor had informed Julie that she might be able to skip Applied Calculus and transfer into Multivariable Calculus.

My, my! It was hard to think of anything more appealing.

Julie surmised that she must have just been radiating derivatives and explicit functions, because she certainly hadn't requested the opportunity to place out. The only reason she'd signed up for calculus was to get her math requirement out of the way as early as possible, because who the hell wanted to be stuck cramming a last-minute math course into her senior year?

Julie crossed her legs and started on the test. She was alone in a classroom with a teaching assistant, who was presumably sitting with her to make sure she didn't frantically call some math-geek hotline. Or Matt. But as she moved through the test, it turned out that she didn't really need any help. Yes, a few of the questions were beyond her, but a lot of the material she knew either from her AP high school class or because she just... knew it somehow.

When she was done, the TA took her paper. "I'll score this and have the professor call you later today to give you the results. If you've passed, Multivariable Calc meets at the same time, so you'll have an easy transfer."

"That's *excellent*! I can't wait," Julie said, not bothering to hide her sarcasm. She wondered briefly if she could refuse to make the transfer if she passed, but that seemed lame. Even if she wasn't aching to devote her life to vector fields, she couldn't justify taking the easy way out.

Intro to Psych proved to be fun, and Dana was in this class with her. The professor, Dr. Cooley, was wildly enthusiastic about the field and even handed out copies of Freudian slip cartoons along with the lengthy syllabus.

Dr. Cooley erased the whiteboard and addressed the class. "I know this is a big group, and I don't want anyone to get lost. You have all my contact information and my office hours. Use them. I want to hear from you. I want to help you." He turned and set his hands on his hips. "I like teaching, and I like students, and I want to learn from you as much as you want to learn from me."

When class was over, Julie and Dana filed out of the large lecture hall. "I can't stand these huge classes," Dana growled. "These stupid required courses are always so congested. I can't wait until I'm in Evolutionary Psych with, like, five other students."

"You're going to be a psychology major?" Julie asked.

Dana smoothed down her already immaculate straight bangs and wiped nonexistent mascara smudges from under her eyes. "I've known for years. Both my parents are shrinks too. Whitney has a really good program, and Dr. Cooley is highly regarded in the field." She glanced at her watch. "Damn. I was supposed to meet Jamie at the student union for coffee ten minutes ago. I forgot how long this class was. You want to come?"

"I'd love to, but I have to get home, get the car, and pick up Celeste. Rain check?"

"I'll hold you to it." Dana buttoned her blazer with one hand and adjusted her stack of folders with the other. "Call me later."

By the time Julie made it home, changed clothes, and packed Flat Finn into the car, she was running a few minutes late to get Celeste. She sat at a stoplight and swore. The gas tank was nearly empty. Dangerously empty. The only gas station she knew was in the opposite direction, and it seemed to make more sense to go there than to hope she passed one before she ran out. Pulling an illegal U-turn seemed a good way to christen herself into the world of Boston driving. She gunned the car down the road, swearing at every stop light, and peeled into the gas station.

As Julie jabbed the nozzle into the gas tank, she simultaneously sulked and panicked: it was the first day of her official Celeste duties, and she was already screwing up. Celeste didn't seem like the typical kid who wouldn't give a damn if Julie were late. Not that Julie could guess how Celeste would react to a shift in schedule, but she wasn't dying to find out. She tapped her foot anxiously as the numbers rolled over in the pump. Had she selected the slowest possible pump in the entire country? Obviously. *Come on, come on,* she pleaded silently. The gas seemed to be trickling into the car, microscopic drop by microscopic drop. Who leaves the goddamn gas tank empty? After what felt like an endless wait, she had managed to drip a few gallons of gas into the car.

She got back into the car and fumbled with the keys. Why was she so shaky? Celeste would be fine. There wasn't anything to be done about being late, and no one to blame. Except Flat Finn.

"I was warned about your frequent failure to refill the tank!" she hollered. "Not only that, but you're *so* inflexible. And I don't mean disciplined. I mean literally inflexible. It takes way too long to get you into the car, and you don't help out in the least. I don't want to hear any complaints about how I smacked your elbow into the spare tire, OK, Flatty? Just deal with it."

Julie flew out of the station and raced to Celeste's school. She pulled into the pickup lane, nearly empty now, and slammed on the brakes, causing the Volvo to squeal loudly. Celeste was nowhere to be seen. She could hear Matthew's voice echoing loudly in her head. *She's rather regimented...You can't promise anything.* Who knew what might happen because Julie was so late? She still hadn't identified what had upset Celeste the other night in Finn's room, but being this late and off-schedule would surely be a bigger deal.

Julie got out of the car and rushed to the sidewalk in front of the building. "Celeste?" she called. She ran her hands through her hair as she scanned a group of girls who sat on the lawn. God, she could feel her heart racing. How ridiculous that she was panicking about being a few minutes late to give someone a ride home. A few straggling students walked past her. "Celeste!" she said more loudly. "Hey!" She grabbed a boy with spiked hair and a ripped Nine Inch Nails shirt by the sleeve. "Have you seen Celeste Watkins?"

"The loser chick with blond hair who talks weird?"

Julie narrowed her eyes and squeezed his shirt in her hand. "I'll accept your insulting description only because I don't have time to argue with you. So, yes, spiky boy who likely has a behavioral problem and outrageously disappointed parents, *that* Celeste. Where is she?"

"Sitting up there." He nodded in the direction of the covered walkway that ran alongside the building. "But you could blow her off and hang out with us." His friends whooped with laughter and made idiotic catcalls.

"That sounds highly entertaining. Really. I'm attracted to you in the most powerful way, but the odds that I might twist your mouthy little head off with my hands is increasing by the minute. So I'm gonna pass." Julie released her grip on his shirt and turned away. *Idiot.*

She held her hand up to her eyes to block the sun as she walked away in search of Celeste, eventually finding her sitting on one of the concrete benches. Her hands were in her lap, and her head hung down. This was worse than Julie thought. If Celeste was having some kind of nutty meltdown, Julie would never forgive herself.

"Celeste!" Julie waved. "Celeste!" *Oh, no.* Celeste wouldn't even look at her. Julie kept walking closer. "I'm so sorry. Stupid Matt didn't put gas in the car, so that's why I'm late, and—"

Julie stopped, a proud smile slowly taking over her worried face. Celeste was not, in fact, collapsed in a depressive state; she was listening to Julie's iPod. And tapping her foot. Talk about worrying needlessly.

Eventually Celeste looked up. "Oh! I'm sorry, Julie!" she screamed. "I like this playlist that you created for me!"

Julie giggled and put a finger to her lips. "Shhhh," she said.

"Oh." Celeste removed the earphones. "I imagine that I was talking too loudly just now, wasn't I? I'm sorry. I had the volume at a very high level, and the world sort of disappeared." She paused, smiling. "It was rather nice."

"Don't worry about it. No one is around." Julie grabbed Celeste's bag. "Come on. There's a coffee shop I saw near your house that I want to check out. Big comfy chairs, weird art, mystical brews. It'll be cool."

Celeste stood up slowly and began to follow Julie to the car. "Perhaps you can take me home first and then visit this place yourself?"

"Nope." Julie kept walking. "The three of us are going in." She heard Celeste's footsteps quicken behind her. "Yes, the three of us. There's nothing to worry about. Move it, or you're paying for drinks."

"You have a very unusual approach, Julie." Celeste caught up to her. "But I am willing to play along."

"Good. So is Flat Finn."

CHAPTER 11

Matthew Watkins *"All one word" should be spelled...Oh, never mind. This joke is stupid.*

Finn Is God *Considering taking freelance job titling potential porn movies. Working on title involving "Oh, Susannah," and "Pie for Me." Thoughts?*

Julie Seagle *Attempting to perfect tricky Boston accent, but currently sound more like Robin Williams than Matt Damon. Dammit. Success is elusive.*

Julie leaned against the counter and looked up at Java Genius's chalkboard menu. "I need a type of icy, frothy, coffee-chocolate concoction," she said leadingly.

The guy behind the counter crossed his arms. "Do you mean a Frappuccino?"

Julie clicked her tongue. "Close. A little less powerful. Something more like...I don't know...."

He sighed. "A Dunkin' Donuts Coolatta?"

"Bingo!"

The barista set his forearms on the counter and leaned in to Julie, smiling. "We have a Mocha Heatbuster that I think you'll like. Anything for your friend? Or friends?" The coffee guy pointed to the couch by the window, where Celeste sat upright on a couch with Flat Finn standing next to her, facing the open room. At least nobody else was here for now, and Flat Finn could easily pass as some sort of garish advertisement for vitamin-enhanced water should other people show up.

"Yes, two smoothies. A mango yogurt for him and a chocolate banana for her," Julie said, straight-faced.

He looked into Julie's eyes, his own glistening as he tried not to smile. "Will that be it?"

"For now. One of us may need another drink in a bit. In fact, one of us may *really* need a drink in a bit. Those two are a lot to handle, but we'll try to keep it down."

"I'm used to it. We get all types in here. This is Cambridge, after all."

Julie watched as he made their drinks. He had nice arms, and she involuntarily lowered her gaze when he turned around. *Oh, my.* He had a lot of nice parts. The styled black hair and green eyes didn't hurt either.

She reached inside her purse, but he stopped her and tipped his head toward Flat Finn. "Don't worry about it. Your special guest entitles you to free beverages."

Julie flinched. Goddamn Flat Finn was making for a perfectly weird flirty exchange. "Thank you, um…?"

"Seth."

"Seth. Thank you, Seth. I'm Julie." She cleared her throat and tried to come up with an excuse as to why she was out for coffee with a flat boy. Telling him that a thirteen-year-old girl needed to cart around a flat version of her brother for a mysterious reason probably wouldn't fly. "I'm doing an experiment for my psych class. Recording people's reactions to the presence of a life-sized cardboard cutout in various situations."

"Sure you are." He stepped back and held his hands out to the side. "In that case, how am I doing? C'mon, what's the assessment? Am I passing?"

Julie tucked her hair behind her ears and tried to look serious. "It's not a question of doing well or poorly. It's just an objective collection of data." She picked up her drink and couldn't help grinning. "But you're doing well so far."

"I'm relieved," Seth said. "Do you want help carrying those drinks? That guy you came with doesn't look very helpful. Chivalry is dead these days, I guess."

"He has his moments. Now doesn't seem to be one of them. And he's not actually *my* guest."

"So does this mean there's any chance you're single?"

She winked at him. "I think it's too soon for you to ask me that."

"Fair enough."

Celeste was poised stiffly on the end of a purple velvet couch, a bustle of leaves from a potted ficus tree dangling just above her head. Seth set the chocolate banana drink on the coffee table in front of her and held the mango smoothie out. "What should I—"

"Just put that one down," Julie advised.

"OK. Hi," he said as he held his hand out to Celeste. "I'm Seth."

Celeste was breathing audibly, but she took his hand. "Celeste."

"Mind if I sit down?"

Celeste sized him up. "I think that decision is up to Julie. You are interested in her romantically, correct?" she said robotically.

"I think it's too soon for you to ask me that," he said. It was his turn to wink at Julie. "But yes, I am."

"Let's let him stay. I'm sure he'll have another customer any minute, and then we can talk about him behind his back." Julie sat down next to Celeste and tried her drink. "As blended coffee beverages go, this one is not bad."

"Maybe you'll be a regular customer then?" Seth dropped into the cushy armchair in front of them. "Maybe all of you will? I would not complain if two beautiful women with a non-threatening guest wanted to stop in every day."

Julie pretended to pout. "Celeste, I think he's hitting on you."

Celeste blushed nearly scarlet red and hurriedly reached for her drink. The pins in her hair had held up, and with the decent outfit on, she not only looked her age, but also looked especially pretty. "*Julie*," she scolded softly, but the tone of her voice had lightened. She couldn't hide her obvious enjoyment at being complimented.

Seth laughed and slouched over, resting his arms on his legs. "Ah, if I were only a few years younger, then definitely. As it is, I'll have to settle for shamelessly hitting on Julie. What do you think, Celeste? Do you think she'll go out with me?"

Normal color had returned to Celeste's cheeks, and she looked seriously at him. "How old are you?"

"Nineteen."

"Do you work here full-time?"

"I'm a sophomore at BU. I work here a few afternoons a week and sometimes weekends. I'm majoring in political stud-ies," Seth said, accepting that an interrogation had begun.

Celeste began firing off questions. "Where do you live?" "Do you have misbehaved roommates?" "Do you have any pets? Do you have any misbehaved pets?" "Are you a good driver?" and on and on.

Seth, to his credit, answered every question thoroughly and respectfully. He lived in one of the dorm rooms and had one roommate, who was a transfer student from Nebraska and so far had not proven to be misbehaved. No pets, as the college wouldn't allow it, but one day Seth would like to have a pot-bellied pig. He had only had one speeding ticket (forty in a thirty-mile-an-hour zone), and he had paid the ticket promptly and had never had a car accident. "No accidents in Boston is a big deal, so I want extra credit for that."

"Noted," Celeste said.

"OK, that's plenty." Julie cut off the line of questioning. She couldn't help noting the irony of Celeste assessing anyone's emotional stability. "I think we've determined that Seth is not a psychotic nut."

"He doesn't seem to be," Celeste agreed. "I think you should go out with him."

Seth clapped his hands together. "Yeah? OK, I have one vote for yes. I just need one more...one more! What's it gonna be? What's it gonna be?"

"Sure, why not?" Julie agreed.

"Yes!" He threw his hands up in victory. "Friday night? Seven o'clock?"

"OK," she said.

"This is going to be a real date, I assume?" Celeste asked. "You are not going to take her to a tawdry, rambunctious college party, are you?"

"No. Definitely not. I promise I will take Julie somewhere nice. Dinner and then something else respectable to be determined." The front door swung open, and a flood of customers came in. "I have to go take care of them, but can I call you?" Seth pulled his cell from his pocket and programmed in Julie's number. "I'm glad you both came in today. You two are much cuter than the stuffy English professor and her mother who were here before you. Julie? I'll talk to you soon." He returned to his job behind the counter.

Huh. Julie had a date. She smiled and put her feet up on the table. Seth was probably going to want an explanation regarding Flat Finn, but he seemed nice, and she could picture him tolerating Celeste's issues. Julie still wasn't quite clear on the scope of Flat Finn's purpose. Well, at least he was an attractive enough cardboard brother.

"We could come here and do homework together in the afternoons. It's pretty quiet here," Julie suggested.

"It is something to consider." Celeste rose and examined the paperback books that sat on a shelf. "Do you think you will fall in love with Seth?"

"I have no idea. I've known him for twenty minutes. That's not something you know immediately. At least I don't think so."

"You said that you didn't want ordinary. How do you know that he is not ordinary? Maybe he will turn out to be dull and uninspiring. Or worse, maybe he will make you adore him and then suddenly disappear and break your heart."

"Nice positive attitude you have," Julie said, frowning. "Those are all possibilities, but I think I'll give him a chance anyway. It's worth the risk."

"I do not know about that."

Julie sunk further into the cushy couch. "I'm no expert. What the hell do I understand about boyfriends and love anyway? The only way I'm going to learn is by trying."

"I think that is valiant of you. Fearless." Celeste took a book of short stories from the collection and sat back down to read. "I find it a good sign that they have reading material here. This is an inviting atmosphere."

Julie pulled out her phone and checked her mail. "Hey, Finn wrote to us. With pictures."

Celeste leaned over excitedly and stared at the screen. "What did he say? Quick! Where is he now?"

"It seems he's on the scuba-diving leg of his trip. Look." Julie angled the screen so Celeste could see the photos of Finn dressed in a full wet suit, snorkel, mask, and air tank. He was saluting the camera in one and falling off a boat in another. The third was taken underwater, and he was surrounded by a school of fish.

Dear Celeste and Julie

In a rush right now, so you both get the same message. Deal with it! You can now refer to me as Scuba Man. My new name entitles me to superhero status, so I expect both of you to give me the appropriate respect. My skills include cutting myself on barnacles, swimming at an Olympic pace to evade sharks, and collecting sand in uncomfortable places in my wet suit. Don't be jealous; not everyone can be as powerful as I am. Future powers to be determined.

–Finn

Celeste beamed. "Isn't Finn funny? I love him."

"Does he ever call the house so you can talk to him?" Julie asked.

"No. Absolutely not," Celeste said sharply. "I asked him not to. It makes it easier for me. I would rather just wait to speak with him in person."

"I can understand that. And at least you have all these messages and pictures, right?"

The door opened again, and more people came in. Celeste tightened her hold on the book in her hand. "I would like to go home now," she said. "I need to go home. Right now. *Right. Now.*"

"Sure. If that's what you want." Julie stood up and went to lift Flat Finn.

"I will do it," Celeste hissed. "I will do it."

"A couple of contractions here and there wouldn't kill you," Julie muttered.

She took their drinks while Celeste moved rigidly, picking up Flat Finn with her usual awkwardness. Julie walked ahead, past two teen boys seated with two girls at a table near the exit, calling out their orders to a friend in line. Her heart sank. They must be the reason for the sudden need to leave. Julie cringed as she held the door open and watched Celeste march stoically past them, careful not to look their way. There was a small hope that the teens had conjured up a sane explanation for Flat Finn's presence. The advantage of being in a major city was that there were weird things to see anywhere. For all she knew, there were cardboard boys riding the T and auditing classes at Harvard. But one of the boys looked at the cardboard Finn and tapped the girl on his left to show her. She turned her head and giggled, her eyes wide and mocking.

Celeste brushed past Julie, onto the sidewalk.

They go to school with Celeste. Julie could tell.

She turned toward Seth at the counter and waved. "Thanks for letting us borrow your display for our theater performance," she said loudly. "We'll return it in good condition!"

Seth looked quizzically at Julie and then nodded slowly. "Yeah. Sure thing. Don't damage it, or you won't get your deposit back."

Julie shut the door and caught up with Celeste. "Do you know them? Those kids?"

Celeste shrugged.

"You know them, don't you?" Julie unlocked the car and took Flat Finn from Celeste.

"Perhaps," she answered sharply. Celeste got into the passenger seat and slammed the door.

Julie gently positioned Flat Finn and shut the trunk. She walked slowly to the front of the car, trying to figure out what to say.

Celeste clasped her hands together. "I have to start a history paper today, so we need to get home."

"We're going." The engine rolled over noisily. God, did anyone take this car in for regular maintenance?

"I have yet to determine which topic I will be doing, so we need to get home right now."

"Jesus, Celeste, we're going!"

Celeste scowled and retrieved Julie's iPod from her bag. She put the earphones in and turned away.

Julie smiled. Well, *that* was damned normal.

CHAPTER 12

Matthew Watkins *My visit to the O.K. Corral was…well…*

Finn Is God *I "Facebook like" you, but I'm not IN "Facebook like" with you.*

Julie Seagle *A typical espresso only has 1/3 the caffeine of a regular-size cup of coffee, so all you snobs can bite me. I can out-caffeine you any day. Of course, I can't pretend to be a giant using a non-giant's cup, but I'll deal.*

Julie checked the clock in Matt's room. She still had half an hour to kill before Seth picked her up, and she'd been hanging out in Matt's room, hoping to distract herself before her date. So far he hadn't been very chatty, but at least he didn't seem to mind that she was in there pestering him. Celeste was reading *The Great Gatsby* aloud to Flat Finn, Erin was having dinner with colleagues, and Roger had already left for his shrimp-study trip. The family was used to his frequent traveling by now, and nobody had made a fuss about his departure. Julie, however, had slipped a *"Have a good trip!"* card into his briefcase. Julie knew that her own father couldn't be with her as much as he would choose, and so she wanted to let Roger know that she was supportive and understanding. Both were fathers who loved their children, but work demands were work demands.

Just as he'd promised, Seth had called a few days after they met to get directions to the house. He was taking her to a restaurant downtown and then to a late showing at the Omni Theater, located in the Museum of Science.

She flopped back down on Matt's bed and tried to pay attention to her copy of Voltaire's *Candide*. It was hard to focus knowing that Seth would be there soon. Julie had never gone out with someone on a formal date before. Not that they were actually going anywhere formal, obviously, but it felt a bit old-fashioned to have a scheduled day and time to be picked up by a boy. High school had been much more about just hanging out together. Everything then had felt so casual and relatively meaningless—based mostly on convenience. This date felt different. Seth had gone out of his way to ask her out, and Julie liked that.

She watched Matt squint seriously at his computer as though at any moment he was about to make a breakthrough discovery that would earn him the Nobel Prize for some incomprehensible scientific digital-magnetic-opti-something or other. Well, if he won, she would valiantly take him clothes shopping so that he could attend the awards ceremony in something besides the awful shirt that he had on.

"Matt?"

"Yeah?" he said distractedly.

"Let's discuss your choice of attire for the evening."

Matt hit the touchpad a few times. "Really? What aspects would you like to discuss?"

"Let's discuss how lame it is."

"That doesn't sound like the opening of a discussion. It sounds as if you've already made up your mind about how you feel, so I'm not sure what's left to discuss."

Julie rolled onto her side. "I'd like to hear the thought process you went through when selecting that shirt. Let's face it, there are thousands of clothing options out there for you to choose from, and yet, despite many stylish shirts that could flatter you, you selected that one. So I'd like to hear what led to the purchase. Ready? Go."

Matt backed his swivel chair from the desk and turned toward her, resting his palms on his knees. "The shirt says *Geek*. What's to talk about?"

Julie looked at the print on the shirt again and groaned. "The shirt is a nice shade of blue. I'll give you that. Otherwise I don't think it conveys much that's positive about you."

"It positively conveys that I'm a geek."

"Ha ha. Very funny."

"You may find my label unappealing, but it could be worse. At least I'm not a font nerd."

"A what?"

Matt smiled. "You know. People who love fonts. There are people who go to a movie and get agitated because, while the movie is supposed to be set in 1962, the restaurant awning shown in the background of some scene is printed in Arras Bold, which wasn't invented until 1991, so clearly the producers of this movie are insane and should be beheaded."

Julie shook her head. "You're totally lying. Nobody cares about that crap."

"I'm not lying. Look." He picked up his laptop and sat down next to Julie on the bed. "A simple search is all the proof you'll need." Within seconds he'd pulled up thousands of search results verifying the existence of these font nerds. "There's even a shirt for them."

"What does it say? *I Brake for Fonts*?"

"No. It just says *Helvetica*, which is a very well-known and well-loved font, but the T-shirt's font is in Comic Sans, which font nerds absolutely detest."

Julie clapped her hand to her forehead. "Wait, there are loved and unloved fonts?"

"For some people, yes. And check this out. There's a font conference called TypeCon." He opened a new web page. "Unfortunately the schedule for the upcoming conference isn't up yet, but past lectures include 'Open Stroke Surgery: A Dissection of Letterform Bodyparts into Modular Elements for a Flexible Prototyping Base.' Julie, you don't want to miss this. I think you had better register early so that you can get into all of the best lectures."

She feigned looking at the web page with grave interest. "Obviously. It's been a lifelong dream of mine to attend a font conference, and I would never forgive myself if I didn't make it this year. Thank God you reminded me in time." Julie put a hand on his arm and looked at him seriously. "Matthew, confess now. Are you a closeted font nerd? Do you go to these conferences? I promise I won't respect you any less if you are. OK, fine, secretly I will, but it's better to get this off your chest and be who you are than to live in deception. Hiding the truth will only cripple your emotional development."

"More than it's already crippled?"

"Yes."

Matt frowned. "Well, I'm sorry to disappoint you. I'm not a font nerd. You can e-mail me in Papyrus and I won't care."

"Fine. When you're hard at work at school one night and you get a whining note from me about my multivariable calc homework and I beg you for help, I don't want to hear any complaints about my chosen font."

"You're taking multivariable calc? That's great!"

She slumped back onto the bed. "No, it's not great. The school figured out that I'd already taken calc in high school, and they made me take some test that unfortunately I passed. So now I'm stuck."

"I'm happy to help if you need it."

"I'll hold you to that." Her phone sounded, and she reached onto the floor to retrieve it from her purse. Seth was calling her. He was probably going to bail, and she'd be forced to discuss geek subgenres for the rest of the night. She answered the call. "Hey, Seth."

"Julie? I'm on your street, but all these houses are buried behind foliage, and I can't see any street numbers."

"Don't worry. I'll come outside and flag you down."

"Awesome. I can't wait to see you."

"Same here. See you in a minute, Seth." She hung up and got off the bed.

Matt moved back to his desk, repositioning his laptop and adjusting the chair. "Where are you off to?"

Julie sighed and waved her hands across her body. "My hot outfit and excessive eye makeup didn't indicate that I have a date tonight? Wow, we need to get you off the computer more."

"I did notice that you look dressed up tonight," he admitted. "Have a good time."

"Thanks," Julie said. "You know, Matt, I can stay home with Celeste sometimes when your parents are out so that you can have a social life. You must have friends asking you to do things. You have to hang out with them sometime."

He shrugged. "I really don't have time for socializing these days. Don't worry about it. Go have fun."

She felt bad that Matt was stuck at home with his sister. He was in college. He should be out having fun. Not that he looked like the sort who was aching to do keg stands at a frat house, but still. There might be a physics bee some Friday night, and he could return home with a nice ribbon for having spelled "*coulomb*" or "*neutralino*" correctly. Why in the world was he catering to Celeste's bizarre needs? Why did it seem as if Flat Finn governed the household? Things were really off here. Matt was a nice guy, and he deserved better. Well, it wasn't as if there was anything to do about this now. Maybe she could figure out something later.

"If he's a monstrous date, I will call you to come rescue me. We need a code word that signals I'm in date hell," Julie said as she walked to the door. "Something you'll respond to. Aha! I'll mention some boring mathematician. So when I call and say *Fibonacci*, you'll know that you have to fly out the door."

"That's kind of an obvious choice, but fine."

Julie glared at him. God, he was annoying sometimes. "Karl Gauss, then."

"Eh, that's all right. Again, a bit obvious."

"Then I'll surprise you. And I'll make it a good one. Just you wait."

Matt leaned back, put his hands behind his head, and smiled. "*With bated breath,*" he quoted.

Julie cocked her head. "Is that the colloquial *baited* with an 'i' or the original, insulting Shakespearean *bated* without?"

Matt winked. "I'll give you the 'i.'"

Huh. So he knew Shakespeare too. Julie paused for a moment and then began to leave. "Bye, Matt. Maybe I'll text you in Webdings later and give you an update on my evening."

Her heels clicked soundly on the floor as she headed down the stairs.

"Webdings one, two, or three?" Matt's voice rang through the stairwell.

"I'll mix and match!"

She went out the front door and down the porch steps. She looked to her left and saw headlights inching down the road. Julie waved. The car sped up a bit and then slowed in front of the Watkinses' house.

Seth stopped the car and bounded out of the driver's side. "Julie! I found you!" He rounded the car and gave her a hug.

"I'm glad you did."

Maybe the first thing one notices on a date should not be how someone smells, but as he wrapped his arms around her, she couldn't help but inhale. He smelled masculine. And not in a stinky, too-much-cheap-cologne way. Masculine in a hot, rugged, delicious way. She liked the feel of his arms around her and the way he hugged her warmly and confidently without being too forward.

Seth moved away and opened the car door for her. "Not that I didn't enjoy my drive around the back streets of Cambridge, but I hope you didn't think I was blowing you off."

Julie got in and buckled her seat belt. "Don't worry about it."

Seth shifted the car into gear. "I'm such a dork. I wrote your address down on a piece of paper, and I have the worst handwriting in the world. I wasn't sure if I was looking for twenty-one or seventy-one or twenty-seven or…Well, it doesn't matter now."

"*You're* not a dork, but speaking of dorks," Julie said as she turned her body toward him, "I just found out the weirdest thing. Did you know there are people who are font nerds?"

Seth grinned. "Let me guess. People who get turned on by the many exciting facets of the world of typesetting?"

"Exactly! It's one of many unique dorky subgenres! Or nerdy subgenres. I'm not really sure exactly how the classification system works."

"I'm a little scared that you know this."

"So am I," Julie agreed. "So am I."

"Please don't jump out of the moving car, but I have to tell you up front that I am not a font nerd. Or much of any nerd, really."

"You've just earned another bonus point."

"Just one?" He flashed his adorable smile as he drove them into the city.

"Fine. Five points."

"Now you're talking."

PART TWO

PART TWO

CHAPTER 13

Julie stood on her tiptoes, desperately trying to retrieve the duffel bag from the top of the closet shelf. She finally looped a finger around the strap and pulled it down, causing it to land on her head. She hated traveling, and if the packing situation was any indicator of her trip's success, she was not headed for a smooth flight. As if navigating an airport wasn't enough of a hassle on the day before Thanksgiving, she was desperately trying to condense her belongings so that she wouldn't have to check any luggage.

She would definitely be checking bags when she went to California with her father, that was for sure. He'd sent her their itinerary a few days ago. Or rather, his secretary had forwarded it to her. Still, he was showing a huge effort by taking her on this trip. Julie could only imagine the hassle it'd been for him to take off three weeks from work for this whirlwind trip. LA, Huntington Beach, San Diego, Santa Barbara…Julie couldn't even remember where else! She couldn't wait to tell her dad all about school and how well she was doing in her classes.

For this trip, she didn't need too many outfits, but hauling her laptop and books home was a drag. How Julie was supposed to celebrate the holiday, visit with relatives and friends, finish a research paper, *and* study for her calculus exam was beyond her. Colleges clearly saw Thanksgiving as a working holiday.

"Knock, knock." Erin stepped into the bedroom, and Julie again admired how poised and together she always looked. The gray tweed pencil skirt and coordinating cardigan were so streamlined and…well, classy. That was it; Erin was classy. Professional and classy. "You must be itching to get home and see your family, I imagine."

"A little bit," Julie agreed as she tossed the duffel bag onto the bed. "I just have so much work to do that it's hard to feel excited about going back to Ohio."

Erin waved her hand. "You'll get it done. There will be time in the airport, on the plane, and at home while you're recovering from turkey overload."

"I guess." Julie grabbed a handful of clean socks and tossed them into the bag. "Although maybe I should have just taken a long weekend earlier in the month instead and avoided the crowds. Oh, I mean, not that I would want to infringe on your family's holiday plans. I just meant—"

"You'd be welcome here for Thanksgiving, Julie. But I can't imagine a day of Chinese food and Scrabble is what you're used to. It'll just be Matthew, Celeste, and me sitting around eating spicy tofu and debating the validity of Matthew's plays. He tends to make up words, but we usually give him partial credit for creativity."

"That actually sounds better than eating sweet potatoes with marshmallows and listening to my uncle retell what went down on Comedy Central the night before."

"It does not!" Erin protested. "There's nothing wrong with a traditional Thanksgiving. Family warts and all. I'm sure it will be lovely."

"Is it strange not to have Roger here for the holiday?"

"Not at all. Roger takes month-long trips several times a year, so this longer trip is not surprising." Erin crossed her arms. "And your friend Seth? What's he doing over break?"

"He and his parents are going to Vermont to see his aunt and uncle. He left yesterday to try to avoid the traffic, and they're coming home on Saturday for the same reason."

"You've spoken highly of him. A political science major at BU, I believe, right? I'm glad you've made some nice connections this fall. You and your friend Dana seem to be getting close too. It's important to have social opportunities that get you out of the house sometimes."

Julie smiled. Dana had become a good friend, and even though both of them were busy, they had a standing coffee date on Tuesdays that they never missed. Dana was still absolutely bewitched by Jamie, and Julie had spent many hours over the semester listening to play-by-play accounts of the progress of their roller-coaster relationship. Of course Julie talked about Seth, too, to some degree, but their status was more of the casual-dating variety than Dana and Jamie's—which at this point was highlighted by frequent dramatic arguments followed by early morning walks of shame. Julie felt that, for a psych major, Dana could use a bit of self-examination. Maybe Julie and Seth weren't full of passion and mega-sparks, but there was something to be said for slow and steady.

"Goodness, Julie, are you planning on bringing all those books with you?" Erin asked.

"I have to. I need to do a paper on Carl Jung for my psychology class, and I need them as references."

Erin squinted at the stack of books. "Those are adequate, I suppose. Julie, you should have better sources."

"I have some online articles, too, but not enough."

"That's ridiculous. I can take care of that." Erin moved to the desk and began writing on a notepad. "This is my user name and ID so that you can access Harvard's article database. This should give you more than you need for your paper, and you'll be able to review critical examinations of Jung's work by others highly regarded in the field."

"Really?" Julie walked to the desk and looked at the paper. Erin had just opened up an entire world for her. "Are you sure you don't mind? I mean, this is a big deal. The only thing I can do through school is get into the library's listings and reserve books."

Erin tucked the pen behind her ear and put her hands on her hips. "Of course not. There's no reason you shouldn't have the best resources accessible to you. I'm surprised Whitney doesn't have more available to you online. You might not want to thank me, though, because I guarantee that you'll quickly get sucked into the system, going from one recommended article to another. So if your mother throws a fit because you're glued to the computer this weekend, don't blame me."

Julie impulsively threw her arms around Erin and hugged her bony frame. "I will take all the blame. I cannot thank you enough."

Erin, clearly not the hugging type, stiffened a bit but laughed softly with surprise and patted Julie's arm with one hand. "No need to thank me. You're the one doing all the hard work. I admire your enthusiasm about your studies." She stepped back and held Julie at arm's length. "But if you'd like to return the favor, you can persuade Matt to start pushing himself the way you push yourself. Then I wouldn't have to nag him so much."

"He seems to work all the time, from what I've seen. We end up studying together a lot, and if he's not at school, then he's on the computer working."

"I'm not saying that he doesn't spend a lot of time working. I'm talking about the quality of his work and his *drive*." Erin narrowed her eyes. "He's spreading himself thin in terms of his coursework and academic interest, and it's getting to a point in his education where he needs to narrow his focus so that he's not floundering when he graduates. That's how he's going to get published one day. He's got one chance to get this right, and I expect more from him than what I'm seeing."

It seemed a bit of a harsh take, but Julie could understand what Erin was saying. She wanted the best for her son. Julie began pulling clothes from the dresser. "What kind of student was Finn?"

"Oh, Finn!" Erin beamed. "Finn was a very well-rounded student. Rather skilled in everything he tackled. He chose a very classic, liberal arts approach to school and so studied everything from anthropology to literature to history. A real creative and dynamic boy, that one. He was deeply involved in political campaigns when he was at Brandeis. Very socially conscious and involved. And he played rugby with a community team on the weekends. Celeste loved going to his games."

Julie smiled. "He sounds like a very interesting person. Hopefully I'll get to meet him soon? I know Celeste is itching for him to come home."

"Everyone would love to see Finn again soon."

"Maybe he and I will overlap at Christmas? He's sure to come home sometime over the holidays."

"That would be nice, wouldn't it?" Erin took a few steps toward the door. "Let me go call Matt and make sure he hasn't forgotten about taking you to the airport."

"I can take a cab, Erin. It's fine."

"I'd drive you myself, but the truth is that I don't actually have my license anymore, if you can believe it. I got so caught up in the whole environmentally responsible acts of biking and walking everywhere that I never bothered to renew my license when it expired. I really do prefer it, though. I'm in better shape now than I was when I was twenty, and I've lost those ten pounds that I carried around for years."

"If I didn't have my bags to carry, I'd feel guilty about not walking to the airport," Julie joked. "I think it's admirable that you're doing what you can to reduce your carbon footprint. I hate that expression. Being politically correct seems to come with the inevitable clichés, doesn't it? I have a quick meeting with one of my professors at school, and then I'll just take the T to the airport. I don't want to bother Matt."

Erin shrugged. "If you say so. Call the house on Sunday and let us know what time your plane will be in. You may end up dealing with delays."

"OK, I will. Have a nice Thanksgiving, Erin. "

"You too. Send your mother our good wishes."

***

Julie set her suitcase down on the floor of the cramped office and sat in the chair across from her psychology professor's desk. The small room could barely contain the few pieces of furniture. Folders and books covered the desk and sparse shelf area. But there was something comforting and cozy about his office, perhaps due to the gentle man who sat before her. Julie loved her psych class and hadn't missed a class meeting yet. Dr. Cooley's lectures were incisively smart and interesting and delivered with genuine passion for the field. His thoughtfulness and compassion when he was presenting case studies made Julie feel sure that he would have something helpful to offer her today.

"Thank you for meeting with me, Dr. Cooley."

"Not a problem. Heading home, I assume?" he asked, eyeing her bag.

"Yes. Ohio. To see my mother and her side of the family. I'm sorry to be bothering you just before the holiday, but I'd like to get your perspective on something."

"Something from class? I went over your test and paper grades earlier today, and you're doing extremely well. Not to mention your frequent participation in class. Impressive in such a large group." He nodded approvingly. "A lot of students prefer to take these larger lecture courses as pass/fail. You stand out."

"Thank you. I enjoy your class a lot. But I actually need help with something else. I'm living with a family this year. The mother is a friend of my mother's. Everyone is really nice, but..." Julie didn't know where to start. "There is something very quirky about the daughter. I thought you might have some insight. I guess I need help."

"Help how?"

"I'm trying to figure out the daughter. Celeste. She's odd. Her oldest brother, Finn, is away traveling this year, and she carries a cardboard cutout of him everywhere she goes."

"You've definitely piqued my curiosity," Dr. Cooley said as he crossed his legs, "but I'd be more comfortable discussing this if you were telling me about a hypothetical family." He looked at her pointedly, but tried not to smile.

"Hypothetically," Julie said slowly, "the flat-brother thing might be alarming to me. And hypothetically, I'm quite worried about her. Some things seem to...I don't know...trigger her. I just don't know what they are."

Julie spent the next few minutes describing Celeste's behavior surrounding Flat Finn, her social limitations, and her generally unusual personality.

Dr. Cooley held up a hand. "Let me stop you for a minute. You're telling me about the daughter, but I want to hear about the whole family unit. Tell me what a typical day or week is like in this house."

"But she's the…" Julie fumbled for the right words. "The one with the issue. Or issues. Piles of them, I'm guessing." OK, Matt had issues too—mostly involving an obsessive need to become one with his laptop and an inability to dress in anything not revolting—but he certainly didn't have any cardboard sidekicks. Well, at least that she knew about. "Everyone else is fine."

"Humor me."

He sat silently while Julie talked for twenty-five minutes about the Watkins household. She told him about Celeste's quirky behavior and her social isolation, quite a bit about Flat Finn, Erin's seemingly endless energy, and how Matt and Finn seemed to be polar opposites of each other.

Julie's professor rubbed his forehead as if in disbelief. "So this family has absent parents and an absent eldest brother. Then we have the younger brother who has been forced into a parental role and is trying to be present and is probably struggling quite a bit. Lastly, a young, socially delayed teenager attempting to manage her emotions through the creation of a substitute, tangible version of her idolized sibling?"

Shit. It sounded really nuts when he spelled it out like that.

"Yeah. That sounds about right." Julie slumped deep into the chair. "Oh my God."

"Listen, I can give you a few thoughts about this family, but I'm not willing to diagnose anyone or give you any hard-and-fast answers based on this conversation. It wouldn't be fair to you or to them. Hypothetically. However, I might be able to get you thinking about a few things."

"I understand."

"My first thought is that this story you've laid out makes me sad."

"It doesn't feel that sad being in that house, though."

"Why not?"

"I don't know." Julie looked out the small window at the gray sky. "Because I like them?"

"They probably like you too. But there's something very sad here. Everyone is in coping mode. Functioning independently. Everyone has defense mechanisms working at full force. And there is a firm level of secrecy regarding…well, we don't know what, do we?"

"Correct."

"They've set their parameters, and I'm not sure you're in the position to cross those."

"Why is Celeste doing this? I mean, her brother is off traveling. Big deal. He has the right to, doesn't he? He can't live at home forever. Tons of girls her age must have older brothers who leave the house, yet they don't react the way she has. I don't get it. She's got so much potential. And I think I can help Celeste."

"Ah. You're a fixer."

"A what?"

"A fixer. You want to fix this for them. Why?"

"I told you. I like them. Especially Celeste. I can't just sit around and pretend that carting around a flat brother is not hideously weird. There's a great kid under the unusual exterior. Nobody is moving. It's like they're frozen, afraid to rock the boat with her."

He nodded. "They probably are. Whatever containment strategies they've developed are working to some degree. At least, working in the sense that they've stabilized whatever they're managing. In their eyes, things aren't getting worse."

Julie held his somber look. "But they will, won't they?"

"Probably, yes. A dysfunctional system like this can't hold up forever. At some point there will be a break."

She felt her stomach knot up. "And then what will happen?"

"I couldn't say. It's not something you can plan for. Tell me your take on this girl."

Julie tossed her hands up. "I've thought about all sorts of things. An adjustment disorder, separation anxiety disorder, reactive attachment disorder? Asperger's? Something to do with seeing Finn as a parental figure? And when he left, she felt that loss more profoundly than made sense. Her defense mechanisms got out of control? She has a chemical imbalance?"

"All possibilities. What else?" Dr. Cooley sat motionless, his eyes fixed on Julie's, waiting patiently as she struggled to find an answer herself.

Julie wriggled her toes inside her shoes, hoping to distract herself from the increasingly uncomfortable feeling that was taking over. But one thought would not be pushed aside. "Something happened?"

He nodded. "Something happened. That's my guess. Something quite major. Something you've clearly been told not to address. And this flat version of Celeste's brother is an extreme response to an incident. A trauma."

Julie stiffened. *Trauma*. She didn't like the sound of that.

Dr. Cooley continued. "The question is, what trauma? But that's a question that you might not get the answer to. Julie, tread lightly," he cautioned. "This is a precarious situation, and you don't know what exactly is going on in this family system. While I admire your compassion, I can't recommend that you take on the task of trying to tackle this."

"I know. I feel like I've been racking my brain trying to understand this kid, and I have no clue if I'm about to do something that will set her off. But when Finn comes back, this should all clear up, right?"

Dr. Cooley clicked his tongue on the roof of his mouth. "Maybe, maybe not. Whatever is causing her anxiety may manifest itself in another way. His return could prompt a significant improvement, sure, but I wouldn't bet on it."

This was a discouraging thought.

"But think about this," he offered, "maybe you're missing something obvious. Don't overanalyze what you see. I have a feeling that you're overthinking things. Give it some time, and the pieces of this puzzle might come together." He laughed. "Of course, they might not. This may be a family that you never fully understand."

"Believe me, that thought has occurred to me."

"And what do we know?" He laughed lightly. "Maybe they're just unusual characters. Not everyone behaves in a traditional manner."

"It would be nice if they were just quirky, wouldn't it?"

"Yes. Unlikely, but nice. Julie, there's another part of this story that I'm wondering about."

Julie sighed. "What's that?"

"You told me a lot about Matt, Finn, Erin, and Celeste." He paused. "I haven't heard much about the father."

"That's because he's gone a lot. Traveling for work. I really like him, though. He's gentle and soft-spoken. There's something earnest about him. He's very normal, but not in a boring way. Really sweet."

"Hmm," Dr. Cooley murmured.

"What's that mean?"

"You said you were going home today. To see your mother."

"Right. So?"

"What about *your* father? Will you see him too?"

"You're implying I have father issues?" Julie scoffed. "I don't have father issues."

Dr. Cooley sat silently.

"This is not about me." Julie shook her head. "This is about a superquirky kid who needs me."

"But why is it your job to help her? Why are *you* the fixer? Why are *you* the one who wants to put this family back together?"

"Because Celeste responds to me. I don't know why, but she does. I can do this."

Dr. Cooley took his glasses off and gently set them down on the table. "Who are you trying to heal?"

"*Celeste.*"

"Are you sure about that?"

"Of course," Julie said, slightly irritated. "This is not about *me.*"

"No," he agreed. "Not entirely."

Julie glanced at the clock on the desk. "I'm really sorry to cut you off, but I should leave now if I'm going to make my flight."

"Of course."

"I can't thank you enough for talking to me," she said sincerely. "I really appreciate it."

"It's a fascinating hypothetical family that you've told me about." He winked. "Remember, Julie. Tread lightly."

CHAPTER 14

Julie's stomach churned while she watched her cousin Damian shovel marshmallow-topped yams into his mouth. She wanted to kill whoever had come up with the sickening idea of combining marshmallows with a perfectly likeable vegetable. As gross as that was, it didn't compare to her aunt's "salad": Red Hots candies suspended in a green Jell-O mold, with carrot bits and canned mandarin orange slices. At least her mother's turkey was devoid of anything offensive. That was something to be thankful for.

"Julie, why aren't you wearing your pilgrim hat? You love the pilgrim hat!" Julie's uncle Pete raised his voice to be heard over the table noise and pointed to his own. "It doesn't feel like Thanksgiving if you don't wear the hat."

Julie scanned the fourteen family members who sat at the table in her mother's house in Ohio. Everyone there wore either a pilgrim hat or an Indian hat that had been purchased years ago at the costume shop on Delacorte Avenue. In other years, Julie had found this tradition amusing, but today the absurdity and idiocy had become undeniable. It was undignified. Not to mention the cultural offensiveness factor.

"Consider me the rebellious relative who refuses to conform. I can't say I'm a fan of supporting stereotypes." Julie jabbed her fork into the heaping mound of green bean casserole. God, the canned fried onion smell alone was enough to give her indigestion for days.

"Pete, she doesn't have to wear the hat if she doesn't want to," her mother said. Kate stood up and reached into the middle of the table for the cranberry sauce. The hideous white dish was painted with country houses. "My daughter is making a statement, I believe." As she moved to sit back down, she tipped the paper turkey centerpiece to the side and into the candle flame, immediately turning the gaudy decoration into a fiery display. "Oh, hell!" Kate shrieked.

Everyone simultaneously backed their chairs up about three feet and—amid hollers to call 911 and prayers to higher powers—Uncle Pete upended his water glass on the flames. "No harm, no foul," he chortled. "Get it? Fowl? Turkey joke."

Julie patted her napkin on the table with one hand and fanned the smoke away with the other. She sighed and sat back down, pinning herself once again between her cousin Damian and her mother's sister, Erika.

"So, Julie," Erika started, "how is school going? Do you love Boston?"

"I do love Boston. It snowed for the first time a few weeks ago, and the city looks even more beautiful at night."

"Eh, Boston," Uncle Pete growled. "I went there once. Dirty city with a bunch of bums hanging all around the Common. It's not that hard not to be homeless."

Julie gripped her fork and considered the pros and cons of stabbing her uncle's hand. Had he always been such a dumb jerk? "I'm sure my Economics of Poverty professor would disagree with you."

"Economics of Poverty? What the hell is that? What's to teach? If you don't have any money, there's no economics to talk about." Her uncle dropped his fork and looked at Julie's mother. "Are you actually paying money for your daughter to take a class on being poor?"

Her mother squirmed uncomfortably. "I doubt the class is just about—"

"The class is about exploring and analyzing poverty and understanding the effects of poverty and discrimination on different populations," Julie explained through clenched teeth. "Currently we're looking critically at different public policies that attempt to combat the cycle of poverty."

"You want to end poverty? Get a job like the rest of us. There. Class dismissed."

"What about the working poor? It's a little more complicated than that." Julie practically snorted.

"No, missy, it's not. Now, we're not rich or anything, but we work hard and pay our bills. You don't need some college class to know that poor people bring it on themselves." Pete's face had started to turn red with anger. "And these government handouts you're talking about? Another excuse for these lazy people to sit on their asses and collect cash."

"So when you lost your job two years ago and tracked down my father for fifteen hundred dollars, he should have told you to suck it up and get a job, the wretched economy be damned?" Julie shook her head and stood up. "Have you even paid him back now that you're employed again?"

"Julie, sit down!" Kate ordered.

Pete's face was now scarlet, and the vein next to his eye throbbed disgustingly. "Your father doesn't give a rat's ass about that money, and you know it! He also doesn't give a rat's ass about—"

"Shut your mouth!" Julie hissed. "Don't you dare." She stepped away from the table. "While you're busy ignoring the systemic, social, cultural, educational, and political contributions to poverty, I have a paper on ignorant, bigoted creeps to finish writing." Julie walked angrily out of the room, up the stairs, and into her old bedroom.

She shut the door and blocked out most of the dinner-table chaos. She didn't care in the least that the cousins and uncles and aunts were probably tearing her apart right now. They revolted her even more than the slew of tacky Thanksgiving decorations that her mother had strewn throughout the house.

She sat at her old desk and logged on to the article database that Erin had given her access to. Julie was about to write the best damn term paper on "the collapse of the housing market as it relates to an increase in suburban poverty."

So there.

CHAPTER 15

Matthew Watkins *At the first Thanksgiving, one of the bloodiest battles ensued when it was discovered that the deliveryman forgot to bring extra duck sauce.*

Finn Is God *is, on this enchanted evening, in love with a wonderful guy.*

Julie Seagle *Going to write a book called "Binge, Screw, Loathe." It will be about a hateful woman who travels across the US visiting all-you-can-eat brothels.*

Julie giggled at Finn's reference to the musical *South Pacific*. She knew where he was now.

It was the Friday night of Thanksgiving break, and Julie was itching to get back to Boston and end the torture that this trip had become. She hadn't bothered to return any of her friends' phone calls and even had her mom tell callers that she hadn't come home for the break. Since the scene on Thursday, she'd pretty much been holed up in her bedroom working, and except for one snarly conversation about her lousy attitude, her mother had left her alone. She had nearly finished her paper on poverty and took a break from spell-checking to go online.

Her e-mail held twenty-some messages from friends in Ohio wondering why she wasn't home; there was nothing worse than *missing the most badass party at Jacob O'Malley's tonight!* Whatever. Nothing from Seth, but his parents had decided that the holiday weekend in Vermont was going to be technology-free.

She and Celeste had taken to studying at the coffeehouse after school once a week, and Seth had proved to be completely unfazed by Flat Finn's presence. He was an all-around good guy: smart, funny, a hard worker, sweet to Julie, and patient. Between classes, homework, Seth's job, and Julie's long days with Celeste, it'd been hard to get together alone more than once a week, if that. So their relationship was on a slower track than normal. While most of Julie's friends from school spent nearly every night with their boyfriends in the dorms, Julie and Seth were taking it slow. Being responsible. Smart. Methodical.

But Julie thought that was a good thing. They held hands and messed around a little in his car, and Julie wasn't rushing into anything else. So far Seth had understood. Not that he wasn't a good kisser, because he was. And not that Julie didn't have raging hormones, because she did. She just wasn't in a huge rush.

A lot of Julie's time was eaten up by the exorbitant amount of schoolwork that she had. She was killing herself to keep up, and it was paying off with excellent grades. Even her calculus class was going better than she'd hoped, and Matt had helped her out more than a few times whenever she'd needed it. For someone so intellectually smug, he was a surprisingly good teacher, and they often studied together at night. So far she hadn't found any opportunity to help him out with anything, of course, but one could hold out hope that there might be an occasion where Matt got stumped.

Julie wasn't holding her breath on that one.

She stretched her arms above her head and yawned. It was only ten o'clock, but she was worn out. This trip home had hardly been energizing. She deleted a few more messages and then saw that there was one from Finn. Julie and Finn had been in touch regularly over the past few months. In fact, she checked her e-mail more often than she liked to admit. He liked receiving her updates on Celeste, and she liked all the cool pictures from his travels.

She read his e-mail because she was fairly confident that Finn was not going to invite her to an annoying party, make her wear a holiday outfit, or proselytize about why those in poverty deserve what they got.

Julie–

Hope your trip home is going well? I'm in the Cook Islands. Fan-freakin'-tastic here!

Wanted to give you a heads-up: I heard that Flat Finn sustained an injury the other day. Nothing major, though. Something to do with Matt, a steaming iron, and maniacal shouts of "There are no wrinkles allowed in this house! You may be flat, but you're not smooth enough yet for this family!" From all reports, Matt Dearest had an alarming, fortunately temporary, reaction to the traditional Thanksgiving moo shu pork. Celeste bonked him over the head with an LL Bean umbrella and he returned to his normal state. I think she should've hit him again, but that's just my opinion.

–Finn

Clearly the Watkins household was falling apart in her absence.

Finn–

Ohio is…not that great actually. Family members are driving me crazy. Thanksgiving was a nightmare. I spent twenty minutes listening to my oldest cousin reenact some stand-up comedian's routine from Comedy Central (not funny and poor delivery), tried to get my aunt interested in what I was reading in my Eng. Class (failure level=high), observed a paper turkey go up in flames (an appropriate holiday sign regarding good taste), and verbally abused my offensive uncle (well-deserved) in an explosive scene that will live on in memory for years to come.

Can't wait to get back to Boston for a million reasons. Need to return to normal. Will assess damage to Flat Finn and berate Matt for his outburst.

How are the Cook Islands? The South Pacific must be amazing. Any chance you're awake now? I need someone normal to chat with. I don't know what time it is there…

–Julie

Two minutes later, she heard back.

Julie–

I'm up. I'm five hours earlier than you are. Turn on FB chat!

–Finn

Oh. By *chat* she hadn't actually meant *chat*, as in instant message chat. She hadn't felt like IMing with anyone in ages. Not only did she now feel so far removed from her old life, but also she loathed all the IM and texting abbreviations and acronyms. She was a snob like that and knew she fell into the minority of people her age. How was she supposed to know that *DQMOT* meant *Don't quote me on this*? And that crap like *CUL8ER*? Blech. It was all so cutesy and corny. *B4N*? Seriously, just say good-bye like a normal person. OK, true she used the occasional *LOL* and *WTF*, but trying to translate an entire sentence that had been abbreviated into a few letters was more than she wanted to deal with. Julie suspected that billions of brain cells were being killed each hour as people shortened language into indecipherable code. As much as she loved technology, this sort of lingo was one of her top pet peeves. And now she was about to do it again with Finn. She'd probably have to pull up some online dictionary to translate this conversation, but she went on to Facebook's chat anyway.

Julie Seagle
Hey!
Finn Is God
Hey, back!

And then she panicked. Well, this had been a dumb idea. Why had she said *chat*? What was she supposed to say now? It wasn't as if she actually knew Finn, and here she'd gone ahead without think-ing and agreed to this. And she couldn't very well back out now.

Finn Is God
I am concerned about that last e-mail. You're quantifying me as "normal"?

Julie Seagle
Only in comparison to my relatives.

Finn Is God
Huge relief. Less pressure to behave now.

Julie Seagle
Go nuts. You can't possibly be that bad.

Finn Is God
Just wait...!

Julie Seagle
Very funny.

Julie tapped her foot during the seemingly endless four-minute pause. Topics, topics...What could they talk about? Ugh, this was a colossal mistake. He'd probably dozed off because she was so excruciatingly boring. Then finally Finn piped up.

Finn Is God
What are you wearing?

Oh. My. God. This had now gone beyond *colossal mistake* to *violently alarming*. What the hell was she supposed to do now?

Finn Is God
Julie? Relax. I'm kidding.

Julie laughed. Not only was he funny, but he wrote using actual whole words!

Julie Seagle
[Delete] [Delete] [Delete] Was just about to give you a full description of enticing bedroom attire.

Finn Is God
Oh. NOT KIDDING! NOT KIDDING!

Finn Is God
Fine. Kidding. Tell me more about Thanksgiving there. First time home should have been fun.

Julie Seagle
You would think. Big fight at the table. Didn't help that I wouldn't wear the pilgrim hat. More settled in Boston than I thought, and this whole trip just feels…disruptive.

Finn Is God
More disruptive than living in my house? You're clearly unbalanced.

Julie Seagle
Hey! I like your house. Your parents are great, Celeste is my buddy, and Matt has been really nice.

Julie Seagle
Even Flat Finn seems to have accepted me.

Finn Is God
sob Fear real family has been abducted and replaced with well-behaved clones. Tragedy. Enjoy new clone mommy!

Julie Seagle
So sorry for your loss, but the difference between our moms? Your so-called clone mom hooked me up w/awesome Harvard intel, and my mom doubled the hay pile display out front.

Finn Is God
Lucky girl. I'd take the hay and run.

Julie Seagle

Ha ha! Don't be mean.

Finn Is God

I'll put it this way: Erin is not as perfect as you may think.

Julie Seagle

Does she make you wear holiday hats too?

Finn Is God

She takes a different strategy to torture us.

Julie Seagle

Really? I have more in common with her than my own mother.

Finn Is God

That's a horrible thing to say about yourself. Appearances are not everything. Case in point: One summer when I was at day camp, I made her an art project. She spent weeks saying how weird it was that I'd made her a woodcarving that said "WOW."

Julie Seagle

???

Julie Seagle

Oh, wait a minute…!

Finn Is God

Yeah. She had it upside down. It was supposed to read "MOM."

Julie Seagle

I'm sorry, but that IS funny!

Finn Is God

That's my mother for you. I think she still has it. And is probably still under the wrong impression.

Julie Seagle

Oh, my. Sort of sweet in a tragic way.

Finn Is God

What about your parents? Love 'em or want to mail them back to Walmart?

Julie Seagle

Costco, actually. Mom is OK. A little...lacking depth, maybe? But nice. Dad is not around much.

Finn Is God

Where is he?

Julie Seagle

They divorced when I was five, and I only get to see him a few times a year since then. He works all over the country, and it's hard to coordinate times to see him.

Finn Is God

Sorry to hear that. You deserve better.

Julie Seagle

Not a big deal. I'm used to it. And it's great when I do see him.

Finn Is God

When do you go back to Boston?

Julie Seagle

Sunday morning. Really early flight. Home by noon, I think.

Finn Is God

You're calling it "home" now?

Julie Seagle

Uh…Apparently.

Julie Seagle

How long are you in the South Pacific? Sounds so exotic.

Finn Is God

Probably three weeks. Just got here last Sunday. Exotic experience started early while on the looooong flight. Ate a distinct meal of fermented cheese on canvas-y crackers.

Julie Seagle

Mmmm…. Yummy!

Finn Is God

Dessert was even more exotic: congealed glob of rice pudding. Can still taste it!

Julie Seagle

Now you'll just keep booking flights all over the world.

Finn Is God

I live for airline food. Nothing gets me off more than small portions of gunk on a tray. And sporks, of course.

Finn Is God

Love sporks!

Julie Seagle

Am making a note of your fetishes.

Finn Is God

It's gonna be a long list.

Julie Seagle

Understood. Tell me the best thing you've done on this trip so far.

Finn Is God

Bungee jumped. So awesome.

Julie Seagle

Ugh. I would NEVER. How was it?

Finn Is God

Complete rush. Phenomenal. You're not a daredevil?

Julie Seagle

No way. Total wuss. I nearly faint on escalators. What other crazy things have you done?

Julie Seagle

Oh, let me guess! Are those your skydiving shirts I saw?

Finn Is God
Yup. Want to go sometime?

Julie Seagle
Uh, let me think…NO!

Finn Is God
Come on! You'll love it. Maybe. It's nothing like an escalator.

Julie Seagle
Again, NO!

Finn Is God
But don't tell my parents. They don't know about my risky activities.

Julie Seagle
Seriously?

Finn Is God:
They'd freak.

Julie Seagle
Understood. Lips are sealed.

Finn Is God
I want to go bungee jumping in South America next. Right by waterfalls. Supposed to be gorgeous.

Julie Seagle
So many bungee jumps to make. Sounds like I won't get to meet the renowned Finn anytime soon.

Finn Is God

Probably not. Pretty committed for a while. We'll see. Hard to pass up these opportunities. Be good to meet you, though. But at least we can chat for now!

Julie Seagle

True. And I kind of feel like I know you already. Weird.

Finn Is God

I know what you mean.

Julie Seagle

Think it's because I'm staying in your room and absorbing Finn vibes?

Finn Is God

The vibes from the stinky monster poop in the closet? Yes, that's it.

Julie Seagle

So that's the funky smell. I've been wondering.

Finn Is God

Apologies. Boys are gross.

Julie Seagle

Not all boys.

Finn Is God

If I'd known you'd be staying in my room, I would have tried harder to make a better impression.

Finn Is God
Will work on bolstering my image!

Julie Seagle
Not necessary. You're very charming.

Finn Is God
You don't need pictures of me in a tuxedo, cleaned up, trying to look suave and presentable?

Julie Seagle
I don't need tuxedos to be impressed.

Finn Is God
Hmm...

Finn Is God
What do you need?

Julie Seagle
Still trying to figure that one out.

And so it went for the next two hours. Finn IM'd her more pictures, gave her more details on his many trips, and asked lots of questions about her classes, her family, her friends. She didn't mention Seth because...well, Finn didn't specifically ask. And she didn't know exactly where she stood with Seth, so there wasn't much to say right now anyway. Was he a real *boyfriend*? Or were they just dating casually?

And, yes, she kept flirting. Because it was harmless and fun, and truthfully, she just couldn't help herself. There was something extraordinarily intoxicating about this Finn.

Finn Is God

OK, so Thanksgiving didn't work out so well for you. Winter break? Will it be a step up?

Julie Seagle

Of course. But I'll be in California with my dad for three weeks, so I'll miss Mom's stockings and trees and lights.

Julie Seagle

Illuminated reindeer statues on the lawn, drunk Santa at the mall, pop stars releasing carol collections, etc. What more could a girl want?

Finn Is God

Hold on. Are you anti-Christmas?

Julie Seagle

Nah. Just kidding! I love Christmas. Mom covers the entire living room in white twinkle lights and puts real candles on the tree.

Julie Seagle

On Christmas Eve, I slide under the tree and look up through the branches at the lights. Hokey, but my tradition.

Finn Is God

Do you lie there and make a wish for the New Year?

Julie Seagle

Exactly. Silly, I guess.

Finn Is God

What do you wish for?

Julie Seagle

Depends on the year. Could be to marry some dopey teen idol.

Julie Seagle

Or to get stranded on a deserted island with Prince Charming and an endless supply of sunscreen.

Finn Is God

So your Christmas tradition is centered on cute boys, huh?

Julie Seagle

I never said they were lofty fantasies.

Finn Is God

Oh, now they're FANTASIES, are they? So you need to be alone for this tradition, I guess…*cough, cough*

Julie Seagle

Very funny. I'll go with "dreams" then. Not just about cute boys (although I guess that has been a theme), but more about being…I don't know…generally satisfied. Content. Complete. I don't know…It sounds lame when I say it. (Or type it.)

Julie Seagle

Dreaming about the future. Wondering what's ahead for me. Coming-of-age nonsense. Corny.

Finn Is God
It's not nonsense. I think that's very cool.

Julie Seagle
Very cool until hot wax falls from the branches and burns my eyeballs. That actually happened. Candles on the tree=dangerous fire hazard. But what's a holiday without a little danger?

Julie Seagle
Oh look! There's the risk-taking behavior you were looking for!

Finn Is God
That's pushing it, kid.

Finn Is God
Maybe you're not cut out for real danger. That's OK. Not all my interests run the risk of crashing thousands of feet. Did the Boston Polar Plunge a few times. That doesn't involve heights.

Julie Seagle
What's that?

Finn Is God
Boston crazies put on swimsuits and plunge into the Atlantic Ocean on New Year's Day. Rather quick swim due to frigidly cold/awful water.

Finn Is God
News crews love this story.

Julie Seagle

groan Yeah, this sounds really fun. Unfortunately I won't be in Boston for this event, otherwise I'd totally do it.

Finn Is God

Liar! You would not! But it's awesome. Sucks going in, but great on the way out. A shock to the system in a good way.

Finn Is God

Would go this year but will be in sunny Puerto Rico. Leading a white water rafting tour. (And bungee jumping, of course.)

Julie Seagle

Boo hoo. That sounds miserable. Poor you.

Finn Is God

I know. Rough.

Julie Seagle

Pit stop in Boston before you go? Celeste is dying to see you.

Finn Is God

I could work on a pit stop.

Julie Seagle

Oh, and could we talk about Celeste for a minute?

Julie waited. And waited. It looked as if he was going to be as difficult about his sister as Matt was.

Julie Seagle

So, Celeste…Tell me why she made Flat Finn.

Finn Is God

Don't know. She needs Flat Finn's good looks to counteract
Matt's lack of?

Julie Seagle

Nice try.

Again Julie waited. She stared at the clock on her computer,
watching as six endless minutes ticked by.

Finn Is God

I can't tell you.

Julie Seagle

Why? She needs help, Finn.

Finn Is God

You're the best thing for her.

Julie Seagle

How do you know that? I don't know what I'm doing.

Finn Is God

You're doing great. She's happy.

Julie Seagle

She's not happy. She can't be. She needs you.

Finn Is God
This is more complicated than I can explain.

Finn Is God
You'll have to trust me on this. I can't say anything else. I need you to drop this. OK?

What the hell? Julie stared at the chat window. Things suddenly felt weird with Finn, and that was the last thing she wanted.

Finn Is God
Please don't be mad. I just can't. I'm sorry.

Julie Seagle
OK.

Finn Is God
So…is Celeste the only one who wants to see me?

Julie Seagle
Your whole family does.

Finn Is God
Only my whole family?

Julie Seagle
Girlfriend back home who is missing you like crazy?

Finn Is God
Maybe.

Julie paused. She hadn't really thought about this possibility before, but for some reason she didn't really like the idea that Finn might have a girlfriend. Not that it was any of her business. It wasn't as if she had any right to be jealous.

Except that she was.

There is nothing more unpleasant than the overwhelming effect caused by jealousy, and she couldn't deny that typing out the word *girlfriend* had made her stomach knot up, her breathing change, and her brain swirl. This was not the reaction she would have expected. She didn't even *know* Finn.

Well, she couldn't suddenly go chat silent now. It would look weird. She held her hands over the keyboard, desperately trying to figure out something normal to say. *How nice for you. I'm sure she's lovely.* No, that would sound obnoxious. Crap. Who was this girlfriend? Neither Matt nor Celeste had ever mentioned anything about her. *She's a curvy Victoria's Secret model with the intellect of a geneticist and the strength of spirit to go cliff-diving, I assume?* No. That was both obnoxious *and* passive-aggressive.

Finn Is God
But no girlfriend. So just my crazy family that wants me to come visit, I guess. I'll confess disappointment.

Julie couldn't help smiling.

Julie Seagle
Would not complain if you came to visit. Must meet the world-traveling, thrill-seeking, adventure-loving idol.

Finn Is God
In that case, I'll do my best to make it happen. Don't tell anyone yet, though, until I'm sure.

Julie Seagle

OK. Fair enough.

Finn Is God

I should go…Dinner soon.

Julie Seagle

And I should get to bed.

Finn Is God

Nice! What are you wearing?

Finn Is God

Sorry. Forgot I already tried that one…

Julie Seagle

Impressed with your persistence.

Finn Is God

Ta da! I impressed you. Success! You've totally made my night.

Julie Seagle

And you've made mine.

Finn Is God

Enjoy the rest of break. Really. You're lucky to have your mom.

Julie Seagle

Will consider it.

✳✳✳

The sound of the train woke Julie in the middle of the night. After sleeping noise-free for nearly three months in the Watkinses' quiet Cambridge neighborhood, she couldn't sleep through the roaring train sound anymore. She threw the covers off and got up. She'd been having a dream that she knew involved pancakes and ski jumping. She couldn't remember the rest. But whatever it'd been about had left her soaked in sweat and hungry. Bleary-eyed, she stumbled down the stairs in her sweatpants and T-shirt and made the familiar walk to the kitchen.

"Hey, Jules." Her mother smiled warmly at her. She was standing at the kitchen island, surrounded by every leftover dish from Thanksgiving. "Hungry?"

Julie nodded and took a seat on a stool.

"Milk?" her mom asked.

Julie nodded again. "What are you doing up?"

"Raiding the fridge." Kate poured a glass for Julie. "How can I sleep knowing there is all this good food just sitting down here? What about you, kiddo? Thought you'd be zonked out from working so hard."

Julie shrugged. "The train woke me."

"Hmm, that hasn't bothered you in years." Kate tousled Julie's hair lightly. "Things are different now, huh? Well, dig in. I'll heat up a plate for you. White meat or dark? Gravy? Potatoes? Green beans?"

"Everything. I need a heaping plate of everything." Julie put her elbow on the counter and dropped her head into her hand. "And I need a pilgrim hat in order to properly enjoy the flavor."

Kate clapped her hands together happily. "I knew it! I knew you'd miss the hat! I happen to have yours right here." She reached behind her and grabbed the black hat from the cluttered kitchen desk, setting it on Julie's head with a satisfied look. "It really suits you."

Julie cracked a smile. "I think so."

"So…," Kate said slowly, "have you heard from your father?"

"He sent me the itinerary for our trip. I can't wait. Thanks for letting me go. It'll be fun, don't you think?"

"Mmmm," her mother agreed. "I hope so."

"What do you mean you hope so? Of course it'll be fun. I can't believe Dad got so much time off to be with me."

"Julie, you do know he'll probably be doing some work during this trip," Kate said gently. "The hotel he works for has locations all over California."

"Oh. Well, that's fine. I mean, we'll still be together, and that's what counts."

"I just don't want you to be disappointed. Your father has never been—"

"It's going to be awesome. Just wait." Julie beamed. This trip really was going to be amazing. She'd never been to California, and she'd never traveled with her father. Their visits were mostly confined to dinners when he was in town, so this was going to be different. "He's really trying. He's prioritizing. What about you? Are you excited for your cruise?" Kate's best friend, Suzanne, was treating Kate to a fourteen-day holiday cruise in the Caribbean.

"Assuming I don't get seasick, I think it'll be lovely. I couldn't bear to hang around the house over the holidays without you. I'm going to miss you, kiddo. Our first Christmas apart."

"Mom, don't cry! I'll miss you too. It's so hard for Dad to find time to see me, and I can't pass this up."

Kate patted her eyes with her napkin and took a huge bite of turkey. "So things are good, living at the Watkinses' house?" her mom asked through a mouthful of food.

"Yeah. I really like them."

"And it's still going well with Celeste? Isn't she kind of old for a babysitter? What's that about?"

"I'm not really a babysitter. More of a…" Julie struggled to find the right word. "A companion."

Kate looked confused. "A *companion*? What does that mean?"

"Celeste is a little quirky." That was putting it mildly, but Julie hadn't told her mother about Flat Finn. She couldn't think of a way to explain him without making Celeste out to be a complete nut case. "I really like her, but she has a hard time with friends. She acts a lot younger than she is."

"So you're less of a companion and more of a role model."

"Huh. I hadn't thought of it like that, but yeah. I guess so."

"She's lucky to have you," Kate said.

Julie shook her head. "I'm lucky to have her."

CHAPTER 16

Matthew Watkins *People in my age group, educational, and financial status don't appreciate generalizations or profiling.*
Finn Is God *I have half a mind to tell you to fu of.*
Julie Seagle *I think that when Twitter says someone has "protected their Tweets," a little picture of a chastity belt should pop up.*

Julie sat curled up on the Watkinses' living room couch with a chenille blanket wrapped around her shoulders. It had snowed heavily the night before, coating the trees and the ground with a crisp, white mask and leaving the city temporarily picturesque before the plows came by and dirtied everything up with black, sandy slush. It was sunny and cold, and Julie liked the feeling of holing up in the house and snuggling into the cushions. She'd been back from Thanksgiving break for five days, and her two classes this Friday had been canceled due to the weather. Matt was also home, but Celeste's private school, Barnaby, didn't cancel classes unless a major natural disaster hit. Erin had put on snowshoes and trekked into her office, saying that if she didn't have classes to teach, she might as well grade papers. Truthfully, the snowfall had been much less than was predicted, and Julie was sure there were pissed-off parents all over the state who were now stuck at home with their kids.

Matt sat in the armchair across from her, his feet resting on the coffee table while he typed at warp speed. Julie dropped her book into her lap. She just couldn't get into study mode, and the idea of blowing off her work for the day was gaining appeal by the minute.

"Matt? I'm bored." She glared at him as he kept typing. "Matty?" He didn't respond, and it aggravated Julie that he could be so narrowly focused on his computer that the rest of the world ceased to exist. Julie took her laptop from the table. She'd have to take a different approach. E-mail.

Dear Matthew Watkins,

Whatcha doing? I'm bored. Let's build a snowman. Or a snow...a snow...a snow magnetic field formula!

Sincerely,
Julie Seagle

Julie sat back and waited until Matt's e-mail sounded. Unlike the rest of the world, he didn't jump to see what Nigerian prince had bequeathed him millions of dollars or which company had a special offer promising to save him piles of cash on his next order of male enhancement products. Maybe he didn't need either. Well, good for him.

"Aren't you going to check your e-mail?" she asked loudly.

"Why?" he muttered.

"It could be an invitation to speak at some exciting math event. Or the long-lost love of your life writing to say that she is desperate to win back your affections."

"I'm sure it's both of those," Matt said, but she saw him click the touchpad.

She watched him as he read her note, expressionless, and then typed for a few seconds. Now *her* e-mail sounded.

Dear Julie Seagle,
While there are a number of charming magnetic formulas to choose from, I have concerns about constructing a concept. I was thinking something more along the lines of replicating the Large Hadron Collider.
You in?

Sincerely,
Matthew Watkins

Julie let out an exaggerated sigh.

Dear Disagreeable One,
I'll meet your counter offer of the Large Hadron Collider and raise you the addition of a snow Clive Owen.
You in?

Slightly less sincerely,
Julie Seagle
P.S. Sorry. I'm sure you don't know who Clive Owen is. Just play along.
P.P.S. Just because you have on that bulky sweatshirt doesn't mean that I don't know you're wearing a stupid, geeky T-shirt underneath it.

Matt read her e-mail without looking up and smiled.

Dear Wardrobe Assessor,
I'm in.

Still sincerely,
Matthew Watkins

P.S. I do not have on a "stupid, geeky T-shirt."

Julie marched over to Matt. She stood in front of him and crossed her arms. "Lift up your sweatshirt."

Matt rolled his eyes. "God, you really know how to turn a guy on."

Julie didn't budge. "If I were trying to turn you on, I could do better than that. Now, lift up your sweatshirt."

Matt looked up at her and tried to look serious. "Julie, I'm completely offended that you have so little faith in my honesty. I thought at this point in our friendship that you would at least—"

"Get up." Julie leaned over and shut his laptop. "Get up!" she said again.

"You're being ridiculous," Matt said, laughing, but he stood up. "I trust you implicitly, and it wouldn't kill you to show me the same respect."

"Show me!"

Matt sidestepped the chair and took a few steps backward. "You have quite the attitude today. Suspicious and mean."

Julie took a step forward, causing Matt to continue backing away. "Lift up your shirt."

"Look, I appreciate an aggressive woman, but this is really getting weird."

Julie grabbed his sweatshirt by the waist cuff and lifted it up with one hand as she pulled down his T-shirt with the other. Matt put his hands over hers, lightly protesting, but she refused to let go. "Aha!" She squinted at his shirt. "OK, I don't even know what this is, but it's definitely geeky."

Matt's hands were still on hers, but he'd given up trying to hide his shirt. "It's a representation of a caffeine molecule. You should love it, considering your addiction to those horrible drinks you're obsessed with. Although they can't really be considered true coffee. How can you like those? A real coffee aficionado would drink espresso, or an Americano, or—"

"Don't try and change the subject. And I'm not having the coffee argument with you again, by the way."

"It's not an argument. I have an opinion on what you drink, *and* I have a right to express that I think it's disgusting—"

Julie groaned. "Oh my God, stop talking!"

"So I should stand here silently while you ridicule my clothing choices?" Matt held her look for a few moments before tightening his hands around hers, pushing his sweatshirt back down. "Not terribly fair."

They stood unmoving. "I suppose not," Julie finally admitted. "But your shirt is still hideously lame." She looked at his hands, holding hers against his chest. "You can let go now."

"Oh. Of course." Matt let go and stepped back. "Sorry."

The house phone rang, cutting sharply through the silence.

Matt went into the kitchen to get the phone while Julie took her seat back on the couch. She yanked the hair tie from around her wrist and pushed her hair back into a ponytail, noting the moisture at the nape of her neck. Final exams were right around the corner, for God's sake, and here she was messing around on what should be a productive day. She should really use this snow day to get work done.

She heard Matt clear his throat in the other room. "Yes. I'll be right there." He returned to the living room. "I have to go to a meeting at Celeste's school, so the snow-building activities will have to wait."

Julie frowned. "Everything all right?"

"It's just a scheduled meeting."

"Oh, OK." Julie halfheartedly picked up her book and then dropped it to her lap. "Wait a minute. Why are you going to the meeting? Where's your mom?"

"She forgot about it, and when they called her, she asked them to call me. So I'm going to go. It's not a big deal."

Julie stood up. "I could come with you, if you want."

"No. Stay here. Get some work done."

"I spend a lot of time with Celeste, so maybe I could help. Besides, you shouldn't have to do this alone. It's not really your job." She crossed the room to the front hallway and grabbed her coat off the hook. "Come on. We have to shovel the car out before we're going anywhere."

"Julie, really, you shouldn't come. It'll be a boring meeting. It's not a big deal."

"Let me give you a little moral support here, OK? I'm coming." Julie zipped her coat and put on fleece mittens.

Matt didn't budge from his spot. "I'd rather you not."

"I'd rather I did."

"It's just that—"

"Stop talking and start shoveling. I'm coming."

Matt cracked a smile. "Bossy, bossy."

＊＊＊

Julie crossed her legs and did her best not to sneer at Mr. Alberta, the guidance counselor. *Bastard*, she thought. This guy totally didn't *get* Celeste.

Mr. Alberta leaned back in his leather swivel chair and patted the bald spot on top of his head. The man had patted his head eight times so far (Julie was counting) in an irksome nervous tic. Julie didn't like his green plaid shirt or his wrinkled khaki pants, both of which seemed an overzealous effort to appear casual and approachable. She didn't buy it, and it didn't help that his eyes kept darting around the room as though he was afraid to look at either her or Matt. He should be afraid, Julie thought, considering that he was flinging insults about Celeste left and right. *Tremendous difficulty with peers, both male and female. Virtually no attempts to engage in social interactions and inappropriate responses to the rare initiative from another student.* Why had he not acknowledged one positive trait? How about the fact that Celeste could do her schoolwork in her sleep? That she was smart as a whip, and interesting, and unique? Did he not notice that she was scared and defenseless and…and so what if she wasn't like every other kid at school? Julie didn't like this man.

Mr. Alberta suddenly flung himself forward. "Here's the thing, Matthew. The school thinks that Celeste may not be equipped to attend Barnaby. It's becoming clear that we cannot meet her needs."

Matt was sitting bolt upright, his face hardened and serious. "Her grades are excellent. Stellar, in fact."

The guidance counselor nodded. "Absolutely. It's not a question of her academic abilities, Matthew. It's her social development that concerns us."

"She's making progress," Matt said unconvincingly.

"I understand the challenges of the Finn situation. With him out of the picture—"

"I know the situation, Mr. Alberta," Matt said quickly.

"I was really hoping to speak to your parents about this," the counselor said awkwardly. "Given what an important role you play in Celeste's life, and your age, I agreed to meet with you, but this is not how I would prefer to handle this. Matthew, here is what it boils down to. I'm not sure what else we can offer Celeste. The truth is that she doesn't have friends. Any. Her social exchanges are markedly odd, and she displays little interest in improving on them. She is withdrawn from her peers and seemingly operating on another plane. I'm sorry to say it like that, but it *is* the case. I realize we are dealing with delicate matters, but I'm quite concerned about her."

"Well, what is it that you suggest we do?" Matthew did not shift his position, but his voice now had a hard edge to it. "How about we take my sister out of here and lock her up in a boarding school for crazy girls? Does that sound like an appealing possibility to you? I'm sure Celeste would thrive. What a good way to get her out of her shell."

"Her shell? Oh, Matthew, is that how you see it? Celeste has more than a shell. There is a whole host of complicated defense systems and coping mechanisms at work here—"

"I have an idea," Julie cut in. "I, uh, I think I have an idea. Let's not make any rash decisions right now. Mr. Alberta, can you give her six months?"

"Ms. Seagle, I appreciate your being here. Really I do. I can see you care about Celeste's well-being, but six months is a long time."

"No, it's really not a long time. She isn't hurting anybody or infringing on any other students' academic experience, correct?"

He nodded begrudgingly.

"So just give it some time. We can get her moving in the right direction. This is all a temporary problem anyway."

"Temporary?" Mr. Alberta tossed Celeste's file onto the desk in front of him. "I'm not sure we can define this as *temporary.*"

"Julie, let's go." Matt got up from his chair and stormed out of the office.

Julie reluctantly got up. She looked pleadingly at Mr. Alberta. "Six months. A lot can happen in six months. She needs time."

Mr. Alberta was quiet for a moment while he considered Julie's request. "Sure. Six months."

Julie shook his hand, now nervous herself. "Thank you. Thank you so much." She tucked her coat over her arm. "Celeste is a really good kid, you know?"

He nodded. "I do know that. I like her. It's just with everything that's gone on…I worry about her."

Julie nodded. Maybe he wasn't such a monster after all? "I had better go after Matt. Thanks again." Julie turned and rushed down the hallway, catching up with Matt just as he slammed Barnaby's front door wide open. "Matt? Are you all right?"

"Not particularly, no. I wouldn't describe that as a successful school meeting, would you?" He stormed down the front steps, and Julie hurried to keep up with him. Suddenly he stopped short, and Julie smashed into his back.

"Sorry." Julie rubbed her nose.

"Wait a minute. What else did he say in there?" Matt demanded. "What did he tell you about Celeste?"

"Only that they'll give her some more time to pull it together. That's good, right?"

"I suppose." Matt started walking again. "And what's this idea that you say you have?"

"It's just a start, but hear me out."

They reached the car, and Julie sketched out her thoughts to Matt on the drive home.

"I think that's a terrible plan. Celeste will never go for it," he said. He turned up the hard rock station so that Julie would practically have to yell to be heard.

She stared out the window. "She might," Julie said hopefully. The sky had clouded over, and the energy she'd had this morning was beginning to fade. She turned down the radio. "Really. She might."

"No." Despite his unflinching expression, Julie could hear the fear in his voice. "She's too fragile."

"She's fragile because you let her be fragile."

"Julie, you have no idea what you're talking about." He was angry now. "You can't begin to understand what she's going through."

"Then tell me," Julie spat back.

"No. Some things are private."

"God, what is wrong with you people? Don't you want to help her?"

"Julie, stop. Now."

"Why? Why won't anybody talk about this? Even Finn won't tell me."

"Finn again, huh?"

"What the hell does that mean?" Julie folded her arms and continued to look away.

"You've been talking about him all week as if he's some kind of gift to humanity. Pretty soon you'll have your own Flat Finn to cart around, right? You and Celeste will have a Finn fan club, with membership dues and monthly newsletters detailing how fantastic he is."

"What *exactly* is your problem?"

"Nothing," Matt muttered. "You should probably stay out of this."

"How am I supposed to stay out of this? I'm with Celeste more than anyone. She needs someone to help her."

"I know." Matt cranked the music back up. "I know she does."

CHAPTER 17

When they got home, Julie jumped on Facebook and saw that Finn was offline. She sent him a message asking if he was around and then stayed fixed on her inbox, hoping to hear back. After only a few minutes he replied.

Julie–
    I'm here. Can't connect to chat right now for some reason. Facebook is acting up. What's going on?
                                                                        –Finn

Julie wanted to feel out Finn and see what he thought about her plan for Celeste. She wrote him back, explaining her idea.

Julie–
    It's risky. I'm not sure what to say. Go easy, though. Celeste has been through a lot.
                                                                        –Finn

Finn–
    So everyone keeps saying. Celeste's school is threatening to kick her out if they don't see her improve socially, etc. I'm trying

to do what I can, but none of you will give me any information. I'm at a loss, and so this is what I've come up with. Either get your butt back here and give me some insight, or at least show some enthusiasm for my plan.

–Julie

Julie–

OK. Easy, girl.

It's not something we really talk about much. Or at all, to be honest.

This is a one-time-only deal, here, OK? Then we're not talking about this again. Ugh, here are the basics: A while ago, Mom went through a rough time. A major depression that was bad. Really bad. It left her not terribly functional. There's a longer history that I don't know much about, but a few years ago she went off her meds and crashed really hard. I guess that was when Celeste got so attached to me. Dad was busy dealing with Mom, Matt was being Matt, and so Celeste saw me as her savior, I guess.

A shrink could probably give you a better picture, but there's a lot that comes along with this stuff. My father travels as much as he can so he doesn't have to deal with this, and my mother has never exactly been the most involved mother even when stable. (Have you not noticed this yet? It's a joy.) So when I left, I guess it hit my sister hard. Mom is back on her meds now, and so you probably can't pick up on the underlying depression. Please don't bring this up with anyone else…it'll just rock the boat.

Flat Finn is about old wounds that are healing. About her attachment to me, and about crazy, unavailable parents.

Enough said on that matter. For real.

What are you wearing? ☺

–Finn

Finn–

Thank you. I know this wasn't easy to tell me, and it means a lot that you did. And it explains things a bit. I never would have guessed your mom has had such a difficult time. She seems so totally together. I'm sorry to hear about this, though. It must have been really hard on all of you.

Your mom forgot about a meeting at Celeste's school today, so Matt and I went in her place. The school is worried about Celeste, so I'm hoping to…Well, I don't know what I'm hoping to do. Get Celeste into the real world? I'll let you know how it goes. Maybe you could send her something for Christmas, especially if you're not going to make it home? Something more portable than Flat Finn that she can keep with her? Of course, don't let this discourage you from coming home…

I'm wearing six turtlenecks, sweatpants over jeans, three pairs of tube socks, and a golf hat.

–Julie

Julie–

When Mom is on her medications, you can't tell. And she works very hard to hide her depression from everyone.

I'll get something to Celeste. Promise. I'll be in Tahiti in a few days, and I'll find a good gift there.

God, I wish I could see you in that outfit. It sounds so sexy.

Gotta run. Might be around tonight to chat later if I can get online. Eleven your time?

–Finn

Finn–

Thought you were going to South America after the Cook Islands? I can't keep up with you!

I'll be around tonight.

–Julie

She was going out for a late dinner with Seth and knew she'd be home by ten at the latest. So much for going to bed at a reasonable hour. But she didn't care if she was up until dawn because messaging with Finn was worth the sleep deprivation. He was entertaining and a nice distraction from her impending finals. Plus, he was now the only one giving her any information on Celeste, even if it was sparse.

***

The roads were clear enough that Julie felt fine driving to the hardware store on her own. Even though she generally loathed navigating snow and ice, she certainly wasn't about to ask Matt to drive her after he'd unleashed his obnoxious attitude all over the place. Granted, he was probably upset about Celeste, but it didn't mean that he had to be such a pill. He couldn't even have a conversation about his sister without getting all weird; either he was rude or mean, or else he deflected all over the place until she just gave up asking.

Julie headed for the stairs. "I'm going to the hardware store. Back in a bit," she called in the direction of Matt's room. "Not that you care," she added under her breath.

She got to the front door before she heard Matt's footsteps clamoring out of his room and down to the first floor. "Wait! Julie, you're going now? I didn't know you were doing this… this *thing* today."

"Stop spazzing," she said calmly. "I'm just buying supplies. Nobody else is doing anything, so I'm going to."

"That's not fair. We're trying."

"No, you're all stagnant. And where the hell was your mother today, huh? This was a big deal."

"I know."

"How could she have forgotten?"

Matt stood silently for a moment. "I don't think she forgot," he said slowly. "She probably didn't want to go."

"Oh, well *that's* a good excuse!"

"I'm not saying it is. It's just the way things are."

"Another great excuse!"

"Julie?" Matt caught the door as she swung it open.

She whipped around. "What? What is it, Matt?" she snapped. "If you have something to say, then say it. If you want to help, help. If not, stay out of it."

"I just wanted to say thank you," he said softly.

"Oh." He wasn't being horrible right now. "Don't thank me yet."

"Thank you for trying."

Julie looked up at him. "Sure thing."

"Do you want me to drive? The roads aren't great," he offered.

"Are you going to behave yourself or are you going to pitch a fit every time I put something in the shopping cart?"

Matt smirked. "I will make a concerted effort to behave. Will that do?"

"No grumbling, no frowning, no disapproving gestures or words of any kind. In fact, no talking at all."

"Do you know how many times you've told me to stop talking today?"

"Do you know how many *more* times I could have told you that?"

"Do you want me to drive or not?"

"I do. I'm a big wimp. You be in charge of driving, and I'll be in charge of shopping."

"Blech. What stereotyped gender roles we've fallen into," Matt said, feigning horror. "The man drives, and the woman—"

"Have you already forgotten the no-talking rule?" Julie marched down the steps. "Let's go, smartass."

Matt bowed formally and waved her through the door. She could tell it was killing him, but he kept his mouth shut the entire ride. He didn't cringe once while she shopped, and he even bagged the items at the self-checkout.

It had started to snow a bit by the time they left, and Julie shivered as she waited for Matt to unlock the door. It took a few tries to start the car, and then they sat for a few minutes, waiting for the heat system to kick in.

Julie took a deep breath. "Why didn't you tell me about Erin?"

Matt fumbled with the radio. "Tell you what?"

"About her depression. Finn told me."

Matt winced. "Look, I don't want to do this now." He turned the dial quickly, filling the car with static noise and commercial clips.

"Matt."

"Julie, not now."

"OK." She leaned back into the headrest and pulled her coat in tightly around her body. "Maybe sometime?"

"You can't let anything go, can you?"

"Come on! It'd be great." She slapped his arm lightly. "We could sit around and have a long, drawn-out conversation about your mother and the impact her depression has had on the dynamics of the family. Then you can pour your heart out about your angst-ridden childhood, and we'd analyze every minute nuance of your personality."

At least he was smiling now. "That sounds like torture."

"Really? You don't want to bare your soul to me? Cry a little? Catharsis at its finest?"

"Intro to Psych has gotten out of hand, I see."

"I need to practice. You don't want me to fail my class, do you?"

"If it means avoiding that nauseating conversation, then yes. I'll tolerate your failing a class."

Julie slapped his arm again. "Jerk."

CHAPTER 18

Matthew Watkins *is brought to you today by the Second Law of Thermodynamics and the letter Qua.*

Finn Is God *I put my pants on one leg at a time, just like everyone else. It's the way I take them OFF that makes me better than you.*

Julie Seagle *Why is luge a sport? You dress up like a giant sperm and go sledding really fast. That's hardly athletic. Phallic and sexy, yes. But hardly athletic.*

"Julie! Julie!" Celeste's voice carried from the second floor down to the kitchen.

Julie calmly took another bite of cereal and set her phone on the table. She was exhausted, having stayed up until nearly three in the morning IMing with Finn, but she'd gone ahead with her plan for the day anyway. There was no sense in waiting any longer.

"Julie!" Celeste stomped down the stairs, and Julie tried not to flinch as she heard her enter the room.

"Yes? What is it?" She kept her eyes on the newsprint.

"I do not find this amusing."

"You don't find what amusing? The fact that you avoid using contractions when you get worked up?"

"Julie, I would like you to take this seriously. I have concerns about your flippant tone. Your behavior is unnerving."

Julie finally looked up. Celeste stood beside Flat Finn, and while his expression hadn't changed, she wore a decidedly irked expression. "Which behavior would that be?"

"You've affixed this unfunny note to Flat Finn's mouth. As though he is expressing a thought."

"*He* thinks it's funny."

"He is not a cartoon, and we find it disrespectful."

"*He* doesn't find it disrespectful."

"How do you know what Flat Finn thinks?" Celeste demanded.

"I spend quite a bit of time with him, in case you hadn't noticed. I can sense these things."

Celeste frowned and examined the bubble-style note written on bright yellow paper that was stuck by Flat Finn's mouth. "I do not even understand what this note is supposed to mean. *I seek a flexibility transformation!!!*"

"He's rather stiff, don't you think? I suspect Flat Finn would appreciate not having his head smacked against the trunk of the car every time he has to go in or out. And perhaps he'd like to sit in a chair properly without having to lean at sharp angles." Julie shrugged and looked back at her newspaper. "He's crying out for help, and I think we should give it to him. He's been suffering in silence for too long now, aching to be bendy and to conform to standard furniture. Plus, I think he wants to take a Pilates class."

"There is that flippant tone again," Celeste said. "Although you might have a point. However, you could have conveyed your enthusiasm for this idea with the use of only one exclamation point. Three is overkill. What would this *flexibility transformation* involve?"

As Julie outlined the idea, Celeste stared back, expressionless.

"I will consider this option and get back to you." Celeste proudly raised Flat Finn off the floor and marched out of the room.

"Take your time," Julie murmured. "There's only a lifetime of good mental health at stake here."

✳✳✳

Julie pushed out the blade from the utility knife and repositioned Flat Finn on the thick towel that she'd spread out on the kitchen floor. "Inhale and exhale, Celeste. Inhale and exhale."

"Flat Finn is having second thoughts! Flat Finn is having second thoughts!"

"Flat Finn is not having second thoughts."

"You are going to cut him into two pieces," Celeste said in a severely accusing tone. "That is a rather monumental injury."

"It's not an injury. It's a modification. I agree that it'll be pretty creepy for a few moments. He will indeed be in two pieces. But I swear to God that I'm going to put him back together." Julie held up the hardware that she'd bought the day before. "See these hinges? They'll hold him together, just like we talked about. Then he can bend at the waist. He can even fold in half, which is a damn good party trick if you ask me."

"Flat Finn does not attend parties."

"He might after this." Julie pushed the metal ruler against the cardboard and checked the cutting line again. She poised the blade at the edge of the cutout. "You ready?"

Celeste moved away from Julie. "I think that I will stay on this side of the room and turn my back to you."

"Fine," Julie agreed. "Why don't you talk to him while I work."

"Talk to him about what exactly?"

"Reassure him. Tell him everything will be peachy. That he'll be happier in the long run. Stuff like that. OK, here I go." Julie pressed the knife into Flat Finn's waistline and etched a cut across the width. "Start talking, Celeste!" She began to retrace the line, sinking the blade deeper into the cardboard.

"This is a great day to increase limberness!" Celeste yelled unconvincingly. "Think of all of the things you will be able to achieve, Flat Finn!"

"He's doing great. Keep going," Julie encouraged.

"Um…It was stupid Julie's idea, and so you will hold her responsible if this surgery ends in tragedy!"

"Very funny. Try again. Tell him that this is an important and necessary step in his development. That he will thank you for helping him fit in with others. This is a challenging time, but you are here for him and will get him through this." Julie finished the cut and separated Flat Finn into two parts. OK, even she had to admit that this was pretty freaky. "There!"

"You did it? He has been divided?" Celeste's voice trembled. "Hurry. Julie, hurry. Please!"

"I am. Don't look." She grabbed the screwdriver and a set of hinges. "Your boy here needs to know that you support this step, Celeste."

"OK, OK…Flat Finn? I support this modification?"

Julie could hear Celeste pacing at the other end of the room. "With a little more conviction, please."

"I support this modification!"

"You will be his pillar of strength!" Julie prompted.

"That is a vile cliché, and I will not say that."

"Then come up with your own phrases," Julie said as she continued screwing in the silver hinges.

"This is difficult. I *cannot* think of the appropriate thing to say." Celeste let out a frustrated, guttural sound that made Julie flinch. "Help me. You talk to him."

"Oh, Flat Finn, my dear. This is nothing to get all stressed out about. I realize that you're having an understandably nervous reaction to this simple procedure. Just because you want this doesn't mean it's easy. You're doing very well. Much less complaining than most flat people. Really. I'm quite impressed."

"Julie, hurry up. You have to hurry up."

"Almost done, kiddo. Just one more minute, and…Ta da!" Julie rolled back on her knees and examined her work. Not bad for someone who could barely identify most tools. "Want to see him?" She lifted Flat Finn to a standing position and turned the small semicircular dial that she had put on the back to prevent him from collapsing in half at inappropriate times.

Celeste turned around and eyed Flat Finn warily. After a few moments, her face softened. "Actually, I quite like his appearance. It's as though he's wearing a belt buckle. You might have selected gold, but the silver isn't terrible."

"Yay! You have some contractions back *and* an added concern for fashion."

"Do I really do that? The thing with the contractions? No one has ever mentioned that."

"You do. It's sort of cute sometimes. You sound like Matt. But you might want to ease up on it. It'd make you sound more relaxed and casual. Comfortable."

"I will try to pay more attention to my speech. I mean, *I'll try.*"

Julie bent Flat Finn forward and back a few times at the waist. "Look! He's exercising. Or practicing to pick up pennies off the sidewalk. Oh my God, he's a cheapskate, isn't he? What a loathsome quality."

"He is not a cheapskate." Celeste cracked a smile. "He is conservative. Thoughtful."

"Yeah? Christmas is coming up. I expect big things." Julie brushed a smudge off his arm. "If this hinge deal works out, maybe we can add more later? At the arms, legs, neck?"

Celeste examined the spot that Julie had wiped off. "Let's not get ahead of ourselves."

"Come on. Let's take him for a test run. Follow me."

"Where are we going?"

"Just follow me." Julie led the way up to the second floor, with Celeste and Flat Finn close behind her. She knocked on Matt's open door. "Hello! You have visitors!"

As usual, he was seated in front of his laptop. "Hey." Matt looked tired, but his eyes widened as Celeste toted Flat Finn into the room. "What's going on here?"

"Flat Finn has expanded his repertoire of possible poses." Julie took Flat Finn from Celeste's hands and sat him up on Matt's bed. "Now you two can hang out and shoot the breeze without feeling socially uncomfortable because you're sitting while he's always standing."

Matt eyed the figure on his bed. "Yes, this will be significantly less socially uncomfortable. Celeste, you're fine with this? This, um, alteration?"

"I am. What do you think Dad will say?"

Julie sat at the foot of the bed. "It should be the first thing he hears when he gets back from his trip tonight. He'll be proud of Flat Finn. And so will your mom."

"If she notices," Matt added in a soft singsong tone.

"So perhaps," Julie started hesitantly, "you'd be willing to hang out with Flat Finn once in a while if Celeste and I want to go out by ourselves and do girl stuff?"

Celeste stiffened. "Wait, you never said—"

"Just assessing the options now available," Julie said. "You could do that, right, Matt? Should the need arise?"

"I guess I could do that," Matt agreed, doing a less than spectacular job of hiding his reluctance. "What's the pay rate?"

Julie smirked. "There is a sliding scale dependent on your enthusiasm. So far, you are at the rate of a penny per hour."

Celeste crossed her arms. "Are you two done entertaining yourselves?"

"I didn't realize we had started." Matt got up from his seat. "You ready for lunch, Celeste?"

"Sure. Will you make egg-and-cheese sandwiches?"

Matt nodded and walked by Julie. "Whatever you want."

"Matt!" Julie hissed.

He turned back, confused. "What?"

Julie tossed her hands up. "Nothing."

She hung back in Matt's room while they went downstairs. God, she had just made a step in the right direction with this hinge thing, and here was Matt acting as if his sister were six years old. Seriously, Celeste could make herself lunch. *Way to inspire confidence, Matt.*

Would someone let this kid grow up, already?

CHAPTER 19

"Hi, Seth." Julie tucked the phone in the crook of her neck while she folded another T-shirt and added it to the pile of clean laundry on the bed.

"Hey, you. I feel like I haven't talked to you in weeks." Seth sounded sweet, but she could detect a frustrated edge.

"I know. With finals coming up, I've been mobbed. Sorry I didn't call you back yesterday."

"It's just that it's the middle of December, and you're leaving soon for three weeks. I was hoping we could hang out some more before then. You know, a little alone time?" Julie could tell he was smiling now.

"You mean you've had enough time with Celeste and me in the coffeehouse?" she teased. "You don't find that romantic, and sexy, and hot?"

"While I very much enjoy watching you sweat over your calculus assignments, and I'm equally fond of Celeste's detailed and ruthless assessments of my beverage-making skills, I'd kill for a night alone with you."

Julie opened the bottom drawer of the dresser and picked up a stack of folded clothes. "You got it. How about tonight?"

Seth groaned. "I can't. I'm leading a study group for one of my polisci classes. Tomorrow? Besides, Friday is a better date night anyhow."

"Works for me."

"Come over around seven and I'll make you dinner."

"OK, see you then." She tossed the phone down and went to set her clothes in the drawer. Finn's skydiving shirts sat in the bottom. She took out the weathered blue shirt that read, *Don't forget to pull*. Without thinking, she lifted it up to her face and inhaled.

"What are you doing?"

Julie whipped around. This was the first time that she had heard Matt laugh uncontrollably. She felt herself blush, but threw the shirt at him. "I found some of Finn's clothes in here and wanted to make sure they weren't all stinky and gross. I just did laundry and don't need my clean stuff next to smelly boy stuff."

"Uh-huh. Whatever you say." He tossed the shirt back to her.

"Shut up!" Julie rolled her eyes.

"If you want to smell Finn's clothes, be my guest. I think there is a pair of his old hiking boots in the attic. Do you want me to get those? I'm positive they'll still have a good Finn scent. Believe me, Odor Eaters never did a thing for my brother's feet."

Julie's phone rang again. "Middle child syndrome," she mumbled as she reached over to answer it. "Hello?"

"I can't wait to see you," Seth said. "I just had to tell you that. Gotta run. Bye!"

She smiled and hung up just as Celeste brushed past Matthew and held her fingers out to Julie. "My polish is chipping. Can I redo my fingernails?"

"Sure thing. Help yourself to whatever color you want. You know where the stuff is."

Celeste turned on the radio, picked up the bag of nail polish, and took a seat on the end of the bed.

"Hey, Celeste," Matt said. "This came for you earlier." Julie hadn't even noticed that he had been holding a bulging Fed Ex envelope in his hand. "It's from Finn."

Celeste dropped the bag and slowly lifted her head. "Finn sent me something?"

"Yeah, sweetie. He did. Here you go." Matt walked the package to his sister and then left the room.

Julie scrambled over the two laundry baskets to reach Celeste, who sat silently beaming at the item in her hands. "Open it! Open it!"

"Oh. Of course. How did he...? I can't...I can't believe that he sent me something. But I *knew*. Look at how far this had to travel." She pointed at the postage marks and strange writing on the front. "I don't know how he..."

"For God's sake, open it!"

Celeste's hands shook as she tore off the perforated tab and upended the mailing envelope. "Oooooh, Julie, look." She held up a silver barrette with beautiful turquoise and amber stones. "It's lovely, isn't it?" she asked breathlessly.

"It really is. It will look amazing in your hair." She peeked inside the envelope. "No card?"

"I guess not. That's OK, though. Will you put it in for me?"

"Of course." Julie gathered Celeste's thick hair at the nape of her neck. As she undid the clasp, she noticed something. "Honey, look. It's engraved on the back."

"It is?" Celeste turned around, her eyes sparkling brightly.

"Yes." Julie squinted at the small etching. "It says, *Love is a portion of the soul itself, and it is of the same nature as the celestial breathing of the atmosphere of paradise.*"

Celeste beamed. "Finn used to find quotes with *celestial* in them for me. That one is Victor Hugo. It's my favorite." She turned around again so Julie could put the barrette in. "Although Finn always liked to tease me with quotes from the Jean de Brunhoff books. Do you know those? The stories about the elephants? King Babar and Queen Celeste?"

"I do know those stories. My mom used to read them to me."

Celeste seemed energized and illuminated by Finn's gift. And while Julie doubted this would eradicate Celeste's attachment to Flat Finn, it couldn't hurt.

Julie sighed softly as she tousled Celeste's curls. Five more months. Julie had told the guidance counselor at Barnaby that Celeste would make significant progress by May. But five months until what exactly? Until she turned into a typical teenager? Julie couldn't see that happening, nor did she want it to happen. Celeste's uniqueness shouldn't be obliterated. What was the marker of acceptable progress? When she ditched Flat Finn? When she had a given number of friends? When she stopped talking like someone from a Victorian movie? Well, *something* would need to change, and Julie figured that she would know it when it happened.

∗∗∗

Matthew Watkins *"One's life should never be so boring that one resorts to making up quotes and falsely attributing them to famous people." –Winston Churchill*

Finn Is God *SAY TAKE FACEBOOK "HOW TASTE YR BRANEZ" QUIZ. SEND BRANEZ 2 ME I TASTE. PS I ARE NOT A ZOMBIES.*

Julie Seagle *If you can't stop thinking about someone's update, that's called "status cling."*

Julie had the car for the evening for her date with Seth. Miraculously she managed to find a parking spot, but it took four tries for her to cram the car into the small space between a huge pickup truck and a beat-up van. It was freezing out tonight, and she sat in the car for a moment before opening the door. She just needed another few minutes.

This was supposed to be a big night with Seth. She knew that. She should be flying up to his place. Maybe she was nervous?

She grabbed her phone and checked her mail. There was a message from Dana: *Have a hot night with Seth! And close the deal already! LOL!* Julie laughed.

And one message from Finn.

Julie–
Did Celeste's package get there? I'm holding a lovely hand-written note that I forgot to put in the envelope. I'm a dummy. Tell her I'm sorry, but that I hope she likes her gift.

Hope you're having a good night.

–Finn

Finn–
I'll tell her. She loved the gift. Very sweet of you. Not the same as having you here, but it'll tide her over for a bit. Gotta run. I'll see if you're on chat later. Although I'm a tired wreck today from being up so late last night. You're evil.

–Julie

She could have just said that she was going to her boyfriend's house. There was no reason not to. But she still hadn't mentioned Seth, and it seemed silly to make a dramatic announcement about it.

Julie got out of the car and walked to the front door of Seth's building, her phone still in her hand. She stood for a moment before ringing the buzzer. Had it sounded stupid to ask Finn if he would be online later? Totally pathetic? It's not as if she was chasing after him or anything, but what if it looked that way? Here she was, heading up to another guy's apartment for a big-deal evening, so she wasn't going to be online later anyway. Why had she even said that?

From now on, maybe she should wait sixty seconds before she sent messages to Finn.

Seth buzzed her in, and she paused in the lobby. Julie had always taken the stairs, of course, and never the elevator, but tonight she was feeling brave. Daring. She could do this. No dramatic fainting or having a panic attack. No more being controlled by this stupid phobia. She would ride the elevator like a completely normal human being. She pressed the elevator button—immediately opening the doors—stepped inside, and hit the button for his floor. She leaned back against the metal wall and closed her eyes, ignoring the handrail that dug into her back. There. There was nothing to be afraid of. Her vision hadn't blurred, the cabin wasn't spinning, and she wasn't going to fall. In fact, the elevator issue felt like the least of her concerns right now.

It didn't really matter what Finn thought of her anyway, right? Who cared if he knew she wanted to find him online tonight? Which she wasn't going to do anyway because she would be busy. Finn was just some boy she would probably never meet anyway. Some boy she e-mailed and chatted with.

Maybe he'd be around tonight, maybe he wouldn't. It didn't matter because *she* wouldn't be free. *She* had important things to take care of. With Seth. Her boyfriend.

Suddenly the elevator slammed to a hard stop, causing Julie to stumble forward. She caught the rail with her hand and froze. The doors didn't open. She knew she hadn't been in the elevator long enough to have reached Seth's floor. Perhaps something would kick into gear in a minute and the elevator would magically finish its trip up? Julie swore and hit every button on the panel but one. The last thing she felt like doing was pressing that nasty red button that would sound the alarm. This was what she got for being a daredevil. She called Seth.

"Where are you? Didn't I just buzz you in?" he asked.

"Yes, I *am* in the building," she agreed. "In the elevator."

"Well, hurry up and get in here. I've got dinner ready, a little wine poured, candles lit. The whole bit."

"That sounds really nice."

"I'll be honest. I'm trying to seduce you, Ms. Seagle."

Julie looked down at the dirty floor, focusing her attention on one particular smudge. "That might be tricky."

"Why's that?"

"Because I'm stuck in your elevator. And it seems to be getting smaller by the minute in here."

"I'll be right there."

Beads of sweat were starting to accumulate on her hairline, and her stomach was noticeably unhappy. The evil metal box with its fluorescent lighting was decidedly uncomfortable, and the thought that she was suspended in the air—by what was probably an ancient cable—was not exactly soothing. It was like being dangled over a cliff or frozen at the top of a Ferris wheel. How did the Ferris wheel even get its name? Had there been a

Mr. Ferris who had sadistically designed such a disgusting, terrifying ride? Matt would probably know. If she ever got out of here, she could ask him. If she didn't faint and smack her head on the wall and give herself brain damage, she could ask him.

"Julie? Julie?" Seth pounded on the top of the elevator doors.

"Don't hit the doors, for God's sake! You'll probably plummet me to the basement!" Julie barely wanted to move in this death trap, and there was her boyfriend trying to snap what was probably the last frayed metal thread holding her up.

"You're stuck between the third and fourth floor. This happens once in a while. I just called the building supervisor, who is calling the fire department."

"Great. That sounds fun." Julie carefully slumped to the floor and tucked her knees into her chest.

"You OK in there?"

"No. I'm not OK. I'm freaking out! I don't want to be in here. Really. Not at all. I'm going to die any minute, I can just tell."

"Um, do you want to do some deep-breathing exercises? Why don't you visualize floating things? Feathers and clouds and bubbles. That might help."

"No, I don't want to do any frickin' deep-breathing exercises! I want the goddamn fire department to get me out."

"Julie, listen to me. I'll count to five, and you inhale through your nose along with me. Then exhale for five counts through your mouth. Ready? One, two—"

Shut. Up. Seth was no help whatsoever. Fine, he had called the fire department, but otherwise he was not helping her to relax one bit. Her phone sounded, and she realized that it was still in her hand, her fingers now white from gripping it so tightly.

Julie–

I should be around later, yes. Where you off to tonight?

–Finn

Oh, thank God. Finn! She checked Facebook's chat from her phone, and he was signed on.

Julie Seagle

Am flipping stuck in an elevator. Alone. Miserable. Help is on the way supposedly, but I am not enjoying this experience. Starting to seriously panic. Sweating, shakes, visions of brutal death.

Finn Is God

What??? Oh, no! Do not panic. Have you forgotten that I am a superhero?

Julie Seagle

I had forgotten! Feel totally safe now. OK, you fly under the elevator and lift me up to safety. Ready? Go!

Finn Is God

Unfortunately my flying powers were deactivated because I abused my superhero status. Apologies. I have other powers, though, that will get you through this.

Julie Seagle

Give it your best shot. Convince me that I'm not a million feet in the air.

"Julie?" Seth called. "You still breathing with me? And... inhale!"

"Yup!" she called out.

"Good! You keep breathing, and I will distract you. Um…I'll sing!" There was silence for a moment. "I don't know what to sing. OK, how about this?" Seth launched into an impressively loud and off-key rendition of "Swing Low, Sweet Chariot." "I don't know why I chose that. It's just what came to mind."

"It's lovely. Keep going," Julie hollered.

Finn Is God

You can't pretend you are not up high, because you are.

Julie Seagle

These are delightful powers you have. Thank you so much. I feel a million times better.

Finn Is God

Accept that you're up high and embrace it. Take control. It's like when I go skydiving. I don't actually love heights. It scares the hell out of me to be in that plane, looking down at the ground. But I jump through that fear and turn it into euphoria.

Julie Seagle

I would never in a million years go skydiving.

Finn Is God

What if I took you?

Julie Seagle

I'd still be jumping out of a plane alone, just like I'm alone in this stupid elevator.

"Swiiiiiing looooow," Seth's singing echoed through the building. "Oh! The fire department is here. Hold on. Let me see what they say."

Finn Is God
You wouldn't be alone. I'd take you tandem, so you'd be strapped to me. We'd jump together.

Julie Seagle
How would that work?

Finn Is God
You'd be in front of me, your back pressed into my chest.

Julie Seagle
That part doesn't sound so awful.

Crap. Did she just write that? There was no *undo* or *delete* button. How totally embarrassing.

Finn Is God
No. It doesn't sound so awful, does it?

Julie Seagle
So then tell me more.

Finn Is God
OK. Pretend we're going right now. Ready?

Julie Seagle
Ready.

Finn Is God
We're in the plane, and it's loud and cold. You see duct tape over parts of the interior of the plane and wonder if jumping is the worst idea you've ever had, but I tell you you'll be fine. We both have on the full skydiving suits, helmets, goggles, chutes. The suit is tight, and it gives you the illusion of being safe, secure. You're full of mixed emotions. Pride, anxiety, exuberance, terror.

Julie Seagle
Nausea?

Finn Is God
That's not an emotion! But yes, nausea.

"Miss? Boston Fire Department here. We'll have you out in about thirty minutes. You hangin' in there?" a gruff voice asked her.

"Take your time," Julie called out as she continued staring at the small screen in her hands.

"Julie, did you hear that?" Seth asked. "Only thirty minutes. I know it sounds like forever, but it'll go by fast. Is my singing helping? It should at least be making you laugh."

"Knock it off with the singing!" one of the firemen ordered. "Miss, even though there will be a bit of banging going on, you're perfectly safe. We'll get you out just fine."

"No rush," Julie muttered.

Julie Seagle
Then what?

Finn Is God

Your mind is racing. Did you remember to turn off the oven at home? Your car needs an oil change. You're out of shampoo. Why do washing machines eat socks? Do they taste good? Should *you* try eating socks? You wonder if you should back out, if this was a mistake. You didn't tell anyone that you were jumping today, and now what if you die? You worry that you'll forget what to do, that you won't remember when to pull the chute. I show you the altimeter. The plane is only halfway up to where we need to be, and it already feels so high. But you're not in any danger.

A loud thud sounded, and the elevator shook. Then metallic noises echoed throughout the chamber. Julie squeezed her eyes shut and couldn't stop the whimpering sound she made.

Julie Seagle

Finn, I'm scared. The elevator is shaking.

Finn Is God

I know you are, but I've got you. You're not in the elevator, remember? You're with me. I stand you up and try to push your body away from mine, reminding you that you are tightly strapped to me and that I won't let anything happen. It's my job to control our jump and my job to pull the chute if you don't. You're safe. Tell me that you trust me.

Julie Seagle

I trust you.

Finn Is God

We're high enough now, and one of the instructors opens the door, sending a powerful rush of air into the cabin. Your heart nearly stops when I start to walk you to the edge. As much as you're terrified, you're also starting to feel the rush, the thrill you get from being on the brink.

The noise from above continued, but Julie barely noticed. The only thing she could pay attention to, the only thing she cared about right now, was what Finn was writing her.

Finn Is God

We're at 15,000 feet now, and when you look down at the ground, you immediately try to step away from the door. You want to bail on this. I back you up, and we let someone else jump first. I put my arms around your waist and pull you in, holding you, letting you know I'm with you. I tell you that you can do this, that you're strong enough and brave enough. I tell you that you can do anything. So you nod and agree to jump.

We move to the edge of the plane again and pause. You cross your arms over your chest and lean your head back into me like I told you. I start to rock us back and forth, getting us ready to jump. And then we go.

Julie's pounding heart and the fact that she was sweating no longer had anything to do with the elevator situation.

Julie Seagle

How do I feel when we jump?

Finn Is God

The minute we hit the air, you are surprisingly relaxed. All of your problems seem to go away. Your stomach doesn't drop. There's no falling sensation. It's just freeing. It's as close to flying as you'll ever get. A calm like you've never known before, and you don't want it to end.

Finn Is God

So we freefall like this for 5,000 feet. We don't want it to stop. We want to feel like this forever, lost in this experience. This is why people pull their chutes late, because freefalling is like a drug.

Julie Seagle

Or something else, I'm guessing.

Finn Is God

Yes, or something else. They do call it an "airgasm" for a reason...

Julie Seagle

I can see why. But we have to pull the chute.

Finn Is God

Yes, we have to pull the chute. So I do it. And it jerks us back—hard—but then we're falling smoothly, softer than before, easily. We're drifting together. It's quieter now, and you can hear my voice.

Julie Seagle

And what do you say to me?

Suddenly the elevator kicked into gear and descended half a floor.

Julie Seagle
Shit. The elevator is working now.

Finn Is God
That's good news!

Julie Seagle
Right now it doesn't feel like it. I'll find you later.

The doors creaked open. From her spot on the dirty floor, Julie stared at the small crowd that faced her. Seth was jubilant, and the firefighters looked pleased with their quick success. Julie was nonetheless annoyed.

"Aren't you going to get up?" Seth asked as he stepped forward. "Are you hurt?" He knelt down in front of her and put his hand on her knee. "Julie? You're all sweaty and flushed."

"I'm fine. Really." She took his hand in hers and smiled. He really was cute, and sweet, and funny. There was nothing not to like about him. In fact, she suddenly liked him—needed him— more than ever. She leaned in and whispered, "We have to get up to your apartment. Now."

Seth looked her in the eyes and nodded.

They quickly thanked the people who had freed her and hurried to the stairwell. Seth practically yanked her up the stairs until they reached his landing. He turned and pulled her into him, pressing his lips to hers and sliding his tongue into her mouth. Julie kissed him back, hard, and they fumbled down the hallway to his door, nearly falling into the living room. He backed her against the wall and slid his hands over the front of her shirt, his fingers digging into her skin, pulling her in closer. Then Julie's hands were in his hair, and she pulled her mouth from his, gasping for air. She closed her eyes and felt his lips move to her neck, his breath hot and ragged, making her lost and dizzy.

His touch was so urgent and heated and the way he kissed her confident and intense. She hadn't been wanted like this before. Jared had been so fumbling and inept, and she didn't have much experience with anyone else.

She wondered what Finn would be like. What would it feel like to kiss him? What would he taste like? Would his hands be gentle? Would he go slowly, smoothly, take his time? How would he sound if she ran her fingers over his arm, up his biceps, down his chest, moving lower? Would their bodies fit together perfectly, molding into each other as they kissed desperately?

Julie opened her eyes. *Oh, no. Oh, no. This was so screwed up.*

She took her hands from the back of Seth's neck and touched his cheek. "Seth?"

"Julie," he murmured, moving to kiss her mouth again.

"Seth. I'm sorry," she whispered in disbelief. She dropped her head to his shoulder. "I'm so sorry."

"Wait, what?" He took a small step back. "What's wrong?"

"I can't…" She took a deep breath. "I can't do this."

"Too much?" he asked. "We've been together a while. I thought you wanted to. You seemed so into everything. It's OK, though."

"No, it's not OK. You're so great. You're wonderful. There's no reason that I shouldn't want this."

Seth took another step back. "But you don't want this, do you?"

She shook her head. Julie hated how hurt he looked. She didn't know what to say. "My head is not where it should be. I'm not *feeling* what I should be. What I wish I were."

He was quiet for a minute. "I pretty much knew that," he admitted. Seth took her hand in his and looked down. "I don't think you've ever been as into us as I have. Is there someone else?"

Julie felt her eyes tear up, and she hesitated before answering him. "I think there might be."

CHAPTER 20

Julie pulled the car into the Watkinses' driveway and turned off the engine. She checked her phone again. Nothing else from Finn.

She called Dana.

"What the hell are you doing calling me from your hot and steamy date? Why are you not rolling around in Seth's bed? Oh, ew! You better not be *calling me* from his bed," Dana warned.

"No." Julie sniffed. "But thank you for implying that I'd do something so creepy. I'm at home."

"What? What are you talking about?"

"Seth and I broke up." Seth had been undeniably understanding about things. *If it's not there, it's not there,* he'd said. But she still felt rotten.

"Julie! What is going on?" Dana demanded.

Julie dropped back against the headrest and looked at herself in the rearview mirror. "I think I'm in love with somebody that I've never met."

"Explain."

"I met him online."

"That's disgusting. You've been frequenting online dating sites? Do you know how many people lie on those things? Oh, man, you didn't go to Craigslist, did you? After your apartment experience, I'd have thought you knew better. Wait a minute. You met him on Facebook, didn't you? That's gross."

"Now that you mention it, I guess I kind of did meet him on Facebook. It's the guy whose room I've been staying in. Finn. We've been talking online for months."

"Oh my God, this is so exciting! And so dirty and wrong! Is he hot? You haven't met him yet? When is he coming home? Did you tell Seth about him?" Dana threw questions at her left and right.

"I don't know when he's coming home. Possibly in the next few weeks for Christmas, but I'm going to be with my father in California then. Hopefully we'll overlap a bit. If pictures say anything, then yes, he's super hot. Gorgeous. Illegally attractive. Seth guessed there was someone else, but I didn't tell him who. It sounds ridiculous."

"And does Finn like you? I mean, *loooove* you? Are you seriously in love with him?" Julie guessed Dana was jumping out of her seat by now.

"Of course I'm not *really* in love with him. I don't even know him." Except that she did know him. At least she felt as if she did. As if she had known him forever. "I have no idea what Finn thinks about me. He'd probably think I'm a lunatic if he overheard this conversation."

"Or he'd be flattered beyond belief that you've fallen for his daily love letters," Dana shrieked. "Months of wooing you online have paid off."

"He's hardly been wooing me. And no love letters." Julie sighed. Although those would be fun. "And I don't hear from him every day. Sometimes he's in remote areas of the world where he can't get online. I don't know. This whole thing is idiotic. I'm idiotic."

"No, it's romantic. You've made an emotional connection that's not based on superficial daily BS."

"Is that your official psychological interpretation?"

"Yes. Now this is all lovely, and I'm thrilled for you, but this raises an important issue for me."

"What's that?"

"Finn has a brother, right? At MIT?"

"Yeah. Matt. So what?"

"Set me up. You've never let me in the house for some stupid reason, but Matt obviously comes from good genes if the parents produced such an online hottie."

Julie laughed. "You don't want to go out with Matt. Trust me. He's not your type. And he looks nothing like Finn. Besides, what about Jamie? I thought you two were still together?"

"He's dumb. There's no way around it. Gorgeous and sex-crazed, yes, but he's a big, dumb stud, and I'm over it. Set me up. I need someone with a brain."

Julie thought for a minute. She might as well. Poor Matt seemed to have no social life whatsoever, and she'd never even heard him hint at having a date. And he definitely had a brain, even if it was slightly warped. She could stay home with Celeste if Erin and Roger were out. Why not? Matt deserved a little fun.

"OK, I'll give him your number."

"Cool. Go find your new boyfriend online, and call me tomorrow."

"Very funny." Julie hung up and blew her nose.

Of all the asinine situations to get herself into. Finn and his thinly veiled skydiving metaphor had just ruined what could have been a perfectly nice relationship with a perfectly nice guy. Seth did not deserve to get dumped for a one-sided, imaginary online flirtation.

But maybe it wasn't one-sided? Or imaginary?

Julie trudged up the front steps and into the house. She just wanted to go to her room. Finn's room. Although it wasn't even late, she was exhausted and stressed out. She was about to open the bedroom door when she heard Erin laugh. Julie leaned her head back and saw that Erin and Roger's door was open. Erin was sitting on the floor by the foot of the bed, smiling and holding something in her hand. She was hardly ever around in the evenings, so it was surprising to find her home.

Julie crossed the floor, then stopped just before she knocked. Erin might have been laughing, but her eyes were red, her face blotchy. A full glass of red wine and an empty wine bottle were on the floor. "Erin?"

"Oh. Hi, Julie." Erin looked up and brushed the hair out of her face. She waved her hand. "Come in. Come in." Her speech was slightly slurred, and she picked up her glass and took a sip. "Would you like some wine? I'll get another bottle."

"No. Thank you." Julie stepped into the room and could see now that Erin was holding Celeste's barrette. "Wasn't that a lovely gift Finn sent?"

Erin turned the clip over in her hand, her lips forming a half-smile. "It's remarkable, isn't it? Amazing that it reached us. Unimaginable, really. From so far away."

Julie knelt down. "You miss him, don't you?"

Erin nodded.

"How long has he been gone?" Julie asked.

"Oh, ages it seems. And yet," Erin swayed forward tipsily, "with Flat Finn around, it's as if he's still here." She giggled. "But I know he's not."

"It sounds as if he's having a wonderful time on this trip. What an opportunity to be able to travel the world the way he is, right? And the volunteer work he's involved with is incredibly generous. Think of all the good he's doing. It must be hard, though, to have your kids grow up and move away from home."

"It's very hard. Finn was always so different. Such a…a light. He was everything. The family glue. Without him here…"

Julie squirmed uncomfortably. "Matt and Celeste are still at home," she offered. "And they're both pretty special too."

Erin bobbed her head up. "Of course. I love them. Although I don't really know what to do with a girl. Poor Celeste." She giggled. "But let me show you the difference between my boys." Erin wobbled to a stand, lurched toward a display shelf on the far wall, and pushed some books aside, digging for something. "See this? Matt made me this when he was a kid. How ridiculous, huh?" She picked up a little woodcarving. "Who makes their mother something that says *Wow*?"

Julie got up and walked toward Erin, who was drunk and confused. Finn had made this for his mother. Julie took the camp project, flipped it upside down, and waited while Erin stared at it.

"Look at that! It says *Mom*." Erin burst out laughing, covering her mouth with her hands and doubling over as her misinterpretation sank in.

"Finn made this for you at camp," Julie said.

"All these years…and I thought…" Erin could hardly speak. She wiped her eyes. "What the hell kind of mother am I? What the hell kind of blind, brainless, disconnected mother am I?" Erin wasn't laughing anymore. "*Mom*. It says *Mom*. Jesus Christ. I'm a piece of work."

"Erin, it's OK. Really." Julie set the woodcarving back on the shelf, the right way.

Erin crossed the room and picked up her wine. "You sure you don't want some? I won't tell your mother."

Julie shook her head. "No. I should get to bed. Where is Roger? Is he home?"

"Upstairs. In the third-floor guest room. He's been snoring with that cold he picked up, and it drives me bonkers."

"Will you be all right? Do you want me to stay with you for a while?" Julie wasn't dying to hang around a tipsy, emotional Erin, but she also felt bad leaving her alone. Hopefully Erin would call it a night.

"I'm fine, Julie. Perfectly fine. Promise. I don't usually drink much. It's making me silly and emotional."

"OK, then. Good night." Julie turned to leave, but Erin stopped her.

"Julie? Thank you for being here. You make the house less lonely."

Julie smiled. "I like it here. I really do. You and Roger are so good to me, and Matt and Celeste are like the siblings I never had."

"So you think of Matt like a brother?"

Julie nodded.

"Huh." She sat down on the floor again. "I love my children, you know. All of them. It's just hard. It's hard for me to be their mother."

Julie didn't know what to say to this. "I know you love them. Just…Just get some sleep. You'll feel better tomorrow."

She tiptoed through the hall to her room. Matt's light was off, and Flat Finn stood at alert outside Celeste's room, reminiscent of the Queen's Guard outside Buckingham Palace. Julie shut her door and kicked off her shoes. She immediately went to the dresser and got changed for bed, pulling one of Finn's skydiving shirts over her head. She touched the worn material, the blue having faded to a weathered, pale color, and the lettering barely readable anymore. *Don't forget to pull.* But it was still Finn's.

She crawled into bed with her phone and sent him a message. She'd already risked an elevator ride today, and despite the mishap, it had actually turned out pretty well. She was willing to take another risk. Julie wrote slowly and deliberately:

I think I'm falling for you.

She set the phone on her nightstand and turned off the light. She pulled a pillow over her head and tried to block out Erin's drunken mood, Seth's hurt feelings, and the stuck elevator. OK, maybe not the *entire* stuck elevator scene.

Too bad Matt had already gone to bed. Julie wanted to see what he thought about calling Dana. Was she even his type? Did he have a type? Was Julie Finn's type? Was having a type bad? It might limit whom you met. Judging a book by its cover and all.

Her phone beeped, and Julie nearly smashed the lamp to the floor as she reached for the phone.

Good. I think I'm falling for you too. Let's not pull this chute.

CHAPTER 21

Julie stared at her computer screen. Considering that it was now just a few days away from Christmas, she'd hoped for good tidings. What the hell was she supposed to do?

She reread the e-mail from her father's secretary for the fifth time, but the message was the same. Julie quickly wiped her eyes as the words blended together. *Unfortunately must cancel this trip...unable to reschedule a number of important business meetings regarding possible merger...apologies...in Boston for New Year's Eve...reservations for 9 o'clock...Let him know if you need airfare to get home to Ohio.*

Her father had just bailed on their trip to California. Anything involving a merger was obviously a big deal, though, and was probably time sensitive. Presumably you can't get companies to schedule major plans around a trip with your daughter. Julie wiped her eyes again and wrote back. *Not a problem. I completely understand. Tell my father that I look forward to dinner.*

It wasn't a vacation with her father, she reasoned, but he was definitely going out of his way to come to Boston to see her for New Year's. And he'd somehow snagged reservations at one of the most upscale, expensive restaurants in the city.

Maybe they could check out some of the First Night activities? Snow sculptures, singers, dancers, theater shows...That would be really fun.

The major issue Julie had now was that she had nowhere to go for winter break. If Julie told her mom about the California plans falling through, Kate would back out of the cruise. Her mother deserved a tropical luxury trip, and Julie didn't want to ruin that for her. Besides, her mother would have something snarky to say about her father having to cancel the trip, and Julie didn't really want to hear it. Her father had been looking forward to this trip too. She was sure.

He loved Julie. She was his daughter.

Of course he loved her.

But Kate would say something derogatory, and Julie would have to defend him again because her mother didn't understand her father the way Julie did. He was driven and successful, and he had responsibilities and commitments that Kate couldn't relate to. Her parents were so different from each other that it was hard to imagine how they'd even gotten together in the first place.

Julie sighed. It would have been nice if she'd had more than a few days notice about having to make other holiday plans. It was December twenty-first, after all.

Well, she just wouldn't tell her mother about the nontrip until after the fact.

So what was she going to do now? Invite herself to stay with the Watkins family? That seemed rather intrusive. Not that there had been much holiday activity around the house. Celeste had pushed Matt to the breaking point until he had taken her and Julie out to buy a Christmas tree, but the tree remained untrimmed. Julie had stuck the presents she had bought for the family underneath the branches, to at least give the tree some semblance of festivity. There'd been no mention of having a holiday party or going to any, and so except for the display of holiday cards on the living room mantel and the empty tree, the house gave no indication that Christmas was only a few days away.

Maybe Julie was better off going to Ohio and spending vacation by herself? But then she'd miss dinner with her father. She could fly back to Boston on the thirty-first. That is, if she could even get a ticket to Ohio at this late date. Great. What a mess.

She didn't want to impose on Erin and Roger more than she already had. Holidays were for family. Granted, Julie had come to feel as if this clan was her family, but this didn't mean she should crash Christmas.

Finn was the obvious exception. She hardly felt sisterly toward him. She felt...Well, she didn't know how to define what she felt. An attraction, a connection, an intensity. And he seemed to feel the same way. Not that he had started writing her long, romantic e-mails where he poured his heart out with confessions of undying love, because that wasn't Finn. Finn was funny and sweet and clever, and he wanted to know about her. Everything from how her day was to what she enjoyed at school and what she wanted to do with her life. But he was not syrupy and corny.

They'd been e-mailing every few days, and she found herself jumping when her phone sounded or her computer beeped. She checked Facebook obsessively, waiting to see his latest status update, waiting to see something that indicated he was thinking about her. She'd liked yesterday's best:

Finn Is God *is striving for terminal velocity. Care to join him?*

Those were the things that let her know he was thinking about her. She didn't need constant notes and texts reminding her. With his crazy traveling schedule, Finn couldn't be in constant contact anyway, and Julie was good with that. They had an understanding.

OK, fine, she didn't entirely understand what they were to each other, but they were *something*. Something more than friends. They had never even met, so he wasn't exactly a boyfriend, but Julie didn't feel the need to define their relationship because she enjoyed whatever they had going on.

But now more than ever, she wanted Finn to come home. At night she'd lie in bed, reading over his e-mails and texts and scrolling through his pictures, wondering if he did the same thing. She could sense his energy and his mood in each message he had written, and she'd come to know him so well that she could practically *feel* him. As if she knew what it would do to her to be with him.

So she would wait for him. Because one day, Finn would be home. One day, they could see what this really was between them.

Julie checked to see if he was on chat. He was signed off. She couldn't remember where he was now. His travel plans were so complicated, and she'd learned that it was easier to stop trying to keep track of where he was going next and just follow along as he reported in.

Finn–

   Thinking about you. That's all.

–Julie

She ran spell check on the paper she had to hand in tomorrow and then started printing. As page fifteen slid out, her e-mail sounded.

Julie—

I hope this message goes through. I keep falling off the network here. Thinking about you too and miss you. (Is that weird? How can I miss you? But I do.)

I'm not going to make it to Boston this month. I'll explain later. I'm so sorry. I don't know what to say.

Glad you're still awake because I have a surprise for you. I know it won't make up for my not being there, but it's all I could think to do:

Go into the living room.

—Finn

She liked that he missed her. She liked it a lot. But she didn't like that he wasn't coming home.

Grouchy but curious to see what Finn was talking about, she walked quietly down the stairs so that she didn't wake anyone and tiptoed to the living room. *Please let the surprise not be another Flat Finn*, she thought. That would be super creepy. Just as she entered the room, she stopped, taking in the scene before her.

All the house lights in here were off, but the room positively glowed. The entire ceiling had been covered in small white lights, and the tree was decorated with real candles. Green garlands with more lights had been tied to the mantel above the fireplace with small red ribbons running throughout the display. Matt stood on a step stool by the tree, lighting the candlewicks on the very top. It was just how she had described her house in Ohio to Finn. Actually, it was better.

"It's beautiful," she said.

Matt startled and wavered dangerously on the step stool. "God, Julie. You scared me to death!"

She laughed. "I'm sorry. I just got a message from Finn, and he told me to come down here." She walked forward and lightly touched one of the branches. "It looks amazing."

Matt lit the last candle and stepped down. "Don't blame me if the house catches fire. This is all Finn's idea. He said it would make you happy?"

Julie nodded, swallowing hard as she slowly spun around. "It does make me happy." She stopped and turned to Matt. "You did all this for me? I mean, Finn asked you to do this?"

Matt stuck his hands in his pockets and looked at the ceiling of lights. "He sent me a list of instructions and included detailed threats of bodily harm if I didn't follow his demands to the letter. I think I got it all." Matt moved to the coffee table where his laptop sat idling. He glanced at the screen and shut the lid. "Yes, OK. Now we're supposed to lie under the tree. *That* does not sound traditional, but he said you would understand?" Matt looked doubtfully at her.

"I do understand. Come on!" She grabbed Matt's hand and pulled him down to the floor with her. "I do this every year. You'll like it."

"Finn owes me," he muttered as he followed Julie and lay down on his back to slide under the lower branches. "Ow! If I lose an eye for this, I expect a massively expensive Christmas present from you both to compensate me for my troubles. Like a bedazzled eye patch or something."

"You have to go slow, silly. Don't fling yourself into the tree. Ease your way underneath. There. See?"

Julie looked up through the branches to see the shadows and highlights that the candlelight created. In this small, private space, things were quiet and safe. The same way Finn had written about skydiving; the real world was gone. It was like when Julie was a kid, and she'd hang her blanket from the top bunk, making the lower bunk into a cozy cave. She did that a lot after her dad left.

"Actually, this is sort of…nice," Matt said.

She turned to him. "I've never done this with anyone before. It's always just me."

"Oh. I thought I was supposed to stay here and do whatever it is we're supposed to do under the tree. Do you want me to go?"

"No, stay!" She grabbed his arm again. "I like the company."

Matt looked at her with amusement. "OK. So what do we do?"

"We think about profound things."

"Ah. Philosophical ponderings and questions? I'll go first. Prove to me that you are not a figment of my imagination."

"Very funny."

"Am I in a computer simulation? Does the door swing both ways? How can something come from nothing? How do you know a line is straight?"

"Matt, stop it!" Julie laughed.

"If animals wanted to be eaten, would it be OK? If time stopped, then started again, would we even know about it? What happens when you get scared half to death twice? What is creationism? What is ethical?"

"*What* is driving me crazy?" Julie asked, still giggling.

"No, *who* is driving you crazy?" Matt corrected her, smiling. "But fine. If you don't like my line of deep thinking, then you lead the way."

Julie paused. "Now it all seems silly and juvenile."

"Tell me anyway."

"It's just…Well, every year I lie under the tree, and…I don't know. Assess my life. Get into a sort of dream state and see where my thoughts lead me."

Matt crossed his long legs and rested his hands on his stomach. "I understand what you mean. Why don't you close your eyes?"

"You close your eyes too."

"OK."

Julie looked at Matt and waited. "You go first."

"No, you go first."

"We'll do it at the same time. I don't want to lie here with you watching me. Ready? Three, two, one, go." Julie shut her eyes. "Now we wait and see what comes to us."

Even with her eyes shut, the light from the candles flickered in her vision, bringing blurry, hazy images into her thoughts. She couldn't believe Finn had arranged this. It was almost as if he were here with her, lying next to her. He had wanted to give her something special, and he had. *What will happen when we meet?* Julie wondered. What if there wasn't that same chemistry—that same draw—that they had now? But she knew there would be. Some feelings just had to be trusted. So she let her mind wander, picturing what things might be like when he was back in Boston.

She'd move out of the house at some point, obviously. Maybe get her own apartment? Maybe Finn would get his own place too? He could take her to his favorite spots in the city, and she could hear more details about his trips. She could tell him about her classes and college life and also drag him to Dunkin' Donuts for Coolattas. He'd probably like them more than Matt. She and Finn could take Celeste to the Museum of Fine Art, and there would be no need to bring Flat Finn with them because Celeste would be whole again. Or closer to whole.

And then that nagging question hit Julie again: What had happened to Celeste to cause her to withdraw from the real world?

Julie turned her head to the side and opened her eyes. Matt was looking at her. "I told you not to watch me," she whispered.

"I couldn't help it," he whispered back.

He was quiet for a moment, and she wondered what he'd been thinking about. He was probably breaking down a boring math theory. That was not what he was supposed to be doing now.

"Julie?"

"Yeah, Matt?"

He waited for a moment. "It's like we're free—"

"Oh my God!" Julie said, cutting him off. "I totally forgot to ask you."

"Um…Ask me what?"

"My friend Dana wants you to call her."

"That's not asking me anything."

"Stop correcting me. She wants to go out with you, you dork!"

"Oh." Matt groaned and turned his head away. "I don't know about that."

"Matty, come on. You never go out!" Julie pleaded. "She's really cool. You'd like Dana."

"I'll think about it. How's that?" he offered.

"Have you ever had a girlfriend?"

Matt shot her a dirty look. "Of course I've had a girlfriend. What kind of question is that?"

Julie shrugged. "I don't know. You never mention anyone."

"I will admit that the romantic area of my life has been slow recently. I simply don't have time to go out with anyone right now. You know what my schedule is like with school and with Celeste."

"So you haven't dated since…you know? Celeste. The Flat Finn stuff."

"Not much. I had a pretty serious girlfriend, but then…" Matt faltered. He was serious now, his face tense and uncomfortable. "Things changed around here."

"With Celeste?"

Matt nodded.

Julie thought about her talk with Professor Cooley. "When something happened?"

Matt nodded again.

"I'm sorry," Julie said. "Because whatever it is, I can tell that you're dealing with it too. Maybe someday you'll want to tell me about it."

"Maybe someday," Matt agreed. "And my girlfriend at the time wasn't interested in staying together. Not everyone can tolerate my life. This house."

"I love Celeste, but she's hurting you, isn't she?"

"Don't say that. I would sell my soul for my sister."

"I know you would." Julie knew she had to be careful here, or Matt would shut down again. "But you must be angry with Finn for leaving. For making whatever happened to Celeste worse."

"I am angry at Finn."

"He has a right to his life, Matt."

"Believe me, I know he does."

"Do you two usually get along?"

"We used to. And then…we didn't. Mostly because of the issues with my mother; he was always the hero. That wasn't easy for me, I guess."

"Celeste thinks you're a hero. Don't you see how she looks at you? She adores you."

"Not the way she adores Finn. It's different. I do the boring stuff. I get her to school, feed her, help her with homework, worry about her. I'm no Finn, that's for sure. He's never given a crap about real life. He cares about fun and horsing around. When my mother was away—that's what we call it, *away*—Finn entertained Celeste, got her laughing, made her wild and free like him. I took care of what needed to be done, and he got all the credit. That's how it's always been."

"You don't sound as though you like Finn all that much."

"On the contrary. He's incredible. He's vivacious and relaxed and unrestrained. Finn gets to do everything I don't, and I envy him."

"So Celeste used to be more like Finn?" Julie asked.

"She did," Matt said softly.

"I think she's doing better, don't you? A little bit? She pitched a fit because I couldn't find the second season of *Glee* the other day. I think that's a good sign."

"What is *Glee*?"

"Don't worry about it. It's a good thing. And she's asking for trendy clothes for Christmas and wants me to take her shopping too."

"So she's becoming devoid of individuality? Exactly what I hoped for."

"Shut up. These are *good* things. Flat Finn is getting another round of hinges in a few weeks. Celeste gave me the go-ahead. Matty, don't you see how much she needs to fit in and needs friends? Can you imagine how desperately lonely she must be?"

"I can." Matt sighed. "You're probably better for her than I am."

"But you do really important stuff. She needs someone like you to take care of her. Your mother is…having a hard time too, I think."

Matt nodded. "I know. She is having a horrible time. Both my parents are. Why do you think she and my father are out of the house so much? They can't stand to be here." Matt ran his hands through his hair. "Julie, I'm tired. I don't want to be Celeste's parent. I can't."

Neither of them said anything for a few minutes.

Finally Julie spoke. "Gee, this lying under the tree routine is really turning out to be fun, isn't it? Aren't you glad you're here?"

"It has exceeded my expectations."

"OK, let's talk about girls again."

"You're interested in girls? I had no idea. I thought you were dating that Seth character."

"You're a riot, Matt. Really. And for your information, Seth and I broke up."

"I didn't know."

"I've moved on. Sort of. I don't know what's going on. I have a crush."

Matt rolled his eyes. "Let me guess. My brother?"

"How did you know?" Julie was surprised.

"Let's see? Could it be the way you go on and on about how fabulously interesting and entertaining he is? How you check your phone for mail every three minutes? Surreptitious, you're not."

"Well, fine. So what? Anyway, we're not talking about me. We're talking about your floundering love life. Call Dana."

"I don't have time for a relationship."

"That's ridiculous. There's always time if you want it. Don't you need a little romance in your life, Matty?" Julie nudged his shoulder with her hand.

He laughed. "I like when you call me *Matty*. It's...cute."

"*Cute?* That's the word you came up with? With that abnormally large brain of yours, I'd think you could do better than *cute.*"

"The smell from the candles sucked all the smart out of me."

"Good. Then you're too dumb now to protest. I'll give you Dana's number, and you'll call her and take her out to dinner."

"No."

"I'll bribe you then." Julie scooted forward until her body was out from under the tree and sat up. "What if I give you your Christmas present now?"

"No," he said again from under the branches.

Julie took his feet in her hands and pulled him out. "It's a good present. Presents, actually. Trust me."

"Yeah?" Matt smiled. "OK, you have a deal."

"Yay!" Julie clapped her hands together. She retrieved Matt's gift from the small pile she had set downstairs a few days earlier and handed him the soft package. "Now, since I'm on a student budget, it's nothing extravagant. It's the thought that counts, though, right?"

"If the thought is cash, then yes."

"Matthew!"

"Kidding, kidding." Matt gently undid the green ribbon and removed the red paper. He looked at the two presents and beamed, pretending to wipe away a tear as he lifted up the first T-shirt. "Han Solo in carbonite," he stated. He lifted up the other shirt, a red one with a picture of a two-stick Popsicle being divided. "*Please don't separate us. We share vital organs,*" he read. "They're perfect. I knew you'd come around to the shirts."

"I have *not* come around to the shirts, but holidays are not about trying to change people into having decent, or even acceptable, taste. Besides, I was fighting a losing battle."

"Do you want yours now? Since you're leaving in a few days?"

"Right. California." Julie nodded in agreement. "I'm going to California."

"You'll have a lot of time with your father. It should be an incredible trip."

"Yes, it should," Julie said. "Wine country, Hollywood, beaches, fancy hotels, gourmet meals. My father will want to hear every single thing about college and my life. I'll probably be so sick of talking about myself by the end that I'll need a vacation from my vacation!" Julie didn't know why she was lying to Matt, but every part of her was stubbornly refusing to tell him the truth. "So, yes, yes, yes! I want my present now!"

"Greedy, aren't you?" he teased. He reached behind him and opened a drawer in one of the small end tables. He handed Julie a red envelope with her name written on the front.

She opened it and impulsively screamed, causing Matt to throw one hand over her mouth and shush her with the other. "Everyone is asleep!" he said, trying not to laugh.

"But you got me a Dunkin' Donuts gift card that will last me for the rest of my college career! How can I not scream? Matty!" She flung her arms around his neck. "You're so sweet!" She sat back down on her knees. "And now you have to call Dana. You promised."

"I guess I did," he said, sighing.

"She's going home for a few weeks, but she'll be back right after the holidays. Isn't this great? We're both starting the New Year with romance. Or at least the possibility of romance."

Matt looked at her. "That would be nice."

CHAPTER 22

Matthew Watkins *thinks the prefrontal lobes are amazing. But then again, it's his prefrontal lobes that enable him to think that, so who knows?*

Finn Is God *See? I told you that was fun! Now, let's go find your eye.*

Julie Seagle *Little-known fact: After his promotion, Rudolph became insufferable. The following year, he was the star of a lesser-known and little-loved Xmas special about humility and not forgetting one's "roots."*

Julie realigned the silverware and took a sip of sparkling water from her glass. It was New Year's Eve, so the restaurant was totally full, of course, and it was fun being in downtown Boston with this festive crowd. She checked the hostess stand again to see if her father had arrived. She had e-mailed him to say that she would be wearing a shimmery pink top and a black skirt and that she would have her hair up the way he liked so he could pick her out in the crowd in an instant. She had so much to tell her father, and she craned her neck to see over the people next to her. Any minute he would be there. It was quarter of nine, fifteen minutes past their reservation time. Hopefully he hadn't had trouble trying to get a taxi from the airport.

So far, winter break had been pretty dreary, but tonight would change all that. It wasn't a three-week trip, but the fact that her father was coming to Boston just to have dinner with her meant something. It had also meant that she'd spent the past week holed up alone in Dana's apartment while she and her roommate were gone for break, which, while somewhat boring, hadn't been too awful. Christmas Eve and Christmas Day had not been great, to be honest, although as an only child, Julie had learned to be pretty good at entertaining herself. Granted, this had been more like hiding out than actual entertainment, but she hadn't had a choice. And she felt sort of shady for lying to her mother and the whole Watkins family about not going to California. Still, that had been easier than getting them to understand what had happened.

At least Finn had been around a lot recently, so they'd been in touch more than ever. She'd had to provide him with fake descriptions of how beautiful the vineyard hotel was and make up details about the extravagant sushi dinner she'd supposedly had the other night, neither of which had felt very good. She wondered what he was doing tonight. He was in Cape Verde working with a turtle conservation group, and he'd sent her pictures of the animals he was helping save from extinction. He and the other volunteers were living on the beach in tents and cooking all of their meals and washing clothes with limited facilities. While this sounded like hell to Julie, he was loving it.

She pulled out her phone and reread the last few Facebook messages she had from him. Occasionally he headed into town to local restaurants, and she had learned that he was not a fan of the local specialty. *"Goat cheese" and "goat and cheese" are not the same thing. Learn from my mistakes. Always read the menus carefully, Julie.* The next one said, *Goat meat this, goat meat that. Barf. Screw the turtles! Based on such high consumption rates, it seems that we'll need to establish a Goat Conservation Group soon.*

Julie scanned the room again. It was OK. He wasn't that late.

It was almost midnight where Finn was. Maybe next year they'd be together for the holiday? She had written countless messages suggesting they talk on the phone and deleted them all. It just seemed too intense, and the possibility for awkwardness was too great. She understood now why Celeste didn't want to talk to him herself until he came home. It was probably better to wait. This online business was good for now. Thank God he wasn't set up to video chat. Ugh. Seeing him for the first time would be nerve-wracking enough.

So next New Year's might bring a long, sensuous midnight kiss. Sometimes when they were talking online, she got this strange vibe. As if she could actually sense him, that she knew what it was like to be with him in person.

Julie stopped herself from going down that road. It was ridiculous. For all she knew, Finn was a horrible, disgusting, messy kisser. They might have no chemistry whatsoever. This silly online game might mean nothing other than foolish flirting.

But she didn't think so.

Neither did Finn, apparently, who messaged her just then.

Almost midnight here. Missing you. Did you get my present yet? I've been waiting for you to find it, but evidently you do not look in the zipped pocket inside your purse very often. Or you hated it. Or Matt screwed up and tucked it in our mother's purse. How repulsively Oedipal. (Uh-oh. Hope Dad is OK...)

Julie nearly dropped her phone as she yanked her purse from the back of the chair. Quickly she fumbled through the messy bag, vowing to clean out all the junk as soon as she got home. A piece of red tissue paper poked out from the pocket. Julie gently took the present in her hand and opened it.

It was beautiful. She lifted the thin cord in her hand and admired the purple stone tied at the end. It was jagged and uneven, but not sharp. She immediately pulled the necklace over her head and held the stone in one hand while she wrote Finn back with the other.

I don't know what to say. It's gorgeous. Perfect. I absolutely love it, and I won't take it off. I wanted to get you something, but you keep moving around!

Julie stared at the screen, waiting for his reply. She couldn't help getting chills every time a new message popped up.

You've already given me enough. Hey, check out the fireworks! It's midnight here!

He must be using a borrowed phone with a camera, because he'd attached an awesome picture of the Cape Verde New Year's celebration. She opened the picture Finn had sent and wished more than anything that she were there with him, standing next to the ocean and watching fireworks explode over the water. It was cheesy and cliché, but romantic nonetheless. Next year, she promised herself. Next year they would be together. She was patient and knew that Finn was worth waiting for. He couldn't be gone forever.

She caught sight of a tall man who stood behind a couple at the hostess stand. Finally!

Gorgeous! Have to run. I think my dad is here. About to have five-course dinner. No goat, though. You around tomorrow?

Finn wrote back:

Yup, fireworks are indeed gorgeous, although I can think of other things I'd rather be doing at midnight. And they don't involve goats. I'll be here.

Julie tossed her phone into her purse and then stretched her arm up, squinting as she waved. Oh. That wasn't her father.

The server appeared, refilled her water glass for what felt like the millionth time, and gave her a sympathetic look.

"I'm sure that traffic is a nightmare. He'll be here soon," Julie said, as much to herself as to the server.

But he wasn't there soon. An hour after their reservation time, Julie called him. She never called her father. Never. There was an unspoken rule that his phone was for business only. Besides, he wasn't the type that liked to get all chatty on the phone anyway. Their conversations were always stilted and slightly uncomfortable, filled with lots of background noise from wherever he was. Julie would blather on for a while with her father saying, "Yes," or "Interesting," when appropriate. From what she remembered, talking in person was better.

But now she had to try his cell. She let it ring until his voice mail picked up and then tried him right back. Still voice mail. Julie stared at the two untouched glasses of champagne on the table, their bubbles still rising festively. Not every table had the tall cooler keeping the bottle cold, and her father had obviously called ahead and arranged for this pre-midnight champagne. She took a few deep breaths and tried to relax.

Twenty minutes later, she checked the time again. He was now officially hideously late. Julie picked up the glass of now-warm champagne and drank half of it. She scrolled through her contact list and found her father's secretary's number. Julie was not a drinker, and so by the time Andrea answered, she could already feel the alcohol in her system.

"Hi. It's Julie Seagle here. Sorry to bother you," she said.

"Julie! How are you? Happy New Year!"

"I'm fine. It's just that I'm at dinner waiting for my dad, and he's well over an hour late. Do you know if there was trouble with his flight to Boston?"

"Oh, Julie." Andrea was quiet for a moment. "Honey, didn't he let you know?"

"Let me know what?"

"He's not *in* Boston."

"I'm sorry, what?"

"He's in New York. He was supposed to call you. Don't tell me that he forgot."

Julie picked up the glass of champagne and finished it off. "He most definitely forgot. You know what? It's more than just forgetting, isn't it?"

"I don't know what…I'm sure he meant to—"

"No. No, he didn't. We both know that he just doesn't give a shit. And that's that. So now I'm sitting here at this stupid, pretentious, overpriced restaurant, and I'm hungry and pissed off and have no way to pay for this bottle of champagne that I plan to finish drinking."

"I'll call the restaurant and have that taken care of. I made the reservation, so I know where you are."

Julie remained expressionless as she held the phone between her ear and her shoulder and refilled her glass. "Thanks, Andrea. Have a good night." She went to hang up and then stopped. "And tell my father he's an asshole. Tell him I'm done." She dropped the phone onto the table. "And there you have it, folks," she said softly.

Within a few minutes the server reappeared. "I understand you'll be dining alone this evening."

Julie nodded and looked up at the man by the table. He was about her father's age, and he smiled kindly at her. She nodded. Yes, she would be eating alone.

"Your meal is paid for, and we'll arrange for a cab for you when you're ready. Have you decided what you'd like to eat?"

She shook her head. "Anything would be fine. You can pick for me. Just something very expensive. No goat, though."

"Excellent. More champagne, miss?"

What the hell? "Sure. More champagne. It's a night to celebrate, right?"

She ate the stuffed lobster with truffle oil that appeared and then ordered dessert. A trio of chocolate something-or-others. She wasn't paying attention. And since the champagne was sitting so well, and the server hadn't carded her, she tried two dessert cordials that both tasted like cough syrup but made her head spin wonderfully after she managed to get them down. She should really consider taking up drinking, because she was totally enjoying herself now.

She wondered how much this meal cost. Probably a good amount, even though it was just her. If only she'd invited some friends, then the bill would have been outrageous.

Julie waved her server over. "You know what? That truffley lobster was bang-up. Could I get five orders of that to go? Thank you. And give yourself a forty percent tip. Then I would like my cab, please. I'm ready to go home."

Forty-five minutes later, Julie stumbled drunkenly into Dana's apartment and threw the two bags of lobster into the fridge. She crawled onto the bed and turned on the television so that she could watch all the New Year's celebrations. Shots of Times Square flashed on the screen. "Screw you, New York!" she shouted and muted the volume. Hey, maybe Finn was still up? It took a little while, but eventually she located her purse, which had landed in the fridge with her to-go cartons.

She fumbled her way back to the bedroom and messaged him. *What are you wearing?* He didn't reply, so she tried again. *I am only wearing thigh-high leather boots and twirling a leopard print parasol.* Still nothing. He must be asleep. Why was he not there? She wanted to chat with him and hear him say cute, flirty stuff. She needed him now. He was funny and would make her laugh.

She kicked off one of her shoes and started to get changed as she pulled up a phone number. Her nylons were halfway off when he answered.

"Hello?"

"What are you wearing?"

"Um…who is this?" he said sleepily.

"Matty, it's me!" she yelled.

"Julie?"

"Yes, Matty! Have you forgotten me already?" She looked dumbly at her tangled nylons, trying to figure out how she had tied them in a knot while they were still half-on. "What are you doing home? You should be out revelrying!"

She heard him laugh softly. "I was sleeping. And *revelrying*? I'm not familiar with that term."

"Yes. It's a term because I say so. I'm creative like that. Oh my God, I'm The Terminator! Get it? Don't you miss me and my delightful banter?"

"I do miss you," he said, yawning. "Sure."

"That's not convincing. You're hurting my feelings."

"Everybody misses you. Especially Celeste. Thanks for all the e-mails you've been sending her."

"Aw, my buddy Celeste." Julie lay down on the floor and yanked on the bunched-up nylons. "There. I did it!"

"You did what?"

"I got myself undressed!"

"I think you got yourself drunk, that's what I think."

"So what? So what if I'm drunk? I'm still funny."

"You are funny," he agreed. "How is California? How's your father?"

"My father is fan-frickin'-tastic. He's clearly aiming for father of the year with the way he's spoiling me. It's a really good trip."

"Er...Are you OK?"

"I'm perfect. Are *you* OK?"

"Yes," he said. "Are you going to make it until midnight?"

"Of course I'll make it to midnight. I'm gonna watch fireworks shoot out over the ocean. Wanna come watch with me?"

"Sure. I'll be there in a minute. Don't start without me."

"I can always count on you, can't I, Matty? You're the best, and you're very helpful. I love you."

"Now I know you're drunk."

"Calm down, silly boy. Not like *I love you*-love you. I just love you. You're so smart. Oh, you love me too, and you know it."

"Have you had any water to drink?"

"See what I mean? *That* is the smartest idea ever!" Julie grabbed the footboard, pulled herself up, and headed to the bathroom. "OK, here I go. Are you ready?" She turned on the faucet.

"Go for it."

"Now, hold on. Don't go anywhere." She stuck her head under the tap and sucked in as much icy water as she could. "Ta da!" she announced.

"You also could have used a glass."

"You didn't say to, and you're the one in charge. Now I have to pee. Don't listen, because that would be gross."

"Believe me, I will not listen."

"You talk, and I'll pee. Talk loud to cover up the pee sound. Tell me something interesting. You always have interesting things to babble about."

"I do not babble. But for the sake of blocking out any noises you are about to make, I will ignore that remark and tell you that Celeste loved the messenger bag you gave her. And she didn't blink twice when she saw the packs of hinges you'd put inside. She even had me add a couple onto Flat Finn, so he now bends at the knees and the neck. Next up are ankles and elbows. Pretty soon he'll fit into the bag like your note told her. It's actually a fairly genius idea that you had, Julie."

"I know, right? I'm a smartie too. Not as smartie as you because you are abnormally smart. I mean, seriously, Matthew Watkins. Do you know how bizarrely intelligent you are? It's pretty freaky. I've never met anyone like you at all. What were we talking about? Oh, yeah. So Celeste can just fold up ol' Flatty and pack him in the messenger bag so no one will see. What about you? Did you like your shirts? They're funny. Han Solo is hot. Everybody likes him because he was already hot and then it was awesome when Princess Leia said *I love you* and he said *I know*. That added to his hotness. That line is timeless. And the popsicles? They're hilarious, right? I will admit that I sorta like all of your shirts."

"Obviously when you get drunk, you lie. And talk a lot."

"I am not lying. They are actually a tiny bit adorable."

"I knew you would come around."

"I'm done peeing now."

"Thank you for letting me know."

Julie shuffled into the hall and caught sight of herself in the mirror. She swayed a bit from side to side and frowned at her sagging hairdo. "I look crazy. I think I should go to bed now."

"Probably a good idea. Happy New Year."

"Wait, don't hang up yet! Tuck me in."

"Tuck you in?"

"Yes. Tuck me in. Come to bed with me. Oh, wait, that's not right, is it? Can you imagine?"

"Imagine what?"

"If we went to bed together. That would be bananas, huh?"

She heard him sigh. "This conversation has officially taken an alarming turn."

"You're just figuring that out now?" She plodded back to the bedroom, shut off the light, and got under the covers. "Matty?"

"Yes, Julie?"

"I have to tell you something."

"Go ahead."

"I like math."

"I think that is wonderful."

"And there's something else."

"Shoot."

She cupped her mouth with her hand, whispering, "I'm a virgin."

"Oh my God, Julie, I'm hanging up now."

"I'm serious. This is important. I'm a freshman in college. How can I still be a virgin, huh? Nobody else is a virgin. Nobody else in the whole world. What about you? You can't be. I mean, you had that girlfriend and everything. And you're old."

"Thank you."

"Well, not old. But older than I am. So you definitely can't be a virgin, right? Tell me. You've had sex, right?"

"I don't think we should be talking about this."

"Come on! Don't be such a baby. It's a perfectly normal question."

There was a long pause. "Fine. Yes, I've had sex."

"I knew it!" she yelled triumphantly. "Have you had a lot of sex?"

Matt laughed. "I suppose it depends how you define *a lot*."

"That means you have! Man, at the rate I'm going, I'm never going to have sex."

"Are you in a big rush?"

"Why wouldn't I be? Everyone says sex is great. It is, isn't it?"

"I don't know that I qualify as an expert, but, yes, it can be great. If you're with the right person." He was silent for a moment. "So you and Seth never...?"

"Ha! I knew you'd want to talk about this stuff! No, we never did. I didn't want to. Seth was cute and nice and perfect and all that, but I didn't want to. He just wasn't *the* guy, you know? I want *the* guy. The everything guy. Not the dumb Prince Charming, nauseatingly perfect everything guy. That's pathetic. I want the flaws-and-all, everything guy."

"You'll find him. Not when you're drunk and slurring, but you'll find him."

"Hey, they're counting down to midnight. In stupid New York where all the stupid cool people are. Let's count together."

"Tell me when."

Julie looked dizzily at the screen. "Seven, six..." Matt started to count with her. "Five, four, three, two, one!" She watched the hordes of people wave their arms and cheer as the famous ball dropped. The cameras panned to couple after couple caught up in kissing.

"Happy New Year, Julie."

"Happy New Year, Matty." She turned off the television and rolled onto her side. "Matty, I have another question for you."

"Uh-oh."

"Are you a skilled lover?"

"And that concludes our evening chat."

"I bet I could be a skilled lover. I'm very energetic. And a quick learner."

"You definitely need to go to sleep."

"Oh, fine." She yanked the sheet up higher. "I can't stay on the phone anymore. I have to get to sleep."

"I think that's a good plan. I'm glad you thought of it."

"I like talking to you," Julie mumbled.

"I like talking to you too. Most of the time. I'll see you when you get back."

"G'night, Matty."

CHAPTER 23

Julie looked at the clock. It was only seven thirty in the morning, and she felt like hell. The expression "death warmed over" came to mind. She had slept horribly, tossing and turning, trying to control the nausea that had woke her up several times. Not to mention the excruciating headache.

Champagne sucks, she thought. *And my father and stupid New York still suck.*

She might as well get up, since there was no use lying around stewing about things. She dragged her hungover self from the bed and plodded to the kitchen, clutching her head with one hand in a futile attempt to keep her brains from smashing against her skull. She grabbed a carton of orange juice and sat down on the couch in the living room to watch TV.

Reporters recapped last night's celebrations and replayed footage of midnight displays and cheers from around the world. Watching this, these masses of happy people, made her feel small and unimportant. Probably the way her father saw her.

She could see it now.

It was quite clear to her that she barely registered on his radar. It was rather unbelievable. She was his daughter, his only child, and he had screwed her over time and again. And she had let him.

Asshole.

Her head was spinning. She flipped through the channels and landed on a local news reporter who had been stuck with the unfortunate job of filming on a windy beach in South Boston. Julie squinted at the television. Why on earth was a crowd forming at the freezing beach at this time of day? Oh my God, they were going swimming!

The reporter yanked her hat down as a gust of wind swirled. "Even with water temperatures predicted to be a painful forty-one degrees, dozens of men, women, and even children are preparing to take the annual Polar Plunge this morning at ten o'clock in Boston Harbor."

Finn had told her about this event. *These people are crazy,* Julie thought.

"Many swimmers will experience an involuntary bout of hyperventilation that can last up to three minutes," the reporter continued. "And these daredevils won't be wearing any protective clothing to combat the icy water. No wetsuits here, folks. Just bathing suits and bravery!"

Julie made a pot of coffee and popped a few pain relievers. She stood by the window, which looked out onto a deserted street. Hardly anyone was out this morning, as if the sullen gray sky had forbidden people from leaving their homes. Julie took a sip from her cup and gagged. Her stomach was a wreck. Every part of her hurt, and she couldn't remember the last time she'd been in such a terrible mood.

She put the cup down and made a decision. She sent Finn a message, quoting one of her favorite In Like Lions' songs, "Shallow Cars."

That should be cryptic enough. In case she backed out.

***

Matthew Watkins *thinks that occasional, in-the-privacy-of-your-own-home binge drinking is unfairly maligned in the media and romantic comedy chick flicks.*
Finn Is God *Can you always do something sometimes?*
Julie Seagle *I had a dream about starting a dating service for fish called solemate.com. In unrelated news, I will never drink again.*

Julie looked around and wondered why everyone was smiling. This was not fun. It was sleeting now, and the wind had picked up. She looked down at her bare legs and questioned what she'd been thinking coming down to the beach. And the only bathing suit that crazy Dana owned was nothing but a small handful of fabric posing as a bikini. Julie felt like an idiot. At least other people in the Polar Plunge crowd looked just as silly, she supposed; the three guys with Red Sox logos painted on their chests, an elderly man in a cowboy hat, the mother dressed as a lobster, and a trio of teen boys dressed as leprechauns all stood out more than she did. Hopefully.

Damn, it was cold, and she wasn't even in the water yet. Julie looked out at the ocean, the waves dark and ominous. Powerful. She didn't understand the crowd's enthusiasm for what they were about to do. It was a chore. A test. A way to prove something. It was scary and awful. But Julie needed to do this. She tried to focus, determined that she would not stop when her foot hit the water. What if she stopped breathing? Stopped moving? What if she panicked and her knees went weak? The force of the waves would push her below the surface, holding her down on the frozen ocean floor. *That is not going to happen,* she told herself. It was mobbed here. Someone would either see her fall or trip over her. She would just have to plow through the first cold shock. She'd run in and out of the water, and then it would be over. Just a few minutes out of her life.

That reporter had said something about involuntary hyperventilating. Yup. Julie was already involuntarily hyperventilating. And who the hell ever *voluntarily* hyperventilated?

Julie caught sight of a girl wearing a Princess Leia outfit and stared at her. Even in her foggy state, something was ringing a bell about this. In fact, screeching, horrible, major-panic kind of alarm bells started going off...

Suddenly the crowd rushed forward, and Julie found that she was running across the cold sand, her feet digging into rock. While she could vaguely hear the whoops and yells from other swimmers, mostly she heard the sound of her ragged, scared breathing. What had Finn said to her? *As much as you're terrified, you're also starting to feel the rush, the thrill you get from being on the brink.*

Julie ran harder, faster, yelling as she hit the ocean, but didn't stop. The water stung her legs, then her waist, making her gasp and struggle for air. The cold was so jarring that she couldn't make a sound. She thought about Finn again: *It's a calm like you've never known before, and you don't want it to end.*

She got it now. As she bent her legs and threw her whole body under water, she got what he meant. Her feet found the ground, and she pushed up, soaring back into the frigid air. She could swear she heard Finn call her name as she went under again. The way her body went numb so quickly was enthralling. Soothing. She was drawn into the sensation. Maybe she could just stay here, here in this euphoric ice water where it felt timeless and peaceful and clear? When she hit the surface again, she turned her back to the beach and stood silently as the salt water splashed against her.

Julie! Julie!

The sky was even darker now. Too dark to be only ten in the morning. The sleet continued to fall. It must be hurting her skin. Her body felt weightless and infallible, and that unfamiliar feeling was riveting. The allure of the deadening ocean was calling her again. She let her legs bend and watched transfixed as the skyline in front of her changed.

Julie!

Someone grabbed her arm. "Girl, you gotta get out. Come on." A burly man took hold of her arm and pulled her up, stopping her from sinking. "Now. That's it. Come on. Make yourself run." Julie noticed he had long, gray hair that he wore in a ponytail the same way her grandfather did. And a full beard. Her legs were moving, but she sensed that she was not going fast enough. As if her steps were in slow motion. She watched fascinated as the man put his arm around her and effortlessly scooped her up. Why was he doing that?

Julie!

The man carried her from the water, then across the sand. "You'll be OK. You just froze up. First time, huh?"

"Yes," she whispered.

The man set her down on her feet, and she leaned forward into a thick blanket. She knew this blanket. The smell and the texture felt like home. As someone swaddled her up in the softness, her body began to shake violently.

"Oh my God, Julie! What were you doing?" She also knew that voice.

"Matt? Did you see me?" she asked without looking up. Her voice sounded far off.

"Yeah. I saw you," Matt said. He did not sound happy.

"Did you see Santa Claus too?"

"That wasn't Santa Claus. That was one of the L Street Brownies who rescued you from certain death. It was considerate of him, after you crashed their event." Matt tightened the blanket around her and started furiously rubbing her back and her arms. "We have to get you warmed up. Dummy. Hey, can you get her sweatpants and socks and boots on? Hurry."

Julie felt someone lift up her foot. "I saw you, too, and I thought you were brilliant! Really stupendous!"

"Celeste?" Julie tried to turn her head. Matt had covered her so thoroughly with the blanket that she couldn't see a thing.

"I'm here!" Celeste said excitedly. "I'm attending to your blue feet!"

Julie's skin felt as if it were burning. "Why are you here? How?" she asked Matt. Her teeth were chattering wildly.

She stood there shivering helplessly, fully aware that she was practically naked. Damn Dana's bikini. At least she was too cold to blush. Matt didn't say anything as he dropped the blanket for a quick moment, pulling a long-sleeved shirt and then a thick sweatshirt over her head. Wow. He looked exceedingly pissed off. She let him swaddle her in the blanket again and wrap his arms around her as he tried to get her body temperature back to normal.

"Finn figured it out. He sent me to get you," he whispered into her ear. "What the hell were you thinking? We could see you standing out there in the ocean, not moving. You're lucky you're not dead. God damn it, Julie. Why would you do that? Why are you here and not in California with your father?" He sounded unreasonably mad.

Julie dropped her head forward and leaned into him. Her toes throbbed. She couldn't control the way her body was trembling. "Because he's a jerk, and I'm a liar." She felt herself choke on a sob. And then she couldn't stop.

Matt didn't say anything, but he kept rubbing her back. Celeste moved behind her and pressed her body against Julie's, hugging her tightly, so that she was pinned between brother and sister. They stayed like that for a few moments, the numbing effect of the cold beginning to wear off and the deep pain setting in.

"Please don't cry, Julie. You were simply wonderful out there," Celeste said.

"She was not wonderful, Celeste. She was a dope," Matt said. "But we're glad you're OK. You are OK, aren't you? I mean… physically?"

Julie nodded. Fine, he obviously thought that *mentally* she was whacked. She knew her crying was making Matt uncomfortable. At least her hangover was significantly less prominent now. The upside to near death. She turned her head to the side and saw the girl in the Princess Leia getup again. Something flashed through her mind. A fuzzy blip…

Uh-oh.

She closed her eyes. Thank God she still had her face hidden. "Matt?"

"Yeah?"

"Did we talk on the phone last night?"

He paused. "We did."

Oh, no. Julie was starting to remember.

This was unbelievable. Maybe she was making this up. "Did I ask you…?" She swallowed hard. "Did I ask you if you were a *skilled lover*?"

Matt cleared his throat and paused again. "You did."

Celeste burst out laughing.

Julie tucked her head down lower. "Sorry."

"Let's get you into the car. It should still be warm."

"Celeste, can you grab my bag?" Julie pointed from under the blanket to the benches on the other side of the beach.

"Absolutely. Hey, Julie?"

"Yeah, kiddo?"

"I'm glad that you're here." Celeste beamed. "Home."

"Me too."

"Meet us at the car, OK?" Matt stepped away from Julie and turned her in the direction of the street.

Her feet were regaining some feeling. She pulled the blanket more tightly around her shoulders and let Matt guide her across the beach. "So, Matt," she started and looked up at him, smiling. "Last night? What was your answer?"

"I'm not going to tell you. Now maybe you won't drink so much again."

Julie sighed. "Believe me. Lesson learned."

Matt got her into the front seat and cranked up the heat. Celeste bounded into the car with Julie's bag, and they started the drive home. Periodically, Julie shuddered as sharp chills ran through her, and she held her hands in front of the lukewarm vents and rubbed them together.

Matt frowned and fiddled with the controls, finally hitting the dashboard. "Come on! Come on, you piece of crap!" He slammed his hand down again.

"It's all right. Calm down. I'm warming up," Julie insisted.

"No, you're not fine." Matt sounded angry again. "That was a stupid thing to do. It was reckless. Seriously, what would possess you?"

Julie leaned back. "I don't care. I'm glad I did it."

"It's called a *plunge*. It's not a *stand-in-the-dangerously-cold-water-and-stare-fixedly-at-nothing* event. A plunge means exactly that. You plunge in and get the hell out. Not that you should have even been doing that."

"Yes, sir."

"I'm not fooling around, Julie. That was stupid. Stupid." He hit the gas and passed a few cars.

"Slow down, Matt!" Julie said hoarsely. "You're going to get a ticket."

"I'll drive as fast as I want. The quicker we get you home, the quicker you can warm up."

"Why don't you just take me back to Dana's? Turn left up here."

"Is that where you've been staying?" He shook his head, looking exasperated with her. "No. I am not taking you back to Dana's. Who knows what other trouble you'll get yourself into?"

"Matt! I can stay wherever I want to. I'm an adult."

"You're not acting like it."

"Why do you care where I stay?"

"Ah, a lovers' quarrel," Celeste said dreamily from the back seat.

"Shut up!" Julie and Matt yelled together.

Trying to ignore his driving for the rest of the ride home was the only thing keeping her sane right now. God, he was so grouchy sometimes. Temperamental. She couldn't keep up with his moods.

He pulled into the driveway and opened her door, moving to help her get out.

"I can walk just fine," she said, although her legs were noticeably shaking. She batted him away.

"Forgive me for not wanting you to collapse on the pavement," he said.

Julie shuffled behind him and Celeste as they walked up the front steps and watched Matt struggle with the finicky front lock. "Wait a minute." She turned back to the car and then looked at Celeste. "Where's Flat Finn?"

Matt froze and also turned to his sister.

Celeste clapped her hand over her mouth. "Oh! He's in the car." She started to walk back down the steps and stopped.

Julie looked at Matt and saw it register with him too. "No, Celeste," he said softly. "He's not." The surprise in his voice was obvious. "Flat Finn is not in the car. We forgot."

Celeste kept her back to them and squeezed her hands.

Matt continued. "We left the house so fast that we forgot."

"I never forget. *Never*," she said.

Julie shivered. She realized that Celeste had not only left the house, but had gone all the way to South Boston, gathered Julie from the beach, and returned home. All without Flat Finn. And all in a more relaxed—and even joyous—state than Julie had ever seen her. "Celeste, I don't think you forgot. I think you didn't need him today."

"That is not *fair* to him!"

Matt moved toward his sister, but Julie grabbed his arm. She didn't want him to rescue her again. "Kiddo? You can take a day off when you want. So can he. It's not a big deal. Some things you need to do without him."

"Besides, it's sleeting and awful out today." He was clearly trying hard to sound nonchalant. "He would have hated the trip."

Celeste unclenched her fists. "I imagine that he would have."

"Speaking of sleet, you need to come in the house, Celeste." Matt got the door lock to open. "Or I'll have *two* icicle girls to attend to."

Celeste whipped around, her long blond curls sparkling from the sleet. "We wouldn't want to overwhelm you, now, would we? Two feeble, dim-witted females such as Julie and I couldn't possibly take care of our delicate bodies. We might have to be carried to the fainting room and revived with smelling salts." She walked back up the stairs and into the house.

Matt looked at Julie, dumbfounded. "Did she just roll her eyes at me?"

"Yes," she said, pleased. "Yes, she did."

"Why don't you go take a hot shower, and I'll start a fire."

Thirty minutes later Julie was bundled up in long underwear and fleece. She scooted closer to the fireplace and stuck her toes as near to the heat as she could without igniting her socks. Matt jabbed a log with an iron poker, sending sparks flying.

"Thanks for the soup," Julie said.

"I'm gifted with a can opener. What can I say?"

"Still. Thank you. And for the water and the orange juice. I feel a little better."

"Good. I'll order dinner tonight from that Vietnamese place you like. You'll be back to normal in no time."

"The fire feels nice. How come you guys don't light more? You have all these beautiful fireplaces in the house."

He threw another log onto the already high flames. "Mom doesn't like the smell much. Since she's not here, I thought I'd take advantage. The house will air out by the time she gets back."

"Where are your parents? They can't be working today."

"They went up to Stowe for a few days. Vermont. We have a house there," he explained.

"They didn't bring you and Celeste," she said softly.

He shook his head. "No, they did not. What about you? What happened with your father and California?"

"He canceled the trip. And then he blew me off for dinner last night."

"I can't believe you spent Christmas alone. Why didn't you tell us? You should have stayed here. My parents are going to be furious with you."

Julie shrugged. "I don't know. It's embarrassing. Don't tell Erin and Roger, please? And Finn. Especially don't tell him."

"Julie, you kind of already told him. I think you have brain damage from that dip in the Atlantic."

"Oh. I did, didn't I?" Julie reached behind her and grabbed a pillow so she could lie down. "How did Finn know where I was?"

"I don't know. He said something about a song. That all you need is the water. Then something about freeing yourself. Finn insisted that while you wouldn't skydive, you might do something like hurl yourself into the Atlantic to prove a point. So I got my mission. As I've said before, I just follow orders around here."

So much for her cryptic quote. She propped herself up on her arm. "I might skydive."

"Sure you would."

"I *might*," she insisted and flopped back down. "With the right person. Depends what you mean by *skydive*."

Matt laughed. "What are you talking about?"

"Nothin'. Hey, Matt?"

"Yeah?"

"I'm sorry your parents left you here alone. That's not very nice."

Matt jabbed the fire with an iron poker. "No, it's not very nice, is it? And I'm sorry your dad left *you* alone. That's also not very nice."

"Thanks." Julie closed her eyes. She was exhausted.

"Tired, huh? Why don't you sleep for a while?"

She heard Matt get up to draw the curtains and then felt him cover her with a wool blanket. *Matt is so consistently inconsistent,* she thought sleepily. *He is always catching me and wrapping me up, and then being evasive and annoying me and then feeding me soup, and then snapping, and then talking about fonts and equations...*It was hard to think anymore.

Julie yawned. "Did you call Dana?"

"Not yet. I will."

The heat from the fire warmed her face. "Thanks for getting me, Matty. I'm sorry," she mumbled.

"Of course. It's not a problem."

Julie wasn't sure, but as the fatigue took over and pulled her into unconsciousness, she thought she felt a hand gently brush the hair from her face. And she thought she heard someone whisper lyrics about being broken, running too far, following the wheels that make your heart move, riding the wave...

But she was probably already dreaming. Because even though she could feel him, Finn wasn't here with her.

PART THREE

CHAPTER 24

Matthew Watkins *was a prototype release only available to developers and had a very buggy pre release cerebral subsystem. Also, no bladder controls.*

Finn Is God *I hope that someday they invent a car that runs on inappropriate thoughts.*

Julie Seagle *thinks that when you comment on NPR's Facebook updates, you should use some semblance of grammar and punctuation. But maybe I'm just a bitch.*

Julie carried glasses and a pitcher of lemonade outside, joining Roger, Matt, and Celeste on the front porch. "*More* hinges? Is Flatty auditioning for Cirque du Soleil?"

"It's quite possible that Flat Finn could now be folded up into a wallet," Roger said. He stood up and pointed at the new hinges that were shining brightly on Flat Finn's ankles. "I don't think there is room for any more. We've done all the other joints. What do you think, Celeste?"

Celeste was lounging in a wicker chair, her head tilted back and her eyes closed as she took in the April sunshine. Slowly, she lifted up a bit and peered over. "You're right. This may be as many as he can handle. He *is* already rather accordion-like, isn't he?" She dropped her head back down.

Roger looked at Julie and whispered, "I have the feeling *someone* isn't so invested in *someone else* anymore."

"I can hear you," Celeste said. "I am decidedly invested. Oh, the mail is here." She leapt from her seat and ran down the front steps.

Roger stared at his daughter as she bounded away. "She looks so…old. Does she look old to you, Matthew?"

Matt poured a glass of lemonade. "Yes. I'm fairly sure that I saw wrinkles on her sagging jowls. Also, she's been downing the Geritol. We should look into a nursing home for her."

"Matthew, relax. She looks good. I think her outfit is wretched, though." Roger frowned. "But I'm supposed to think that. Right, Julie?"

Julie nodded. "Yes, you are. Fathers should hate what their teenage daughters are wearing."

"Mission accomplished," he said somewhat despairingly. "The too-short skirt and those dreadful earrings are your doing?"

"Guilty."

Roger shook his head with acceptance and took a seat on the steps.

Celeste returned with the mail, tossed it onto the small table, and plopped back onto the cushioned chair. "My *Seventeen* arrived. I don't care for the horoscopes or quizzes, or truthfully, most of the articles, but I do enjoy the suggested fashion pieces."

Julie sat down next to Celeste so the two could debate shoe styles and prom updos. Celeste looked radiant and, for her, relaxed. Something had changed over the past few months. It was subtle, but Julie saw differences.

Matt scowled as he rooted through the mail. "Are you two honestly concerned with that stuff?"

Julie glared at him. "There's nothing wrong with it. It's not as if coveting the perfect pair of strappy sandals negates our interest in political and social concerns, does it, Celeste?"

"Ooooh! Look at her hair!" Celeste pointed to a picture. "Do you think you could do that to mine? I find that *very* flattering. And, no, Matthew. I agree with Julie."

"You're smart," he said. "You don't need all that."

"Yes, I know. I'm the smart girl. My identity has been overtaken by that label, and perhaps I would like to be seen as something other than 'the smart girl.'"

Julie smiled at Matt. "So *there*."

Celeste looked up. "I apologize. I don't intend to be rude, Matty. But you are not a girl, and you do not understand the societal pressures that someone my age must contend with."

"Contractions," Julie reminded Celeste with a singsong tone.

"Oh, yes. Right. Sorry. Anyway, attractiveness is probably just a social construct, but succumbing to selected norms is not always a negative move. Julie, for instance, is a good example of someone who is both highly intelligent *and* socially skilled."

"Fine." Matt frowned at a pink envelope. He looked furtively at Celeste, who was now buried back in her magazine, and crossed the porch.

Julie watched as he opened the envelope, scanned a card, and started to tuck it between pages of a store flyer.

"What's that?" Julie asked loudly.

"What? Nothing. Junk mail."

"No, it's not. What is that?" Julie got up and marched over to him. "You do not get letters in pink envelopes, so hand it over."

"Julie!" he hissed.

"Matt!" she hissed back.

She snatched the card from his hands. The envelope was addressed to Celeste, and the card was an invitation to a birthday party, a sleepover the following weekend.

"Hey, Celeste! You got invited to a party. For Rachel. Is she in your class?"

"Julie!" Matt grabbed the card back. "Don't!"

Celeste let the magazine fall into her lap. "I did? She invited me?"

"She did?" Roger turned around and looked at his daughter.

"Yes, she did. Everyone can stop acting so ridiculously flabbergasted. Here." Again, Julie swiped the card from Matt and handed it to Celeste.

Celeste looked intently at the invitation, her mouth beginning to form a wistful smile. But then she set it down on the table. "That was incredibly generous of Rachel to invite me. She's been awfully nice to me. I can't go, of course."

"Why not? Go to the party," Julie insisted. "Have fun, hang out, eat cake, gossip."

Roger stood up. "Julie, this might not be—"

"Celeste, do you want to go?"

"We can't consider that an option, can we?" She glanced at Flat Finn.

"It's OK." Roger waved Celeste up from her seat. "Why don't you come inside with me? I want to show you the results from that study I did on combating the spread of harmful algae."

Celeste didn't look at Julie as she got up and handed over the invitation. "Please don't worry about this. I understand that it would not work."

Fuming, Julie crossed her arms. Celeste's demeanor had changed, and she no longer looked relaxed. This was Matt and Roger's fault entirely.

Matt put his hands in his pockets and looked down. "I know what you're going to say."

"Do you? Do you really? Goddamn it, Matt! How could you do this to her?"

He looked up, surprised. "Do what?"

She sighed. "Ever heard of a self-fulfilling prophecy? You're setting her up for failure. She knew you hid that invitation from her, and that told her you don't believe in her."

"She knew it because you made a spectacle out of it. She can't go. You know that. That's why I didn't want her to see the invitation. It's just another reminder of something that she's not ready for."

"Maybe you're the one who isn't ready? Maybe your parents aren't ready? Huh? You mother had her wearing fricking pinafores, for God's sake, until I took the kid to the mall!"

"Shhh! Stop yelling!" Matt warned. "This is not your decision."

"It's not yours either. It's Celeste's. She should be able to go if she wants to," Julie insisted. "She's ready."

"She's not ready."

"She needs friends, Matt. When was the last time anybody asked her to do anything?"

Matt was silent.

"She needs friends," Julie said again. "And so do you. You need her to expand her world so that you can have yours back."

He nodded. "I know. But this Rachel's parents probably made her invite *everyone*. Including Celeste."

"Every girl in that entire huge class was invited to stay at their house? I don't think so. Celeste got asked because this Rachel girl wanted to invite her. It's just a party. If you don't make a big deal out it, she might not either. You're her brother. She looks up to you, and she needs to know that you believe in her." Julie waved the invitation at him. "That you trust her, and that you think she can succeed. Don't you get that?"

Matt avoided her eyes. "She doesn't look up to me. She looks up to Finn. And you."

"*And* you. She loves you."

He shuffled his feet. "You really think she can handle this?"

"Yes. I do. I know it."

"What about Flat Finn?"

"She'll fold him up and stick him in the bottom of her overnight bag. No one will know. She's gone shopping with me a bunch of times without him, and I don't even have to take him in the car when I pick her up from school anymore. Yes, he still has to stand by her bed or outside her door at night, and she still obsesses about him some of the time, but it's not like it was. She's getting busy with other parts of life. With *life*, for that matter." Julie looked pleadingly at Matt. "She can do this. She's dressing better, she's into normal music, she picks out cute boys on television. Shut up!" Julie cut off Matt before he said anything. "This stuff is normal. She's even talking less…less like someone who just graduated from an advanced articulation class. Well, sometimes. Let her grow up. She's got to take a risk."

"She doesn't even want to go, Julie," he said feebly. "Really."

"She does too. You saw how she looked at that invitation."

Matt let out a big sigh. "I'll talk to my parents."

"And call Dana. I gave you her number months ago."

"She had mono."

"So what? You could have brought her soup. Tended to her needs, if you know what I mean." Julie gave him an exaggerated wink.

"I did call her, and she said she felt awful and that she'd call me when she was less plague-like."

"I talked to her this morning, and she feels better. She's been holed up in her apartment for ages, and she's ready for some fun."

"If you wink at me again, I will never call her."

"Fine. Stop being so uptight."

"Did it ever occur to you that I might have to be? I have a lot to manage."

Julie put her hands on her hips and took a breath. "Sorry."

"Anything else you want me to do? Should I start a list of all of your assigned tasks?"

"That's it. For now. But call Dana, and go on a date like a regular college boy. And don't wear a weird shirt."

"Define *weird*."

"Nice try."

✳✳✳

Julie lay down on her stomach, her fingers poised over the keyboard. The only light in the bedroom came from the glow of the laptop, but she didn't need to see anything right now except the online chat between her and Finn.

Julie Seagle
OK, so I told you about Celeste's upcoming sleepover and Matt's possible date. What else…?

Finn Is God
I project that the sleepover will be a success, and the date will not. Matt tends to get gassy when he's nervous and, well, you know…That doesn't usually go over so well with the ladies.

Julie Seagle

I gather he did actually have a girlfriend for a while, so presumably he can maintain control of his bodily functions for short periods. You should wish him well!

Finn Is God

I wish this poor Dana girl well, poor thing…I'm joking! I'm sure they will be engaged by the end of the date. Aha! And then we can dance at the wedding. I will wear a purple tuxedo so that I stand out and can be identifiable next to Flat Finn. (Must make sure FF does not wear similar suit. Disaster!)

Julie Seagle

You're warped.

Finn Is God

You are not the first, and will not be the last, to say so. I wear my "warped" label with pride. On my lapel. A lapel label!

Finn Is God

You have no impending events yourself?

Julie Seagle

I've been taking it easy since the Polar Plunge. A frail girl like me only has so much stamina, you know.

Finn Is God

Ha! Weak you are not. I was very impressed by your daring feat. Terrified, but impressed. But maybe you have a date yourself…?

Julie Seagle
Nope. Not interested in anyone here.

Finn Is God
Good. Just checking. I mean, you should go out with whomever you want, of course.

Julie Seagle
Oh.

Finn Is God
But I don't want you to go out with anyone. Is that unfair of me?

Julie Seagle
It would be unfair if I were not going out with anyone else just because you didn't want me to. I'm waiting.

Finn Is God
Waiting for what?

Julie Seagle
Just waiting. Maybe waiting for you. (Which, as it turns out, is a lot like waiting for Godot.) But that sounds crazy.

Finn Is God
I'm glad you're maybe waiting for me, crazy girl. (FYI, that play is based on one of my past lives, but I totally didn't get any financial kickback. Publishing bastards!) And Julie,

my dear, you get to see me all the time…in flat form. I'm dashing, yes?

Julie Seagle

A regular heartthrob, although I'm dying to catch sight of a three-dimensional you someday.

Finn Is God

Believe me, I've thought about a three-dimensional you plenty.

Julie Seagle

I'm hoping that just sounds creepier than it actually is. Hey, Finn?

Finn Is God

Yeeeeeessss?

Julie Seagle

Remember when I was stuck in the elevator? We got interrupted.

Finn Is God

We did.

Julie Seagle

I want to know how the skydiving story ends. What you say to me and how we land.

Finn Is God

OK. I was hoping you'd ask. I'll tell you.

Finn Is God

When we last saw our hero and heroine, they had just pulled the chute and were drifting. What will happen next, concerned viewer? Will our brave couple have their chute torn to shreds by a savage vampire seagull? Will a freakish tornado appear and suck them into a swirling wind current? Stay tuned…

Julie Seagle

Finn!

Finn Is God

Ohhhhhh. You want the good version.

Julie Seagle

Yes.

Finn Is God

The slow version.

Julie Seagle

Yes.

Finn Is God

The hot version.

Julie Seagle

Yes.

Finn Is God

I gotcha. I like that one better too. Ready? Here we go…

So we've pulled the chute, and we're drifting, riding the sky. It's just you and I. You can hear me now that we're falling like this, remember? I tell you that I don't want this to end. I don't want to land and reach the real world because I like our world up here better.

Finn Is God
I tell you that I like being this close to you and how you feel against me. But now even I'm hesitant. I'm afraid that when we hit the ground, this will be over. We'll land, and this feeling between us will vanish. That you won't feel it any longer. I can't stand that thought.

Julie's hands shook as she wrote.

Julie Seagle
I'll still feel it.

Finn Is God
You think?

Julie Seagle
I know.

Finn Is God
Then we can land now. I wait until we are just the right distance from the ground. We're coming in hard, so I tell you to start moving your legs like you're running. You feel your feet hit the grass, and we run together for a few feet, before the force of our landing throws me forward. I fall into you, pushing you down. I'm afraid I'm going to crush you, but I

catch myself with my hands, holding my weight up. We're both breathing hard, the thrill from the jump still coursing through us.

Well, now he'd done it: Julie was riled up. This was getting too heated to deny, and she wasn't going to pretend that what he was writing was not totally turning her on.

Finn Is God
Landing feels different than you thought it would. You'd pictured what it would be like and how you might react. As many times as you'd gone over this in your head, it's completely different. All the signs were there telling you how it would be, but it's not what you thought. It's just as good— maybe even better—just not what you expected. You can look back now and see how you should have known, but you were focusing on the facts instead of the feeling.

Finn Is God
I reach between us and release the buckles that are holding us together. This is when I really panic. The ride up in the plane didn't scare me. Or the height or the jump or the noise. None of that scared me. Right now, only one thing does.

Julie Seagle
Tell me.

Finn Is God
I'm terrified that when I undo that buckle and release you, that you'll get up and walk away from me. I can't think of anything more excruciating.

Julie Seagle

I told you I wouldn't do that. I won't leave.

Finn Is God

I'm still worried. If I roll you over so that you're facing me, you won't stop me?

Julie Seagle

I definitely won't stop you.

Finn Is God

Then that's what I do. I tell you to close your eyes. You listen while I tell you how I feel about you. That I think about you all the time, and I can't get you out of my head. I ask you to ignore everything you think you know and to listen only to your heart, without doubting anything. Can you do that?

Julie Seagle

Of course I can.

Finn Is God

Then I kiss you, and I make you feel everything that I feel.

Holy....

Julie was pretty sure that she stopped breathing. What she wouldn't do to have him here with her right now, telling her these things and kissing her...

Julie Seagle

You have to come home.

Finn Is God
I know. Let me think for a minute.

The wait was interminable. Then finally he wrote.

Finn Is God
This summer. I can't make it happen before then.

Julie Seagle
I'll take it.

Finn Is God
Don't tell anyone, though. Just in case. I'd feel bad enough letting you down, and it would be worse with Celeste.

Julie Seagle
Got it. But you'll try? I mean really try this time? Not like at Christmas.

Finn Is God
Yes. Tonight, I'd do just about anything for you. Unless, of course, it involves getting out of my seat right now. I don't want to creep out my host family.

Julie laughed, and it took her a minute to type without hitting the wrong keys.

Julie Seagle
OK, well…ahem…take your time. I should get some sleep. Or try. It's late here. (I can't remember where you are!)

Finn Is God
I don't even know where I am anymore. Get some rest. I'll talk to you soon.

Before she shut down the computer, she copied and pasted their chat into a text file. Yes, it was embarrassing and sort of silly, but she liked having all of their chats so that she could reread them later. This one she would be rereading for sure. Many times.

CHAPTER 25

"It's midnight. What do you think the girls are doing?" Julie asked Matt. "I bet they're giggling and doing each others' hair." She spun around in his swivel chair while he lounged on his bed, adding music to his iTunes library.

"Oh my God, probably!" Matt said in a stupidly high-pitched voice. "Or, like, maybe they're talking about Robert Pattinson! Or Justin Bieber! Oh my God!"

"I can't believe it. Matthew! You made a reference to pop culture." Julie clapped her hands to her cheeks, feigning utter delight. "Actually two references. I'm stunned and so proud."

"I'm incredibly well-rounded. And it's almost one, not midnight."

"Really?" Julie couldn't believe how late it was. She'd been hanging out in Matt's room for hours, listening to music. It turned out that there was, shockingly, some overlap in their musical taste.

"Seriously, I think things went well. You can't deny that your sister was completely excited for this party. She looked awesome, and she got the best gift for Rachel. Plus, Flat Finn is totally hidden in that bag. Nobody will know."

"She did look happy," Matt admitted. "Maybe you were right. I met Rachel for a minute when I dropped Celeste off. She actually seems like a nice girl."

"Will wonders never cease? I would've assumed Rachel was a complete hellion." Julie smirked. "Why aren't you out tonight? Celeste is gone for the first time, so you should be taking advantage, don't you think?"

"Not with my parents gone for the weekend. I wouldn't feel right."

"I'd be here! Where'd they go again?"

"I don't remember. A Harvard retreat in Maine."

"Oh." Julie stopped spinning in the chair. "I'm sorry. You must be fed up with being left in charge."

"Well, once in a while they get tired of the local takeout and need to venture elsewhere to assess the culinary situation in other cities. I understand that."

"I accept your deflection and raise you another question. How was your date with Dana last night? I haven't heard from her all day. Where did you take her? You should be out with her again tonight."

Matt put on a new song. "We had dinner together."

"And?"

"And what?"

"Details!"

"We ate at a Portuguese restaurant in Central Square. I had codfish cakes for an appetizer and then stewed octopus with potatoes and red wine sauce."

Julie sat patiently, waiting for him to say more. "That's it?"

"I don't think that I'd order the octopus again. I'm still tasting the tentacles."

"Come on, Matt. Did you like her? What did you wear? Are you going out again?"

"I'm not sure."

"I can see I'll get nowhere fast on this subject. Like most subjects with you. God forbid you spontaneously produce informative dialogue on your own." She glared at him. "Excuse me, I have to make a phone call about a study group."

"At this hour?"

"College students don't go to bed until at least three. It's a college requirement. You sign a contract when you're accepted."

She pulled her cell from her pocket and dialed.

Dana picked up right away. "Hey. You calling for info on last night?"

"Of course."

"It was interesting."

"Elaborate."

"What did *he* say?"

"I don't have my notes in front of me. Sorry."

"Matt is standing right there, isn't he?"

"Absolutely."

"We had dinner. He paid, which was nice. It's true that he's not physically my type, but I couldn't have cared less. You know, there's something rather sexy and mysterious about him. He had excellent manners and was totally sweet and polite. And you were right. He is smart as hell. I don't know why you've never let me come over to the house, because he's not completely abnormal. Fine, he is a little bit, but I liked him."

"So you found the article I gave you helpful. How did the study group end for you?"

"You want to know if we messed around?"

"Yes."

"He is a *delicious* kisser."

Julie nearly dropped the phone. "I'm sorry. I didn't quite get your interpretation. I've never heard that fact before."

"Seriously. He's totally fantastic. We made out in the car in front of my apartment. He's got great hands too. He did this cool thing where he slid his fingers under—"

"OK, OK. I get the gist. That's…That's very good to know. When is the next group getting together?"

"Oh, lord, I'm not going out with him again."

"The study group is losing members?"

"Hell, yes."

"Even after the good grades?"

"First of all, he talked the entire time. The *entire* time."

"Really? About what?"

"That leads into the second issue."

"Which is?"

"And before you say anything, no, it wasn't the *Evolution is Following Me* shirt." Dana laughed. "Jules, you have a major problem."

"I don't understand."

"You'll figure it out. That's all I'm saying. Look, he's a great guy, he's just not for me. Anyway, I have to go. I'm outside Jamie's dorm."

"Are you kidding me? That sounds like a dumb idea."

"Hey, I'm weak. Sue me. I'll call you tomorrow."

Julie hung up. Matt had loaded a new playlist and was tapping his foot. Why had Dana said that thing about his hands? And his kissing? Ugh. How was she ever going to look at him again? She wasn't supposed to know stuff like that about Matt.

"Sorry," she said. "Important stuff about my study group."

"Sounded like it. I'm going to get something to drink." Matt stood up. "And how's Dana?"

"Oh." Julie looked away. His stupid hands seemed to be ridiculously noticeable all of a sudden. "Ahem. She's fine. Sorry."

Julie groaned to herself after Matt stepped out. How mortifying. And now she had to erase the image of him engaging in anything other than pecking at the keyboard, making sandwiches for Celeste, or folding geeky T-shirts.

Julie heard the house phone ring, and she quickly sat up.

A few minutes later she heard Matt race down the stairs, and then noises echoed up to his room. What was he doing?

Julie hurried downstairs. "Matt?"

She found him in the kitchen, furiously checking all the cubbies on the wall. "Where the hell are my keys?" He touched his jean pockets and then scanned the countertops.

"I think they're hanging by the front door. Where are you going?"

Matt brushed past her, and she followed him into the hallway.

He stopped as he grabbed the door handle and then turned around and faced her, furious. "I told you. God *damn* it, I told you, Julie!" He was screaming at her now.

She took a step back. She'd never seen him look like this. "What are you talking about?"

"Rachel's mother just called from the party. Celeste is having a meltdown."

"What happened?" Julie took her sweatshirt off of the coat rack and started to follow him out. "She seemed so sure of herself."

"No!" he said pointing at her. "You are not coming with me."

"Matt? Please. I can help. I can talk—"

"No! *You* did this, *I'll* fix it."

Matt slammed the door behind him.

Frantic, she walked back and forth, roaming from room to room. *Finn.* Finn would know what to do.

She messaged him, praying he was around.

Finn, are you there? I screwed up. Really badly. The sleepover I told you about went terribly. Matt is getting her now, and I don't know what to do. They'll never forgive me. Maybe you won't either.

Finn was nowhere to be found online. Julie couldn't even remember where he was now. Back in Africa? Yugoslavia? Turkey? The Netherlands? Libya? Oh, for Christ's sake, that wasn't it. Nobody goes to Libya. She waited another few minutes and then sent another message, her hands shaking as she tried to get the words out:

Please, Finn. I need you. I don't know what to do. Maybe you're angry with me now too, but tell me how to make this better. Or at least less dreadful.

Peeking out the window every few minutes was not bringing Celeste home any faster, so she sat on the couch in the living room. Maybe it wasn't that bad. Matt had a tendency to overreact when it came to his sister. He didn't give her enough credit. Still, Julie felt her stomach knot up with dread because as much as she wanted them to get home, she also didn't want to face them.

Finally, the Volvo pulled into the driveway. Julie swung the door open and watched as Matt rounded the front of the car and opened the passenger door. She couldn't stand this, and she looked away for a moment, trying to regroup. Then Matt was walking toward her, Celeste in his arms, an awful mix of rage and fear in his eyes. His sister—her friend—looked like a little kid, her arms around his neck and her head buried in his shirt, her body trembling as she sobbed uncontrollably. The anguish in her crying was crushing.

Julie's heart broke.

Celeste had come undone.

CHAPTER 26

Matt pushed past Julie and carried Celeste up to her room. Julie followed them but heard the bedroom door shut before she had even reached the landing.

Flat Finn. He was still in the car. She raced outside and returned with the messenger bag. Outside Celeste's room, Julie fumbled with the zipper and hoped that this would help a bit. She set Flat Finn onto the carpet and slowly started the process of unfolding him, carefully securing each hinge in the open position. She rubbed her arm across her eyes and moved Flat Finn to standing. As the sobs from behind the door grew louder and more pained, Julie bit her lip and looked at Flat Finn, imagining that the real Finn was there, about to comfort his sister and make this hell disappear.

You have to come home. You have to come home, she repeated to herself. *I know damn well that this is about more than just missing you, but you have to come home for her.*

Julie slumped to the floor and pulled her legs in, dropping her head down and rhythmically rocking her body. It seemed an eternity until Celeste's moans subsided, and she could hear Matt's voice comforting her.

The door opened, and Julie jerked her head up. "Matt? Oh, God. I don't know what—"

He held his hand up. "Don't say anything to me. She wants to talk to you."

She stood up and delicately lifted Flat Finn. He looked so fragile now with all of the hinges. Like a puzzle that had been taped together. Just like Celeste. She walked past Matt and into the bedroom, setting Flat Finn down next to the bed. A head full of blond curls rolled over, and Celeste reached her hand out. Julie took it in her own and knelt down. "I'm so sorry. This is all my fault." She fought to keep back tears as she brushed the hair from Celeste's face.

"I am *much* better now." Her voice was surprisingly calm. "Julie, you have nothing to be sorry for. I do. I need to apologize to you."

"What? What could you possibly have to apologize for?"

"I let you down. You must be horribly disappointed in me."

"Never. You could never disappoint me. You were so brave. Braver than I am. I just pushed too hard."

"No, you did not." Celeste pulled her blanket up. "You *didn't*. I wanted to go."

"I know you did. But I made a mistake. It wasn't the right time. Too many hinges too soon."

Celeste yawned and looked at Flat Finn. "No. The hinges are debonair, but folded-up, hidden Finn is not always the same. Especially at night. The night appears to be the hardest for me without him. For now. He makes me feel better, Julie. I understand that his sort is not for everybody, but I find him comforting."

Julie nodded. "I know. I find his sort comforting too, if you can believe it."

"I do. Now, I must get some sleep. Please tell Matty that I really am less convoluted. I am significantly calmer."

"I will." Julie leaned in and hugged Celeste tightly. "I'll see you in the morning." She let herself out, blowing kisses from the doorway as though she were tucking in a small child.

Matt was leaning against the wall in the hallway, his expression icy and distant. "Stay away from me. I can't deal with you right now."

"Matt…" Julie pleaded.

"I swear to God, don't talk to me now. Don't."

"I'm so sorry. You have no idea."

"I don't want to hear it. I don't want to hear anything from you."

"Matt, you know I love Celeste, and I would never have done anything to hurt her."

"Well, you did."

"If you would just let me explain again why—"

"You don't stop, do you? You want to get into this? Fine. Let's get into it. You thought you could just show up here and insinuate yourself into our lives? You can't. And you also can't act like I'm the bad guy. Like everything I do for her is somehow totally brainless." He moved so that he was facing her, placing his body inches from hers. "I've busted my ass to keep Celeste in a stable place, and you just ruined it. You ruined *her*. God, Julie. You're here for a few months, and you think that you know what is right for Celeste? Nobody asked you to fix anything. You can't." He ran his hands through his hair as he continued to unleash on her. "You can't change this. And your constant reminders that you think we're all completely crazy are not helpful. Do you get that? What is wrong with you? Don't you have your own life to attend to? Or is this how you make yourself feel better about your crappy father, huh?

You excuse the way he treats you for no good reason, and you love him based on nothing more than a few lousy e-mails a year."

His words cut deeply. "That's not fair." Julie felt herself breathing hard as she tried to deal with his anger. His disgust.

"It is fair. And Celeste is not your job. *We're* not your job. We're not your family."

"I know that. I never...I never said you were." Julie knew her lip was trembling, but she was not going to cry in front of Matt again.

"And you know what the most unbelievable part of this is? I listened to you! I knew better, and yet I let you barrel ahead and do what you wanted anyway. *I'm* the one to blame for what happened tonight."

Julie shook her head. "No, Matt. I know I did this. I'm sorry. Please know that. I couldn't possibly feel worse. But don't you see that Celeste can't spend the rest of her life avoiding the real world? And neither can you."

"Why not, huh?" He was still shouting, and Julie winced with each word. "The real world *sucks* for her."

"What about for you?"

"Sometimes, yes."

"So when are *you* going to start living, Matt?" Now she was the one screaming. "You're taking the easy way out. You use Celeste as an excuse to do nothing except drown in theories and calculations. You bury yourself online and—"

"You're one to talk about burying oneself online." His laugh had a nasty, horrible tone. "*I'm* taking the easy way out? I'm not fawning over someone I've never met, someone who isn't even here. You're the one playing it safe because you're too afraid of something real."

"Don't go there," Julie said sharply.

"Now who's the one with boundaries, huh?" He started walking back and forth. "When it comes to Celeste, you don't even know what you're dealing with, so stay out of it."

"No, I don't know what I'm dealing with. I don't understand anything, because none of you will tell me! Why are your parents never here?" she exploded. "Why does she have Flat Finn? Why won't you tell me?"

"I can't, Julie! I just can't! It's none of your business. How many times do you have to hear it?"

She looked helplessly at Matt. She'd never seen him like this. "OK. OK. I'm done." She held her hands up. "I'm out of it. I just…I just wanted to help. I shouldn't have." She was quieter now, giving in. "You're right. You handle this however you want."

"Obviously, Julie, you don't like the way I do things, and you don't like me the way I am. Fine. I couldn't care less. But stop trying to change me. You don't get to pick which parts of me you find acceptable and throw away what you don't. I'll never be what you want. You don't like me? Then stay out of my life."

She was so confused. This conversation was all over the place, and she didn't even know what was happening. "How could you say that? I do like you, Matt."

He turned away and walked toward his room. "I'm exhausted. *You're* exhausting me."

"Matt, please—"

"Go to hell, Julie."

Frozen, Julie could not move from her spot in the hall. She could barely breathe. What had happened? How could Matt have said all those things?

Maybe she *had* been pushy and nosy and should have left things alone. Just because she was staying in their house didn't mean she had the right to meddle into their affairs. Truly, her intention had never been to be intrusive or disrespectful. But she obviously had. Her professor had pointed this out to her too. *Why do you have to be the fixer?*

She didn't. She shouldn't. She was just a guest here. A boarder, a babysitter, a driver.

Eventually she found herself in her room, lying on top of the blankets, unable to sleep. Finn's room felt different now, empty and lonely. Her emotions were on overload, and the sounds of Celeste's cries and Matt's awful words echoed in her head.

He could be right about her father. It was true that she had given him far too many chances, only for him to prove over and over again that he was a dreadful parent. He had never given her any real reason to love him. But she had.

It was different with Finn, though. Matt was wrong about him. He did care about her.

She checked the clock. It was almost four in the morning. The night had been so peaceful until that phone call. Now everything was in shambles.

After another forty-five minutes of anxiety-ridden attempts to sleep, she gave up. She checked her computer, and there were no messages from Finn. Of all the times for him to disappear. Her heart ached. She missed him and needed him now. Summer couldn't come fast enough. Finn *would* be here, and he'd stay here. And Celeste would be better. Maybe not completely, but she would be better.

Roaming the room and staring out the window at the night sky got her nowhere. She couldn't tolerate this. She hated fighting. It made clear thought impossible for her. Everything was in chaos.

Julie left her room and went into the dark hallway. She hesitated for a moment before she knocked lightly. There was no response. She couldn't stop herself and opened the door anyway. "Matt?"

Julie walked softly across the floor and sat down on the edge of his bed. "Matty," she said.

The moonlight was enough that she could see he was awake, just not answering her. He was on his back, one hand folded under his head and the other resting on his chest. He turned to look at her. At least he looked as miserable as she felt.

"I'm sorry. Please. You have to forgive me." Her voice was breaking. She knew that she was on the verge of falling apart, but she couldn't help it. "I'm so sorry. I'm so sorry," she kept repeating. "Matty, please. You can't be this mad at me. I can't take it." Julie leaned forward, dropping her head onto his chest and slipping her arms under his shoulders, trying to make him hold her. The Matt she'd seen earlier tonight had been a stranger. She hugged him tightly, wanting nothing more than for him to come back to her, to be himself again.

A few minutes passed, and then she felt his hand on the back of her head, gently stroking her hair. She closed her eyes.

"Shhh…" he said. "I'm the one who's sorry. I didn't mean any of the things I said to you. You didn't deserve that."

Julie turned her head, resting her cheek against him and listening to his breathing. His voice was soothing, his touch relaxing, and Julie's pain began to lighten a hint. She didn't know what to say, so she said nothing, staying where she was as his hand continued to move through her hair and then to her back. He lulled her into a place where nothing hurt anymore, and this whole dreadful evening started to feel like a nightmare that she was coming out of. His stroke traveled over the straps of her tank top, brushing against her skin, making her shiver and curl into him more.

"I was awful," he continued. "Your relationship with your father is none of my business. Of course you love him, and you have every right to. What I said was unforgivable." Matt was sincerely upset. She could hear it. "You're the best thing to happen to Celeste. She was lost before you got here. As if she didn't belong anywhere. You're saving her. I *never* should have said what I did."

"No, I pushed her too much," Julie said quietly. "And you. It won't happen again."

"You've been perfect. I wish I could tell you everything, but I can't. Not yet."

"I know. That's all right." She kept her tight hold around him, as if letting go might break his absolution, and he would again let loose with more cruel blame.

The rush and tension from their earlier scene had started to wane, and she was feeling drowsy, settled into a postfight haze. Like she'd been drugged with relief.

The air felt chilly, and his touch was giving her goose bumps. Julie shivered again.

"Cold?" he asked.

"Yeah. A little."

As Matt moved his legs over in the bed, she eased in next to him, sliding under the blanket, onto her side and into the crook of his arm. His hand was still on her back, his fingertips starting to trace the curve of her shoulder blade, moving up to brush the nape of her neck, then traveling up and down her arm. She took his free hand in hers, intertwining their fingers, and squeezed.

He squeezed back.

"So we're still friends?" she asked.

"Yes," he said after a moment. "We're still friends."

He didn't hate her. They were fine. Celeste would be fine. This would all work out, and there was no irrevocable damage. Nothing else mattered.

Now fatigue took over and Julie yawned. She was so completely tired and so emotionally spent. The night had drained her of any ability to reason, but she felt peaceful for the moment, grounded. Eventually Matt's touch against her skin slowed, and his breathing changed, and she knew that he'd fallen asleep. It was impossible to fight the heaviness that was drawing at her now, so she let the sound of his slumber pull her into her own.

Later—still in his arms, her hand still in his—she stirred.

She felt him lightly kiss the top of her head and say something. He was so quiet that she could barely hear him.

Julie sleepily tilted her head up.

"God, I'm so sorry, Julie," he said.

"Me too."

And then without realizing it, without thinking, she inched up just a little until her mouth was close to his. She had no idea what she was doing, as though she were following some instinct that she couldn't control. Maybe she was still asleep. Maybe this wasn't happening. She moved a tiny bit closer, barely touching her lips to his. His mouth was warm and tempting, luring her in. Neither of them moved.

Then his hand was firmly on her side, guiding her body up higher and bringing her mouth closer to his. Matt pressed his lips against hers, and he kissed her.

His mouth was soft and unhurried. Teasing, even. His tongue just brushing hers and making her tremble. She kissed back, tasting him, breathing him in. Julie was dizzy and shaky and inundated with his heat. He made her temporarily lost, not able to see beyond the way this kiss felt. In the moonlit light, it was smooth, easy, instinctive. She moved her leg over his, bringing them closer together.

She couldn't possibly be awake.

Her chest was pressed against his, his hand on her lower back, his fingers digging into her skin. She didn't want this to stop. She moved one hand to the back of his neck, kissing him harder.

But then Matt tightened his hand around hers before gently resting his head back onto the pillow. He pushed the hair from her face and tucked it behind her ear. Julie didn't move for a second. *This was nuts.* She lowered her body and nestled back into his chest. As bleary-eyed, stunned, and out-of-it as she was, part of her knew that she should get up and go back to her room. Even though that was the last thing that she wanted to do. And part of her knew that what had just happened was unexplainable. It must be a dream.

It had to be.

But she didn't care too much, at least for right now, because the horrible rift between them was healed. That was the most important thing.

I should go, she told herself. *I'm supposed to leave.* Julie shut her eyes. *Why don't I want to leave? Why don't I want to leave?*

But she simply couldn't stay awake long enough to persuade herself to get out of his bed. Julie surrendered to sleep, letting her body shape against Matt's as he held her closely.

CHAPTER 27

Matthew Watkins *took the "Which random number are you?" quiz and the result was: 3. Which is lame, because 3 is, like, the least random number there is.*

Finn Is God *So much for Earth Day. I totally screwed things up and started celebrating the wrong planet. Now I have to collect all these stupid trademarked dog figurines that I distributed all over the yard. At least it's better than last year's mistake when I had butt statues everywhere.*

Julie Seagle *I like the gritty intensity of* Jaws 4. *There is a simple honesty to the storytelling that is utterly compelling. Plus, the shark roars.*

Julie rolled over and opened her eyes, squinting against the sunlight that blasted her in the face.

Holy...

She was in Matt's bed. Alone, thank God. At least there was no tragic wake-up-in-each-other's-arms moment. She yanked the sheet up over her head and ran over what had happened last night.

This didn't have to be a big deal. They had both been emotional, and so things had taken an unexpected turn. Nothing major. People hook up all the time, right? And not that she and Matt had even really hooked up. A tiny little kiss between friends.

Shit.

"Julie?"

She pulled the sheet down and peeked out. Matt was leaning into his room and quite obviously avoiding making eye contact.

"Celeste is cooking breakfast." He cleared his throat. "You went for a run, and you just got back. That's why you weren't in your room when she went to wake you up."

"When exactly did I take up running? I never knew this about myself."

"Next time you can come up with something better." He paused. "Not that there's going to be a next time. I just meant… Maybe you should…you know…"

"Got it. Getting up now. I was never here." Julie rubbed her hands over her face. "Tell Celeste that I'm in the shower, and I'll be right down."

"OK."

"Wait a minute." She sat up. "Celeste is making breakfast? She's feeling all right?"

"Apparently."

Matt disappeared, and she scrambled to her room. Julie made a face at her unruly reflection in the mirror, grabbed some clothes, and hit the shower. Hopefully Celeste had made a giant pot of coffee too, because four hours of sleep was not going to cut it.

By the time she took a seat next to Flat Finn and Matt at the kitchen table, the smell of a full breakfast had filled the house. She eyed the bowl of cut-up strawberries, the tray of scrambled eggs, bacon, and sausage, and the butter, syrup, and carafe of coffee suspiciously. The table had been set with the good dishes and cloth napkins. Why was Celeste in such a good mood?

"Good morning," Celeste chirped as she ladled pancake batter onto a skillet.

"Good morning," Julie answered hesitantly. "This is very nice of you to cook all this."

"I wanted to. Let me finish with the pancakes, and then we can discuss things."

"Looking forward to it," she lied.

Julie kept her head down and pretended to be captivated by garage sales listings in the newspaper.

"Go ahead and start eating. The pancakes will be ready in a second."

Julie and Matt both reached for the eggs at the same time, causing a flurry of apologies and "go aheads."

Ta da! This is why you don't kiss platonic friends whom you live with. Or sleep in their beds. Or let them run their hands all over your arms and shoulders and make you tingle inappropriately…

Julie stuffed her mouth with food so that she wouldn't have to talk and continued not reading the paper. There was a way to make sense of what had happened last night: After months of being all fired up about Finn, she had transferred her pent-up physical frustrations to Matt. And Matt had probably been in the mood because of his date with Dana the night before. Of course it was sort of disgusting and tacky that she'd kissed the same guy her friend had been making out with the night before. What was wrong with her? And what the hell had Matt been thinking? Perhaps Matt was just a big old slut who ran around Boston kissing every girl he met, and he'd been waiting for the right time to add Julie to his list. At least that way, the kiss would be as meaningless to him as it was to her.

She glanced up for a second and caught him looking at her.

This is all understandable, she reasoned. They *did* have a certain comfort level with each other, so it was not completely freakish that they had blurred the lines for a moment after an emotionally trying evening.

And Julie had probably done the typical girl thing, which is to try to make things better by giving a guy what he wants: physical contact. That's what guys understand, right? It wasn't as if they'd gotten naked or anything, but she was probably responsible for the kiss. She'd been desperate for him to forgive her, and in her weak, drained state, she'd tried to patch things up with something sexual. Well, not *sexual*, meaning that they had almost had sex. Not even close. And not that either of them had been thinking about it. Ridiculous. She was certainly not attracted to him that way, and Matt was probably more turned on by megabytes and firewalls and bit torrents than he was by her.

Of course, he had been the one trailing his fingers across... Whatever.

Matt had to be just as regretful as she was.

Besides, he'd said that everything he had yelled at her wasn't true; therefore, that meant she was, in fact, like family. Making him a brother figure, the way she'd always thought. Except that you don't kiss your brother on the mouth. Especially with tongue. And you don't press your body into his and get all momentarily hot and dreamy. At least you're not supposed to.

Again, *shit.*

But it wasn't like he'd tried to do anything else. His hands hadn't moved anywhere good. Well, not *good.* She didn't mean that. *Improper. Indecent. Lewd. Vulgar. Naughty.* Christ, now was not the time to turn into a thesaurus. The point was that it wasn't as though he'd been grinding against her and whispering dirty things into her ear. Although now that she thought about it, maybe she should be offended that he hadn't. Not that she would have let him.

Wait a minute. *She* had moved her leg over his, and *he* had stopped kissing her first.

Oh. Matt thought she was a terrible kisser. *Bastard*. She was *so* not going to look over at him now.

Julie slugged down half a cup of coffee. *Finn*. That's really what this had been about, she was sure. Finn and his steamy messages had her in a perpetually needy state. Plus, it had been a while since she and Seth had broken up, and she was just some horny college student using whatever guy she'd crawled into bed with.

No, that wasn't right either. Julie wasn't like that. She was just talking in circles.

Celeste set a plate piled with pancakes on the table and sat down. "Wow. You are both quite hungry today, I see. You didn't leave me any eggs, and there is only one piece of sausage left."

Apparently the mutual method of stuffing face to avoid talking that she and Matt had been employing had gone too far.

"Sorry," Matt said with a full mouth.

"It's OK. I can make more. I wanted to talk to you both."

"Sure. That's a good idea," Julie said.

"We need to discuss what happened between you two last night."

Matt started to choke on his food, and Julie knew her face blanched. It seemed that Celeste hadn't bought Matt's dumb story about Julie going running.

Ugh. Julie didn't want anybody to know about this, least of all Celeste. And Finn, of course. Matt wouldn't tell Finn, would he? Was *she* supposed to tell Finn? *Dear Finn, I accidentally sucked face with your brother. Apologies! How are the*

Venezuelan orphans? She touched her hand to the stone that rested on her chest. The necklace was a near-constant reminder of him. Apparently she hadn't paid any attention to that last night.

Flat Finn seemed to chastise her from his position at the table. Julie stabbed her eggs and glared at the arrogant cutout. *Shut up.*

Celeste casually drizzled syrup over her plate. "I'm extremely upset with you two."

"It's really not a big deal," Matt mumbled.

"Totally not," Julie agreed and busied herself selecting strawberries from the bowl.

"It is indeed a big deal. Everything has changed between you two, and I don't like it one bit. I heard everything, and I'm extremely displeased."

Julie and Matt both stayed silent. What exactly had Celeste heard? Had there been slurpy kissing sounds? Inadvertent moans of ecstasy? Oh my God, Julie had not been that out of it, had she? It was one silly, insignificant kiss. There had been no lusty heaving. Definitely not.

Matt rubbed his eyes. "Celeste, what are you talking about?"

"What are *you* talking about?" She looked at them curiously. Annoyingly hopeful, even. "Did something else happen?"

"Nothing. Um…nothing," Julie muttered. "Go ahead."

"I heard that entire terrible argument you two had."

"The argument. Yes, that," Matt said.

In the wake of the sleep-in-Matt's-bed incident, she had almost forgotten.

"I'm furious with both of you. But mostly with you, Matt." Celeste jabbed her fork in his direction. "I have never known you to be so malicious. Julie has been nothing but a saint, so don't you ever scream at her like that again. And Julie, you were frankly not all that nice either. Matt is doing the best that he can with me, and I have not made things easy for him. I love you both, but there will be no more disputes regarding Flat Finn and me. While I am infinitely grateful for all that you have done for me, I'm going to take a more active role in managing myself. It's time. Understand? There will be no more talking behind my back. I may be in junior high school. You two aren't. Act like it." Celeste looked back and forth between them and raised her eyebrows. "Are you still mad at each other? Do you need to kiss and make up?"

Julie shook her head violently. "No. I don't think that's necessary. Matt and I are fine." She looked across the table, finally looking Matt in the eyes. "Right, Matt?"

"Yes. We are." He looked truthful enough.

"Don't ever fight like that again. Ever," Celeste instructed. "The unexpected good news is that I had a remarkably good time at Rachel's. Well, until the end, of course."

"You...You did?" Matt asked.

"Yes. I really did." She helped herself to more pancakes. "Rachel is a very nice girl. She and I actually have some things in common. It's true that she is not the most popular girl at school, and I guess I like that about her. She's in almost all of my classes and scored better on our last history exam than I did. I think I did a nice job of blending in last night. I was even asked to recap one of the first episodes of *Pretty Little Liars*, which I did to perfection, I might add. Anyway, the night was quite enjoyable until it was time to sleep. The dark does funny things to me, and my head gets besieged with unsettled thoughts. Rachel's mother found me in the bathroom crying, and she was nice enough to offer to tell the other girls that I'd come down with a stomach bug and that's why I left. Anyhow, I have a few things to tell you."

"Go ahead," a stunned Matt said.

"First of all, I would like to start walking to and from school by myself. So Julie, that means that you won't need to drive me. I'm ready. Flat Finn won't need to come with me. I still need him, just not all the time."

"Oh. Sure." Julie did her best to look supportive despite being unnerved somehow.

"The second piece of news is not necessarily information one would typically present at the breakfast table, but now is as good a time as any to say that I got my period yesterday morning."

Matt groaned loudly and covered his ears. "Celeste! Really? You need to tell me about this...development?"

Celeste shot him an annoyed look. "Matthew, it's not a big deal. I simply thought I should let everyone know. And, no, I do not need any information on what it means to be a woman. It's a biological change that has occurred, and I thought it important to inform you."

"Do you, er, think that's why you were so, you know...?" Matt fumbled for words pathetically.

"No," Celeste said. "Nobody gets her period for the first time and has a nervous breakdown next to a Kohler toilet. Men have such stupid ideas about menstruation, don't they, Julie? But it *is* an indicator that I am maturing, and it brought up other issues for me. Thus the dramatic crying and Flat Finn freak-out. Also, speaking of growing up, I really need a bra. Even though I am not exactly billowing out of my clothes, there is finally something happening there. The silly sports bras Mom bought for me are ugly. Unless *you* feel like taking me shopping, Matt, I would like to go to the mall with another girl."

"Um...Absolutely. Yes. I mean, if that's what you think should...er, happen. If there is a rush on this...purchase necessity." Poor Matt was really struggling with what to say. "Julie could, I assume, assist in the buying of…"

"We can go to the mall. Sure." Julie tried to shake herself out of her state of shock following Celeste's slew of revelations. She looked cautiously at Matt. "You don't mind my taking her?" Considering that last night she had promised to stay out of things, she was hesitant to help Celeste in any new endeavors.

He averted his gaze, but shook his head. "Of course not. You should."

"Or maybe your mother would prefer to take you when she gets home?" Julie offered.

"I suppose I could ask her. I'll try, although she's not terribly interested in me. And," Celeste continued, "I would like to have Rachel come to the house some day. She wears unattractive wire glasses, and her hair is a frightful mess. I might be able to help her. Plus, she knows nothing about the Phanerozoic eon, and I know quite a bit because Finn was a dinosaur nut when he was younger."

It was hard to know what to say following this unexpected outpouring. So much had changed in the past twelve hours with Celeste. And between her and Matt. Everything felt different.

"Maybe this summer we could all go to the beach together? Plum Island is lovely as long as it's not horsefly season. And I'd like to paint my room. Yellow. Or fern green. That would be a nice summer project. Julie, I could use your assistance in choosing the right color."

Before she could answer, Matt jumped in. "I'm sure Julie will be busy this summer, Celeste. She'll probably have her own place by then, right?"

Julie startled. Getting her own place would make sense. It just hadn't occurred to her. *Of course* she'd have to move out. Roger and Erin had generously put her up for the year, but what was she going to do? Stay here until she graduated? That was ridiculous, and they were too polite to ask her directly to move out. Besides, she was taking up Finn's room, and he would be home soon enough. "Yes, I assume so."

Celeste frowned. "Will we still see each other?"

"Absolutely. We can make a weekly girls' date."

"It won't be the same, will it?"

"No. It won't. But it will still be special."

"There's probably a bunch of apartments opening up for July first. Or June, even," Matt said.

"Great. Thanks," Julie said weakly.

An unpleasant feeling in her chest grew as she started to absorb the idea of not living at the Watkins house. This had become her home.

Except it felt less like home if Matt didn't want her here.

Stupid kissing. Stupid roaming hands. Stupid boys.

"I'll start looking for an apartment today. I could probably be out of here just after classes end. I'll try for June first."

"Julie, I didn't mean—"

"Obviously I'm moving out, Matt," she said sneering. "Obviously."

Matt looked everywhere but at the two girls while Julie urgently checked on those garage sale details again in the paper.

Celeste maintained a rather bemused look on her face. "This is an unusual morning we're all having, isn't it?"

Julie stood up and took her plate to the sink. "Were you thinking more Lady Grace or more Victoria's Secret?"

Matt nearly fainted.

CHAPTER 28

Matthew Watkins *I need an afternoon pick-me-up. I accept cash and/or prizes that can be exchanged for cash. Also, hobbits.*
Finn Is God *If you get off your high horse, you'll notice that it, too, poops.*
Julie Seagle *Mixed emotions regarding Twitter continue. Am again facing warnings about unprotected Tweets, but it's not my fault the condom won't fit over the laptop. "A" for effort and whatnot, I think.*

Finn–

I hope you're sitting down for this: Your mom, Celeste, Celeste's FRIEND Rachel, and I are all going to some ritzy spa to get our nails done. It was Celeste's idea to do something with Rachel, and I thought we should start out of the house first. Less FF temptation that way. When I asked Erin about taking the girls, I suggested maybe she'd like to come along, and after a bit of prodding, I got her to agree! I feel weird driving them around in the car like I'm some sort of chauffeur, but at least we're going somewhere. And lest you start moaning (like Matt) that I've turned Celeste into a shallow teen, you should know that our postmanicure events include a trip to the Institute of Contemporary Arts and dinner at some Mongolian restaurant.

Flat Finn is not coming. Boys are not allowed, according to your sister. He is taking the day off (again) in the front hall closet behind what is either a badminton set or a fishing net.

You won't believe how different Celeste is when you see her. Yes, she's still extremely quirky and unusual (in a loveable way, of course), but she's different. She's happier. Your parents had a meeting at the school with that guidance counselor whom I unreasonably hated so much, and he was "extremely impressed and relieved" at how nicely her social skills are coming along. Finn, she is so much more grown up now. Really self-sufficient. Don't take this the wrong way, but she hasn't been as obsessed with you and when you're coming home. (I, however...) I think other parts of her life are taking over. True, she still only has this one real friend, but it's a start. And she's going online now and searching for normal teenage stuff, which totally annoys your dad, not to mention Matt. She wants to go to the movies and shopping, etc. Don't worry, though; she still curls up on the couch with The Iliad or something equally snooty.

To be honest, I miss her sometimes. The "old" Celeste, I mean. I'm still with her plenty, it's just that she is so much less dependent on other people. I get nostalgic for the Celeste who was so glued to me, the one who looked up to me, the one who freaked out over lip-gloss and a simple trip to the grocery store. That sounds awful, doesn't it? I don't want that for her. I want her to be who she's becoming, you know? Lighter and freer. It's like she was locked in one place, and now she finally sees that movement is possible. She's not sure which way to turn yet, but she can see the options.

To answer your question from the other day, Matt is fine. I haven't seen him a lot recently. We've both been mobbed with end-of-semester work, but I could use his help with Calculus II with Calculations. I'm dying in that class. He always explains stuff so clearly. Things have still been off since the night of Celeste's meltdown. Ironically, she came out of it somewhat healed, while it drove a wedge between Matt and me. I feel bad because we were friends. I guess we still are...It's different, though. We used to hang out all the time, and now I barely see him. Not that he's mean to me or anything, but I don't get the impression he wants to be around me anymore. He keeps leaving me little notes with information about apartment rentals. Obviously he can't wait to get me out of here. I don't know. Maybe he's just trying to be helpful. I wish things were better between us. It feels...It just doesn't feel right like this. It's abnormal.

You know what's funny? You've almost become some diary that I write to. A figment of my imagination. But you're easy to talk to. Write to. Whatever.

There is no need to panic; I'll take all of my teddy bears with me and remove the sparkly heart curtains before you get home.

Miss you,

–Julie

Julie–

See if Mom will get little pictures painted on her nails. I think she'd look fab with looooong painted talons, don't you? It's totally her.

From everything you've been telling me this year about Celeste, I'm not surprised to hear that she has made so many changes. You came into her life and shook up her world in a way that allowed her to still be who she is. You saved her, Julie.

I don't know what to tell you about Matt. Maybe you feel things are abnormal because HE'S abnormal? Kidding. I shouldn't joke because I can tell you're upset. I'm sorry if your

*feelings are hurt. He's as mixed up as the rest of the family. I
do know that he cares about you. I can promise you that. If he's
being awful, I'm quite sure that it's not because of anything that
you've done. He's just not good at handling people. Or himself,
for that matter. Wait it out. Trust me.*

*Don't you DARE take the stuffed animals and adorable cur-
tains with you. I am so overloaded with testosterone (grunt!),
and those items will help me to embrace my feminine side. A
kinder, gentler Finn.*

*I miss you too, and I have so much to tell you. I know you
think that you already know me—and I love that you can say
anything to me—but I just hope that you'll feel the same way
when reality kicks in.*

–Finn

Finn–

*There is nothing you could say that would change what you
mean to me.*

–Julie

Julie–

I'll hold you to that.

–Finn

✳✳✳

The neon red nail polish was slightly alarming, but Julie
didn't protest as the manicurist continued lacquering her toe-
nails. Celeste had chosen the shade and insisted that the four of
them all get their fingers and toes done in the same color. She
had said, "Sharing the same color will indicate that we are all
connected."

"Like gang colors," Erin had added.

Despite Erin's reluctance to spend part of the afternoon holed up in a salon, she looked moderately relaxed as her feet soaked in a soapy bath next to Julie. She even tilted her head back into the soft neck rest.

Julie looked across the room at Rachel and Celeste, who were peering at the pages of a magazine in between giggling at something on Rachel's BlackBerry. Was there any possibility they were snickering over boys? Rachel's top-of-the-lungs demonstration that she knew the entire periodic table of the elements confirmed that Celeste had been right about Rachel being a bit of an odd duck. But anything other than that wouldn't have made sense. This pair of awkward, struggling kids had found each other for a reason.

Erin lifted her head and squinted. "Do you suppose I'm required to get Celeste a handheld device of some kind?"

"I don't think there's a parental law, no," Julie said.

"I haven't been very in tune…attentive, really…to Celeste's needs. I do realize that. I'm starting to, and I know that I need to. I enjoyed taking her shopping last week. Thank you for suggesting that. And for today."

Julie smiled softly at her.

"I was pondering taking Celeste down to the Cape with me one weekend this summer. A mother-and-daughter mini-vacation. Do you think that she would like that?"

Julie nodded. "Very much." She glanced at her electric-colored toes. "Maybe even a vacation for the whole family?"

"Mmm…That sounds lovely. I'll look into that. I don't remember the last time we've all spent a longer span of time together." Erin dropped her head back again.

A family vacation. A foreign concept to Julie. Her father had left her two voice mails and sent three e-mails in the past few months, all via his secretary. Julie had ignored the first batch of messages, and finally had her own secretary—a Miss Celeste Watkins—respond with a terse e-mail explaining that Ms. Seagle was currently engulfed in important business matters but would be arranging a never-to-happen dinner appointment shortly.

"So," Erin said, "Matt says that you're looking for an apartment?"

"Oh. Yeah, I am. I figured it was about time I got out of your hair."

"Nonsense. You're welcome to stay as long as you like, although I imagine you're ready to expand on your collegiate experience."

Julie felt that stabbing pain in her chest again. It *was* all Matt's idea for her to move out. "It might be easier for me to be closer to campus," she said quietly. "Dana asked me to live with her. Her roommate will be gone right after finals, and I can move in then."

"That's so soon. But I know that we've kept you cooped up more than could have been fun. You've spent your whole year attending to Celeste and studying with Matthew. We've been selfish with you." Erin sighed. "It's your fault for being so damn special. I do hope that you'll come around for dinner on occasion. It's not going to be the same without you."

Julie bit her lip and then closed her eyes. She felt lonely and awful and couldn't think of anything to say that wouldn't send her into a crying fit.

"When you have your own place, you can paint and decorate as you like and not worry about other people in the house. You and Dana will have fun together. Just the way that your mother and I used to. Matthew's old room could hardly have been as female-friendly as you would have liked anyway."

"You mean Finn's room," Julie corrected.

"What? No, you've been in Matthew's room. He moved into Finn's old room a while ago, so his was empty until you got here. It's been nice having a full house again."

"I guess I misunderstood…" Julie started. This didn't make any sense. For a lot of reasons. "I thought—"

"You know what?" Erin said happily. "Coming here was a good idea. I rarely just sit and do nothing. It's given me a chance to think. I've missed my family, Julie. Whether you intended to or not, you've helped bring them back to me and me back to them."

Julie inhaled and exhaled deeply and tried to untangle her thoughts.

Then Erin's hand moved on top of hers and rested there, her wordless touch both disquieting and consoling.

CHAPTER 29

"You're not taking the car today?" Matt looked up from his laptop as Julie crossed the living room. He was on the couch, wearing a surprisingly text-free red shirt, with his feet kicked up on the coffee table.

"No. I'm going to walk to the T. It's so nice out." The words felt slow coming from her mouth, heavy and falsely normal.

"May and June are usually nice, but just wait until summer. Hazy, hot, and humid."

Julie sat down in one of the hard-backed chairs and rifled through her school bag, making sure she had everything she needed for her last day. After taking one exam this morning and handing in a term paper, she would be done. Most people in her position would feel elated. Instead, a looming sense of uneasiness stayed with her, as it had for the past few weeks.

She flipped through the printed pages of her paper. Even though she had written the paper, her words looked unfamiliar. The letters blended together and swam across the page into meaningless jumbles. She let the paper slip from her hand and fall to the floor.

"Julie? Are you OK?" Matt asked.

"I'm fine," she said.

"You seem a little off today."

"I told you that I'm fine."

Julie put her term paper back into her bag and walked to the front window. She lifted the heavy old pane and didn't move as a soft breeze blew the sheer curtain against her. The sky was totally clear, and the world had that fresh, unsoiled smell that late spring brings. That precious scent would likely last only until the July heat and stench tore it away.

She turned and watched Matt as he continued working. "Matty?"

"Yeah?"

"Look at me."

"What?" he asked.

"Look at me."

Matt lifted his head. It felt like ages since he had looked right at her, and that spark she often saw in his gray eyes was gone. There had been no back-and-forth banter between them in weeks, no joking about his shirts, no struggling to get her to understand asymptotic methods for her calculus class. She studied his face, trying to figure him out. Trying to understand. He tilted his head to the side, his expression turning solemn as he let her think. But he didn't turn away.

He looked tired and vulnerable.

He probably had reason to.

Neither of them said a word. She could feel the shift between them, the awful change in dynamics. The loss. She knew he felt it too.

Finally Julie reached down for her bag. She turned and walked through the front door and into the glaring sunlight.

✳✳✳

Dana crossed her legs and tore off a piece of the chocolate croissant. "Want some?" she offered.

Julie shook her head. Her stomach didn't feel good, and the coffee from Au Bon Pain was not sitting well. She and Dana had been lucky to snag a small bistro table at the packed outdoor café in Harvard Square. It seemed that everyone except Julie had that end-of-the-year high.

"Julie, what's wrong?" Dana asked. "Something is going on with you. Do you not want to move in with me? It's not a problem if you don't. Just because I went ahead and repainted the bedroom for you doesn't mean that you should feel at all guilty if you've changed your mind." She smiled. "Seriously. It's fine."

"No, that's not it at all. I can't wait to move, actually. Less than a week now."

"Something is wrong. You're not in a good mood."

"No," she agreed. "I'm not."

"Tell me."

Julie stared at the chess players next to them. A college student and a gray-haired man concentrated on the black and white pieces that sat on the concrete chess table. *King, queen, rook, bishop, knight. King, queen, rook, bishop, knight.*

Pawn.

Julie stared at the chess piece. *Pawn.*

"I should get home and pack some more."

"If you say so. Hey," Dana said gently, "you'll call me if you need me, right? I'll be there when you're ready to talk."

Julie looked at her friend and nodded. "I will." She picked up her bag to leave and then stopped. "If I need to move in a few days early, would that be all right?"

"*What* is going on?" Dana leaned forward. "Is this about Matt?"

"Would it be all right or not?"

"Of course. " Dana sat back. "Whatever you need. You know that."

"Thanks. I'll call you later."

Julie pulled her sunglasses down over her eyes and waded through the crowded sidewalks. She walked past the Dunkin' Donuts/Baskin Robbins ice cream on the corner and smiled. This was the *How do you like them apples?* location from *Good Will Hunting*. It was also the place that she and Matt had stopped in the day he had taken her to look for apartments. She passed the subway station and crossed Mass Ave, disappearing into the maze of Harvard's store, The Coop. Wandering in a fog seemed to help her feel better. Julie let herself drift through the store for a while, eventually exiting out the back onto a side street. Clothing boutiques had racks of dresses displayed on the sidewalk, and Julie fingered through sundresses that she wasn't going to buy. Across the street there was a small shop that sold local crafts. She momentarily emerged from her haze and wondered if she might find a little something there for Celeste.

For so many reasons, it was going to be hard moving out. There was no pretending that it wasn't. The emptiness loomed over her, powerful and unrelenting.

Julie found herself scanning the shelves and then moving to the display cases with jewelry. She tried to focus. A small gift for Celeste would be a nice thing to do, for both of them. A memento of their year together. Her eyes skimmed over beaded necklaces and gold bracelets, none of which was right. She walked to the far end of the case.

Something silver caught her eye. Maybe she should have been surprised to see it, but she wasn't. It was almost as if she was expecting that it would be here.

A saleswoman appeared. "Did you want to look at something?"

Julie kept her eyes on the case and pointed. "Yes. That one. Right there."

The woman unlocked the sliding cabinet door and handed Julie the item.

Julie looked down at her hand and studied the familiar silver barrette. Celeste's barrette. The one Finn had sent from far away. She turned it over in her hand a few times. This one had a yellow stone instead of turquoise. Otherwise it was identical. "Everything here…," she started. Did she really want to ask this question? Yes. She had to. "Everything here is made by local artists, right?"

"Absolutely."

"Nothing is imported?"

"No. We're here solely to support New England artists. We have very limited quantities of each item. No two are exactly alike. That hair clip is made by a woman from Martha's Vineyard. It's beautiful, isn't it? We've sold a number of her pieces."

"I bet you have. It's lovely." Julie set it down. Her hand was trembling, and she turned and rushed out of the store.

The walk home felt both eternal and not nearly long enough. The volume on her iPod was set high, and she tried to stop herself from thinking, losing herself in the music as she slowly walked home. Or to what would be her home for only a short time more. Dr. Cooley's words replayed over and over in her head. *Maybe you're missing something obvious. Don't overanalyze what you see.* She'd missed everything. It had all been right there, but she hadn't been able to see the big picture. Maybe she had known for months now, and she just had not wanted to accept what the world had been screaming at her. Denial had made her blind and stupid. Perhaps pathetically so.

The Watkinses' house looked strange to her today. The front lock gave her the usual trouble, and the stairs to the second floor made the same creak that they always did, and yet nothing felt right. Matt was at school, which was good. Julie opened her laptop and scooted the chair close to the desk while she typed.

Finn–

I'm so crazy about you. You know that, right? This thing between us over the past year has been everything that I never knew I wanted. You made me brave and adventurous. You made me laugh. You were charming and sweet and charismatic, and you pulled me in.

I fell in love with you. I couldn't help it, and I couldn't stop it. But now I have to.

We both know better than to pretend any longer.

We both know that this is over.

I had such a strong sense that I knew you and what it was like to be with you. Because I did. Maybe a part of me knew all along. I don't know when I realized it, but there had to be a point where I figured it out. Maybe I didn't want to see what was right in front of me because I wanted more than anything for this connection between us to be real. It's so clear to me now, and the truth is more painful than I imagined. You must think I'm incredibly foolish to have fallen for this charade. I am. It's true. I took a risk—I jumped—and you let me fall alone. I wanted to land with you, Finn. You.

I'll miss that boy who sent me pictures, protected me from monsters, and talked me through deadly elevator rides. I'll miss the stories about protecting wild animals, coaching football in Ghana, and scuba diving in exotic places. I'll miss the way you make me laugh and comfort me and heal me. I'll miss all of that. Mostly I'll miss you. The way we feel together.

But I suppose that I've already started missing you over the past few weeks. I could tell that I was losing you. Now everything is about to get so much worse.

I needed to write you just one more time before this all blows apart.

–Julie

She turned off the computer and went to the bottom drawer of the dresser. The T-shirt was old and washed-up, and she touched the fabric with her fingertips. She felt numb. There was one more thing that she had to check. Just to make sure. Just so she would really believe.

Julie left the bedroom and went into Erin and Roger's room. She stood in the center of the room and turned slowly, looking for what would bring her proof. It wasn't in here. But the wood-carving sat on a shelf, right-side up now. *Mom.* Julie thought about the little boy who had made that for his mother and how disconnected and oblivious Erin had been.

The house was eerily quiet. *Hollow. Isolated,* Julie thought as she walked to the living room. She started at one corner of the room, looking closely at all the books on the tall shelves. Slowly she stepped to the side, making sure not to miss what she knew must be here. When she reached the last shelf, she saw it. The photo album sat on the very top shelf, just below the ceiling. She pushed a chair over to the shelves and reached up, pulling the dark leather book from underneath an atlas. The other books on this high shelf were dusty, but the album cover was clean.

She sat on the couch for a while, just holding the book and putting this off.

Finally she opened it, gingerly turning the pages as she looked at the photographs. She knew these pictures. She had seen some of them before. It was hard not to smile at the ones of Finn. His handsome face, the way his clothes hugged his lean build, that mischievous smile. She touched one of the photos. She would miss the thought of those arms around her. The versions of the photos in her hand were slightly different from the ones she had looked at so many times this past year, but she still knew them.

As much as it hurt to turn each page, she was grateful that Erin and Roger were not the sort to store all their pictures digitally. Not like Julie was.

And not like Matt was.

It was too hard to keep looking, so she shut the album.

An hour passed, maybe more. Julie wasn't sure. He would be home soon. He would check his e-mail and come home.

Finally the front door opened.

"Julie."

She stared at Matt and waited. He took his time before speaking again.

"You know, don't you?" It wasn't really a question.

"Yes. I know."

Matt hung his head. "I don't know how this got so out of hand. I never meant—"

"I want to hear you say it."

"Julie—"

"Say it, Matt," she said loudly. "I want you to say it."

"I've been trying to figure out how to tell you for months." He looked at her now, both fear and melancholy shadowing his face. "I tried at Christmas. And then after New Year's. But I was in too deep. I thought maybe it would be easier after you moved out."

"Screw you." Julie stood up and hurled the photo album at him. "Screw you! Enough with the bullshit. Say it, Matt!" she yelled. "Tell me the goddamn truth for once!"

He stood silently for a bit, trying to delay this moment. His eyes glistened as he spoke. "Finn is dead."

She nodded, calmer now that he had confirmed what she knew. "Your brother is dead. That's why Celeste has Flat Finn."

"Yes."

"You've been pretending to be Finn. Everything he wrote to me was from you. You pasted old pictures of him into other photos."

"Yes."

Julie shut her eyes. She had been piecing this together, but the confirmation hit her hard.

"Do you want to know how he died?"

Julie nodded.

"Two years ago, during the winter. In a car accident. My mother was driving, and the car slid off the road on Memorial Drive, just outside Harvard Square. She hit a tree. The car crumpled from the impact, and Finn was thrown through the windshield. He died instantly." Matt inhaled audibly, bracing himself before continuing. "Her airbag went off, so she wasn't hurt, really. So that's why nobody drives except me. And we don't walk past the river." Matt tucked his hands in his pockets, waiting for Julie to say something. But she didn't. He reached down and picked up the photo album from the floor and flipped through a few pages before tossing it onto a chair. "You know what's really unfair? As if this weren't unbearable enough by itself? As if this weren't cruel and awful already?"

"What?"

"Did you know that Celeste used to play the piano? She was very good. She used to take lessons. In a gorgeous old building near here, off Memorial Drive."

Julie couldn't figure out where he was going with this.

"Guess who was walking home from her lesson just in time to see the accident?"

"Oh, Matt…" Julie could hardly speak.

"Yeah. It was perfect timing, really. Celeste got to see the fire trucks and ambulances. She got to see the smoke billowing out of the family car, and best of all, she got to see her brother's lifeless, bloody, mangled body." Matt was speaking quickly now, the words spilling from his mouth as if pausing for too long would leave him even more unprotected than he already was. "The smoke? That's why Mom doesn't like having fires in the house. Or matches. We can't light matches when she's in the room because the sulfur smell gives her flashbacks. Airbags, I guess, have a similar odor. Ironically, Celeste likes having fires in the house. They make her feel closer to Finn."

Julie stood up, and Matt walked away, turning his back to her. He leaned his shoulder against the window frame and stared outside.

"So the perfect family with the perfect son fell apart. Mom's depression got totally unmanageable, and she checked herself into a psych unit for six months. Dad disappeared into his god-forsaken ocean studies, and Celeste became nearly catatonic. I did what I could for her. I got her up in the mornings, I helped her get dressed, I fed her. I loved her. But it wasn't enough. Don't get me wrong. Celeste was never your typical kid. She's always been eccentric. But Finn's death destroyed her." All Matt's walls were crumbling. All the secrets and the emotion that he had worked so hard to protect this year were coming out. Julie almost didn't recognize the person in front of her. "And then, smart girl that she is, she ordered Flat Finn. Unbelievable. She just went online and ordered a replica of her brother. And that stupid cardboard thing brought her back. When Mom got home from her inpatient treatment, I tried to get her and Dad to do something for Celeste. Get her help." He shook his head. "But they loved Flat Finn almost as much as Celeste did. Maybe part of me did too. Because it kept him alive for us, in some sick, insane way. At some point, Celeste insisted that Finn would be on Facebook, so I did that for her. The *Finn Is God* name was probably my jealousy. He was so damn perfect. Everybody worshipped him."

"What about you, Matt? What happened to you?"

"Me? Nothing. I didn't get to grieve because I had to take care of everything that my parents couldn't. I don't hold them accountable for that. There is no right way to react. Mom, in particular, didn't like when I did anything that reminded her of Finn. He hated math and physics. In fact, he hated school. He wasn't a bad student. Academics just weren't where his heart was. So I did, and do, the opposite. I excel at school in ways he never could have."

"Celeste made up the story about him traveling?" Julie asked.

"Yes. It's actually something Finn would have done. He was just as great as she says he was. Those made-up stories about Finn helped her, and Flat Finn gave her something tangible to hold on to. And at the same time, while that goddamn two-dimensional picture has been keeping her afloat, he's wrecked all of us. When we're around Celeste, we have to act as if Finn is alive, as if his brains were never smeared all over the sidewalk."

Julie flinched. "I don't know what to say."

"There was no obituary in the paper. My mother claimed it was because she would have felt obligated to print his real name, Anatol Finneas Watkins, and she wouldn't do that to him. Finn hated his first name and only went by Finn. There was a tiny private funeral.

"Nobody comes into the house. I know you've noticed. How could you not? Whatever my parents can do to keep up the pretense that their son is just away, that someday he'll be home… Other people would ruin that scenario. My parents don't talk about Finn's death, and friends of the family and colleagues know not to bring him up. Mom and Dad pretend they're doing it for Celeste, but it's for them, too." Matt spun around and let out a sad laugh. "It's insane. I know that. It's all entirely insane."

"Why did your mom let *me* come into the house that first day? Why did she ask me to stay?"

"She felt a loyalty to Kate, I guess. I don't know that I understand it. Maybe she was…I'm not sure. Looking for a way out of this. Looking to get *caught*. She could trust you because of her connection to your mother. You know how you feel about Dana? If you two didn't talk for twenty years, you'd still be there for her if she needed you, right?"

Julie nodded. "Of course."

"I didn't mean to lie to you. I didn't think you'd be here that long. Nobody stays in our lives anymore. We're all alone. So when you e-mailed Finn, I wrote back. You were easy to talk to, and I needed to feel close to someone. To you."

"You should have told me. After you knew I was staying, you should have told me."

"I know. My mom and I fought about that. I didn't want you living here because she didn't want you to know the truth, and I thought you should. But she saw what we all came to see. That you are brilliant with Celeste. With all of us. You were this life force that we needed so desperately. I didn't stop things between you and me—you and Finn—because it was the first time that

I'd felt anything in so long. I got to be myself for the first time in years, with no constraints and no labels. You freed me."

Julie crossed the room until she was standing in front of Matt. Her heart broke for him. She stepped in closer and took his head in her hands, making him look her in the eyes. "I'm so sorry."

He didn't say anything, and she could feel him trembling. God, he looked so drained.

"Why aren't you yelling at me? You have to be angry," he said quietly.

"I'm too sad to yell. I don't get to be angry with you, do I? Your brother died, so I don't get to be angry."

He reached up and put his hands on her arms. "I never meant for this to become so complicated. I didn't plan this." His voice shook.

Julie touched his cheek softly and then ran her fingers over his lips. "This was never going to end well. You realize that, don't you?"

"It could."

"No. This is too messed up," she told him.

"I know," he said.

"And you're so broken." She wiped a tear from his cheek.

"I know."

"And you hurt me."

"I know. I never, never wanted to hurt you. You have to believe that."

"I understand. I really do," Julie managed to say. "But what Finn and I had was real. And you wrecked that."

"There was no you and Finn. There was you and me."

"No."

"This," he said gesturing between them, "is real. You and I are real."

"No, we're not. We're not anything, Matt. Not after this."

"Don't say that. Julie, please don't say that. I fell in love with you. And you fell in love with me."

She brushed the hair from his face and stepped in closer. There wasn't anything she could do to fix this—she could put hinges on Flat Finn, but there were no hinges for grief and deception. Anyway, she was too shattered now to pick him up from this. Her heart was broken. She missed Finn. She missed the Matt she used to know. He looked so completely spent, so full of anguish. She stroked his hair as she cradled his head in her hands. If there were a way for her to take away his suffering, she would. He would do the same for her, she knew that.

She lifted her mouth to his, kissing him deeply. Deliberately this time. She knew what she was doing. Matt's lips moved with hers, his emotion tangible, his aching too much. Julie let herself disappear into the moment. It was easier than thinking, than trying to understand what had happened. The words he had written to her as Finn played over and over: *You can look back now and see how you should have known, but you were focusing on the facts instead of the feeling.* Matt had been trying to prepare her.

But now she didn't know who this boy was, this damaged, lost boy who was kissing her as if he'd never see her again. As if she was everything he wanted. Now her own tears poured down her face. Julie kissed him harder, endlessly, not wanting this to stop but knowing it had to. For just a few more minutes, she let herself drown in the feel of him, because his mouth, his lips, his tongue, his kiss...This moment overshadowed the real world and took her away from misery. His hands roamed her back and her arms, desperate to show her how much he wanted her. She fought back a sob and pulled her mouth from his, kissing his cheeks, his neck, snuggling against the fabric of his shirt. Her hands moved down his chest, then wrapped around his waist, hugging him. She just wanted to hold Matt, even if this was the last time. His arms encircled her body, and he hung on to her. There had been days over this past year when he had made her feel safe and protected when he had held her. It had been so natural to let him hold her, so easy. So easy that she had stupidly never questioned it. None of those times mattered, though, because everything before today had been a lie.

He whispered in her ear, his voice breaking. "Julie, tell me that you fell in love with me too. I know you did. I can feel it."

"No, Matty," she said, crying. "I fell in love with Finn. I loved that boy, that imaginary, wonderful fantasy boy. That boy wasn't you. He was someone else, someone who never really existed. And…maybe part of me did fall in love with some version of you too, but that wasn't real either. And now I've lost you both. You've broken my heart twice."

"Please. I meant everything I wrote to you. Everything." Matt was pleading with her now and squeezed his arms around her tightly. "I used to go skydiving and bungee jumping. Finn and I did those things together. After he died, I couldn't take any more risks like that. It wasn't fair to my parents. Or Celeste. I used to be different. My life was about more than managing and coping and keeping everything together. There was more to me. You started to bring that back. We have something here, Julie. You know that."

"We don't have anything." She wiped her eyes on his shirt. It killed her to say this to him. She knew better than anybody how fragile Matt was right now and how much of himself he was giving to her. "Please don't make this harder. Please don't make me hurt you more. But Matt…Nothing that happened has been true."

"I need you," he begged. "You're everything I'm not."

"And you're everything I don't want." Julie pushed away, breaking his embrace, and shook her head. "If you loved me, you couldn't have done this. You couldn't have been so careless with me. You know pain and loss and hurt better than anyone." She hated each word as it came out of her mouth. "And that's what you gave me. I know that it's not the same. I know yours is worse. I'm so sorry for you, Matt. For your whole family. You've all been through hell. And you've been braver than anyone could. But I hurt now too. And I can't love you."

CHAPTER 30

The alarm clock went off, filling the room with a hideously syrupy old Lifehouse song. Cursing herself for forgetting to turn the alarm off last night, Julie rolled over and yanked the cord out of the wall, but the music kept playing. *God damn that battery backup!* She had been in bed since seven the night before, having mumbled something to Erin through the door about not feeling well. Her eyes burned, and her head and heart ached. Everything hurt. There was really no good reason to get up except to finish packing. She was moving to Dana's tomorrow. She wanted out of here as quickly as possible. But the idea of mustering the energy she'd need to pack was further debilitating. Even with the torturous music, the dark room was safe. The world was on hold.

Holing up in her room since the dreadful talk with Matt was childish perhaps, but she didn't care. Of course, it wasn't really her room. It was Matt's. He must have moved out so that the family didn't have to deal with the agony of Finn's empty bedroom. She threw her arm over her eyes. Poor Matt had taken on the brunt of the family's grief.

After lying in bed for another hour and suffering through "Romance Hour" on the local radio station, she finally dragged herself from the sheets and sat in front of her computer. There was one more thing that she had to do. She clicked on *Finn Is God's* page one last time and reread his status updates. *Matt's* status updates. It was so hard to reconcile the truth with what she had believed for so many months. She moved the cursor to remove him from her friends list and then stopped. Under his profile picture she saw it. It was his birthday today. It was the real Finn's birthday. She couldn't take this; she deleted him immediately.

Julie didn't understand why she was feeling such a loss. It's not as though she'd actually known Finn. It had been Matt the whole time. Technically she hadn't *lost* anyone. But it felt as if she had. To amp up her misery was the fact that she had hurt Matt so terribly yesterday. That might be the worst piece of all.

Julie heard the house phone ring, and moments later Matt's voice filled the house. "Julie! Julie!"

She hadn't seen him since yesterday, when she had dropped from his embrace and fled to her room. The last thing she wanted was to face him now, but the tone of his voice let her know something was wrong.

"Julie!" Matt flung open the door. "Celeste is gone."

"What? What do you mean *gone*?"

"She didn't show up for third period today. My mother just called. She and Dad are heading over to the school now to see if anyone has seen her. Today is…today—"

"I know." Julie stood up. "It's Finn's birthday." This day must be intolerably painful. She rushed to the closet and yanked a shirt from a hanger. "We'll find her."

"I don't know where she could be. Something is wrong. She has never skipped class."

"Go start the car. I'll be down in a minute."

Matt nodded. "OK. Julie? Thank you. I know you hate me right now."

He disappeared before she could protest.

Ten minutes later, Matt and Julie were in the car and heading toward Celeste's school. It seemed worthwhile to drive around the area on the off-chance that she might be nearby. Julie had tried Rachel's house; however, her mother hadn't heard from Celeste, and Rachel was most definitely in class today. Julie was hoping the two girls had ditched school together. Rachel's mom promised to call if she got news.

Matt tapped the steering wheel. "Where could she be? Where could she be?"

"She'll be fine. She wouldn't have done anything stupid. It's got to be a hard day for her. For all of you."

"Yes, it is." He kept his eyes straight ahead. "I had to tell her about our...talk. She would have wondered what was wrong. I don't imagine that helped her."

"I'm sorry. I didn't mean to sound so...callous yesterday. I just can't..." Her words trailed off. "I understand why you did what you did."

"You don't have to explain. Really."

Julie tapped her leg. She didn't want to think about yesterday. Matt looked totally spent. Even worse than she did. And he had shut down on her again. That whole pouring-his-soul-out routine was over. But the only thing that mattered right now was finding Celeste. She stared out the window as Matt drove around aimlessly, desperately hoping to come across his sister. Julie closed her eyes. *Think. Think. Where would Celeste go?*

"Matt, take a left. Here. Here!"

"Why?"

"I know where she is."

He yanked the wheel and steered them toward the Charles River. "She couldn't have," he said in disbelief. "Why would she go there?"

"She went to the site of the accident. She must have."

They sped down Memorial Drive. It was beautiful out, with comfortable temperatures, blue skies, and a wonderful breeze. The irony of them all feeling so dreadful was undeniable.

Suddenly Matt pulled the car over the curb and hit the brakes. "There she is."

They both got out and raced toward her. Celeste sat on a wooden bench, looking out at the sparkling water. Matt and Julie crossed a grassy area, walking between students reading on blankets and bikers taking a break, and sat down on either side of Celeste.

"It's a lovely day for boating, isn't it?" Celeste finally asked. She put her hand in Matt's but continued staring at the river. "I've always thought it would be such fun to go for a ride down this river in a boat."

"We could go sometime. They rent canoes here, you know?" Julie kicked her feet back and forth. "I would love to do that with you."

They sat silently for a few minutes, watching the boats go by.

Finally Celeste turned and looked at Julie. Her eyes were red and puffy, but her voice was clear. "I'm not crazy, you know."

Julie nodded. "I know that."

"I am aware that Finn is dead. Despite my seemingly unbreakable association with Flat Finn, I have always known that. I'm not delusional."

"I understand."

"I loved Finn so much. You would have really liked him, Julie. He was magical, wasn't he, Matty?"

"He was," Matt agreed. "Finn was someone special."

Celeste leaned her head on his shoulder. "You're magical too. I love you, Matthew. I know that you think I liked Finn better than you. That's not true. You are just as much a part of me as Finn is. I utterly worship you both. Always and forever. If you had died, there would have been a Flat Matt. I would have laughed endlessly at the silly rhyme."

Matt dropped his head back and looked into the blue sky. "Sweetie, don't…just don't."

"I'm terribly sorry, Julie," Celeste continued. "I chose to create Flat Finn, and I chose to believe that Finn was traveling. This is my responsibility. I have an overly powerful imagination, and I made everyone abide by my fantasies. We didn't mean to trick you."

"You don't have to apologize for anything," Julie said.

"You're leaving tomorrow. I won't see you anymore."

"I think I'll leave tonight, actually. It seems best." She could feel Matt staring at her. "But you'll see me all the time. You and I will meet once a week in Harvard Square. Promise."

"And Matt. Matt could come too," Celeste suggested.

"We'll see," Julie said.

"Please don't be angry with him. It's because of me that Matt did what he did. He is totally enamored with you, Julie. Captivated. I see it in his eyes. Even though he looks tremendously demoralized today, I can still see it in his eyes. If you're not totally disgruntled with me, you can't be with him either. That's not fair."

"I'm not disgruntled." Julie refused to look toward Matt. It was too confusing. Her emotions were exceptionally raw, and she could hardly tolerate being around him. It was only for Celeste's sake that she was with him right now.

"I am asking you not to dismiss something with this sort of intensity. It's rare."

Julie had to stop her. "I can't hear this right now. I'm sorry. Not now."

"You have to leave her alone, Celeste. She's had enough." Matt put his arm around Celeste's shoulder. "Are you OK? We were worried about you."

She tried to smile. "I will be. Will you stay here with me, Matty? Just for a while? I feel close to Finn here."

"If that's what you want, sure."

She snuggled into her brother's arm. "Tell me again about the time you camped out in the backyard, and how the fabric caught fire when Finn decided to roast marshmallows inside the tent."

Julie stood up. She reached down and took the car keys out of Matt's hand. He looked up at her. It was impossibly brave of him to sit there with Celeste, on a bench right next to where their brother's life had been violently and unforgivably taken away. She couldn't stand the sadness in Matt's eyes, and so she focused on the keys now in her hand. "I'll take the car home and call Erin and Roger."

"Julie." The crack in his voice gutted her. "Thank you. For everything."

"Matt…" Unable to say good-bye, she turned and ran to the car, telling herself that her eyes were stinging from the sharp wind that came off the river.

* * *

There was just enough tape left to seal the last cardboard box. Dana and Jamie would be there in a half hour to help her move. There really wasn't much to load into his Jeep, so at least this should go quickly.

There was a knock on the door, and Erin stepped into the room. "You look as if you're just about set. Can I do anything to help?'

Julie shook her head. "No. I think that's everything."

Erin sat down on the bed and took a deep breath. "You've been crying."

Julie nodded.

"I had a long talk with Roger and Matthew this afternoon. Thank you for finding Celeste today. We were in quite a panic, as you can imagine."

"I'm just glad she's all right. That's all that matters."

"Physically, she's safe. But she's not all right. None of us are. Julie, I'd like to tell you a few things, if you don't mind." Erin clasped her hands together. "Matthew told me that you know about Finn. About the accident."

"Yes. I'm so sorry." Julie sat down next to Erin. "I'm not sure what to say. I can't begin to understand how hard this has been."

"There are some things about the accident that you don't know and that might help you begin to comprehend why I never stopped this whole Finn charade."

"Erin, you don't owe me an explanation for anything. Really."

"I want you to hear this. It might take the edge off what you're going through." Erin rubbed her hands over her knees, pausing before she began. "The accident was entirely my fault. I never should have been driving that day. I killed Finn. I am solely responsible for my son's death."

"It was an accident. Nobody blames you."

"It was an accident, yes, but there's more to it. I doubt Matthew told you this piece of the story, because he wanted to protect me. I gather you know that I have a history of severe depression? It's all right. There have been enough secrets. Depression is nothing to be ashamed of. I know that, but I'm still working on it. I had been doing well on the medication I'd been taking. I was functioning, happy even. Then I did what many people do. I went off them. I was content, enjoying life, and felt so strongly that I didn't need them anymore. I would be fine. Well, I couldn't. Nobody with my sort of depression could. I spiraled downward so quickly. It must have been terrifying for my family. Roger couldn't persuade me to start taking them again. I know that sounds strange, but in as depressive a state as I was in, I just could not see things rationally. I refused. I was hopeless and tired of fighting my despair.

"That day in February, I was completely out of touch with reality. Detached and dissociated, really. I got into the car with the vague thought that a drive might give me a sense of escape. I don't remember this happening, but apparently Finn heard me start the car. He raced after me and jumped into the back seat. I drove by the river. Now I can hear hints of his voice, what he was saying to me, how he was trying to get me to pull over. But that day, as I drove, I had no awareness that Finn was with me, Julie. Can you believe that? I was so out of it that I forgot my own son was with me. I couldn't see him or understand what he was saying to me. Nothing. My depressive fog blocked out everything except the concept of relief, even if it was only temporary. It was easy just to let the cloudy feeling take over for a while. Driving around aimlessly and letting my depression be in charge felt as if it would help. I should never have been behind the wheel that day. The car hit a patch of black ice, spun full circle, and smashed into a tree."

"Erin…"

"You don't need to hear the details of the accident. Suffice it to say that it was gruesome. I'll be haunted forever by what I saw that day." Erin touched a hand to her cheek and closed her eyes. "It was incredibly icy. There had been accidents all over the city. The police considered my crash a result of the weather. Plain and simple. Which was true, to a degree, but my having gone off the medication was the real reason that I lost control of the car. Roger arranged for me to get inpatient help. Matthew didn't know at the time that the accident was a result of my having stupidly stopped taking my meds. We told him later. He didn't tell you because he didn't want you to think less of me. Maybe there would have been an accident even if I'd been clearheaded that day. But Finn wouldn't have been in the back seat without a seat belt on, and he wouldn't have died. The hard truth is that I killed my son, Julie. That's why I have avoided my family since that day. I don't deserve to be a mother. I cannot be responsible for Matthew and Celeste after what I've done. I don't know how."

Julie put her hand on Erin's back. "You are still their mother. You will always be."

Erin nodded vigorously and opened her eyes. "Eventually I will see that. I'm going to get there. I need to get some help, though. Having these amazing blinders on for so long has made it possible to keep going. Flat Finn let me pretend. From now on, I need to do better. I will do better. We all have to find a way to get through this."

Everything that Julie could think to say felt beyond inadequate. She wrapped her arms around Erin and held her while she cried.

CHAPTER 31

It was late August. Julie opened another packet of sugar and poured it into her coffee. The café was quiet today, which was nice because it meant she'd be able to hear everything Celeste had to say without distraction.

Just as she had promised, she'd been meeting Celeste here every Monday afternoon since Julie had moved out of the Watkinses' house. Sometimes Celeste walked here alone, and sometimes Roger or Erin came with her. Never Matt, though. Julie hadn't responded to any of Matt's e-mails except once when she asked him to please never be the person who came with Celeste. She wasn't ready to see him. Maybe one day, maybe never. It had been three months since Julie had said good-bye to him on that bench by the river. He had stopped writing her last month.

Dana had been pushing her all summer to talk about Matt, but she just couldn't. The last time Dana tried, Julie had nearly dumped a bowl of cereal on her head. After that, her roommate had the good sense not to bring him up.

The summer had been nice. Quiet, uneventful, and perhaps a little boring. Precisely what she had needed. Julie had been doing an internship at a small publishing house in Cambridge, a position that she figured would look good on her resume. And it had kept her distracted. Kate had come to visit for a long weekend in July, but Julie was surprisingly less homesick than she would have imagined.

"There she is!"

Julie looked up just as Celeste threw her arms around her neck in a hug. "Hey, kiddo! How was the Cape? I missed you last week."

Celeste flopped into a chair and tossed her hair back. She had a light tan, and her hair had lightened even more in the summer sun. She was radiant.

"Hi, Julie." Roger leaned in and gave Julie a kiss on the cheek. "Nice to see you."

"You too."

"Celeste has been dying to get together and tell you about her triumphant fishing expedition."

Celeste beamed. "We all went deep-sea fishing, and I caught a sizeable bluefish. Even the captain was impressed. The beast put up a tireless fight, and Matt had to take over for me a few times. In the end, I successfully reeled in the clichéd catch of the day. I'll show you pictures next time."

"She really was amazing," Roger said proudly. "The captain filleted the fish for us, and Erin cooked it for dinner."

"Erin cooked?" Julie asked, shocked.

Roger laughed. "Amazing, isn't it? My wife has become obsessed with cooking, and not a takeout carton has been seen in the past three weeks."

"I'm speechless."

"You'll have to come for dinner one night. I can't guarantee that the meal will be entirely edible, but it *will* be homemade."

Julie nodded politely. She hadn't been back to the house since she had left.

"I'm going to be in a recital in two weeks. Would you come? Rachel is playing the trumpet, and I'll be playing the piano. As you can tell, it's an unusual sort of duet, and Rachel is not particularly gifted when it comes to any musical instrument." Celeste paused. "Most notably the trumpet. She makes up for lack of talent by a frequent use of exaggerated facial expressions when blowing into the mouthpiece."

"Of course I'll come to the recital," Julie said. "I'm glad performing arts camp has been such a success."

"Attending has compensated for having to be present at weekly individual *and* family therapy sessions. I find those challenging and draining."

"I would think so."

"As much as I loathe the experience, you can guess how Matty feels about therapy." Celeste grinned.

Julie laughed. She knew exactly how much Matt must hate going.

"Didn't you have something else to ask Julie?" Roger tousled Celeste's hair.

"I do. Julie, this is serious." Celeste reached into the small purse she had over her shoulder and pulled out an envelope that she set on the table. "This is an invitation. I'm having a going-away party for Flat Finn."

Julie was stunned. She took the envelope from Celeste and opened it. The details of the party had been printed on expensive stock, and a small ribbon was tied at the top of the card. "Really?"

"Yes. I was inspired by the party that your mother threw for you when you left home, and this party is in the same spirit. Except that I want a brunch. Finn loved bagels and lox. The only guests will be you, Mom, Dad, and Matty. It's a private party, for obvious reasons. It won't be sad, though. The plan is for the day to be a celebration. Flat Finn served a crucial purpose, and it's important to show our gratitude."

"Where will Flat Finn go?" Julie had visions of Flat Finn being burned to ashes over the grill or hacked to bits with a carving knife. That would be dreadful. She had a fondness for the cutout brother, however dysfunctional and immobilizing he may have been.

"He's just going up to the attic." She shrugged. "Just in case. And maybe a time will come when I will find the entire Flat Finn experience amusing. I might want to show him to my grandchildren one day. *Back when I was a highly disturbed child...*You know. It might be entertaining."

"Yes, it might."

"So you'll come, right?"

Julie couldn't say no. "Absolutely. There is no way I would miss this." She could face Matt for one day.

"Excellent. So next Saturday at eleven we will celebrate. Please note that it's casual attire. Flat Finn wouldn't want anyone in ball gowns or tuxedos."

"Understood."

Roger snapped his fingers. "Damn. And I was hoping to wear my lime-green suit and matching tie that day."

Celeste groaned. "Mom would never allow that. She has impeccable taste. I'm going to go get us some drinks. Back momentarily." She headed to the counter to order.

Julie looked at Roger. "I cannot believe that is the same girl I met almost a year ago. She seems incredibly happy."

"She is. She's doing well. There are hard days still, but she has surprised us all."

Julie leaned forward. "Truthfully, I'm glad she hasn't lost all her Celeste-ness. I like her unique personality."

"I do too." Roger fiddled with a sugar packet. "How are you, kid? You seem...subdued."

"I'm fine. Just distracted, I guess. Busy. Gearing up to head back to school."

"Uh-huh. If you say so." Something caught his eye, and he reached his hand out. "Julie? Where did you get this? Is this Matthew's?" He held the stone of her necklace in his hand.

"Oh." She sat back, pulling it from his grasp, and clasped her hand to her chest.

As much as she couldn't bear to think about Matt, she hadn't been able to take off the necklace. It was part of her—her and Finn—and she wouldn't feel like herself without it.

Roger squinted. "It *is* Matthew's. Did he tell you what this is?"

Confused, she shook her head. She hadn't really thought about where it had come from. Obviously not from Finn's worldly travels, though. She assumed Matt had picked it up at a store nearby.

"Wow. I haven't seen that in years. When Matt was a kid, rocks and minerals fascinated him. He was actively involved in the Boston Minerals Club."

Of course he was. Julie felt that same twinge of wistfulness that hit her more than she liked to admit. She knew Matt so well that it hurt.

"I used to take him on weekend outings with the club," Roger said. "We'd go on hikes in New Hampshire and Vermont. Once to the Berkshires. And the kids would dig and whatnot, looking for rocks. All little boys love that stuff, but Matthew in particular. He kept copious notes about his findings and made charts and graphs that he kept in a binder. Rock and mineral-wise, this is not a terribly exciting part of the country to live in. Nonetheless, Matt held out hope that he would find that special item. And God love him, he did." Roger pointed to her neck-lace. "That's a fragment of purpurite. Not the sexiest-sounding mineral, I guess, but Matt was over the moon when he collected this. He wouldn't let anyone touch it, and he kept that thing in a locked display case for years." He tipped his head to the side. "I can't believe he parted with that. You mean something very special to him, Julie."

She looked down and squeezed her hand around the necklace.

"Look, this is none of my business, and I don't know exactly what happened this year, but I know something fell apart between you two. I've tried to talk to him about it…Well, you know Matt. He has a hard time opening up. I do know a bit about him posing as Finn online." He held up his hand to stop Julie from interrupting him. "I agree. It was a seriously peculiar thing to do, and it wasn't right. However ticked off you may be about that, I hope you can appreciate the lengths he went to in order to keep your attention."

Julie looked up. "I guess."

"Can you imagine how much time he spent doctoring all those pictures? Inventing new volunteer opportunities? And when he sent Celeste the package, the poor guy had to track down an old friend overseas, mail the package there, and have that person mail it back to the house so that it would have the right postage. Not to mention all the work it must have taken to keep his stories straight." He smiled. "Come on, Julie. Effort has to count for something."

"This has been hard on me," she said. "I feel stupid saying that, considering what your family has been through, but—"

Roger stopped her. "You're allowed to feel the way you do. Matt was an idiot. And maybe you have other reasons for hold-ing back. Reasons that don't have to do with Matthew."

"I don't know what to trust...whom to trust."

Roger tipped his head to the side. "Look, Finn was good with all this girl stuff. He was cool and suave and...magnetic. He was *absolutely magnetic*. But Matthew is exceptional too, just in a different way. It must have been rough competing with Finn before, and now that Finn is gone, it's probably even worse for him. You can't beat out memories of the dead. Sweetheart, Matt is not the smoothest of young men, but his heart was in the right place." Roger patted her hand. "Aw, Julie. Matt's execution might have been disastrous, but don't forget about his heart."

Images from the past year flashed through Julie's head: Matt picking her up in front of the nonapartment. Explaining font nerds. Reluctantly taking her to buy hinges for Flat Finn. Trading e-mails about possible snow sculptures. Lying under the tree. Arguing, bantering, defending his silly T-shirts. The hours spent hanging out in his room. She thought about how he had held her when she had come out of the freezing ocean. And that night after Celeste's sleepover, touching her tenderly in his bed. How he looked when he finally poured his feelings out. The way it felt just to be near him. The way the world stopped when he kissed her.

And that's when she knew. Julie looked at Roger and smiled. She felt whole for the first time in weeks.

CHAPTER 32

Matthew Watkins *When I screw up, I'm just going to think of it as the group disbanding. And by "the group" I mean "brain function." And by "disbanding" I mean "failing miserably."*

Julie Seagle *"The best way to hold a man is in your arms." –Mae West*

Celeste Watkins *thinks the expression should be, "Free to be you OR me," because "Free to be you AND me" makes one think of a dissociative identity disorder.*

Her heart was pounding uncontrollably. Julie had to muster every scrap of courage she had just to ring the bell. She was on time for the party, but she hoped that she wasn't too late for the most important thing.

Erin opened the door. "You're here! Look at you! You look wonderful!"

Julie leaned in for a hug, smiling at Erin's typically awkward embrace. "It's a big day, huh?"

"A long overdue day. Come on, we're all in the backyard." Erin waited for Julie to step into the house. "Well, come on. Don't be shy. This is practically your house too."

Julie forced her feet to move. *Breathe, breathe, breathe.*

They walked to the dining room. A platter with bagels and spreads sat in the center of the table underneath a mass of balloons, and ribbons had been tied to the backs of the chairs. The room was lighter and cheerier than Julie had ever seen it.

"Tell me about your summer, Julie. You and I have barely seen each other in months, and I don't like not knowing what's going on with you. And have you registered for fall classes yet? I'd be honored to look over your course options with you." She pulled out a chair. "Here, sit down. Coffee?"

Julie nodded. She spent twenty minutes trying her best to pay attention to Erin's advice about the upcoming semester. She had missed Erin and was so happy to see how engaged and genuinely cheerful she was. But her mind was elsewhere.

Celeste bounded into the room and practically toppled her with a hug. "Why is it that nobody told me you had arrived? Oh my gosh! Are these for me?"

Julie nodded and handed her a massive bouquet of flowers. "Congratulations, pal. I know this day means a lot to you. It does to me too."

"I'm going to find out if Roger is ready," Erin said. "He has been in the basement for two hours, and the house is still sweltering." She fanned herself with her hand as she left the room. "August in Boston never fails to infuriate me."

"My dad is fiddling with the AC system," Celeste explained. "Don't go near him until he has finished because he's not very adept and has already given himself two minor shocks. Did you see Matt yet? He's hiding in the backyard. I think he's nervous."

"Join the club."

Celeste touched Julie's arm. "Do not be nervous, Julie. This is going to work out marvelously. I believe in you. Both of you."

"We'll see."

Julie went through the kitchen and out through the back door to the porch.

He was there. Out on the lawn, standing with his back to her, his hands tucked into his shorts pockets. He looked amazing. Everything about him pulled her in. Julie touched her palm to her chest, reminding herself again to breathe, to calm down. "Matt."

Matt turned around hesitantly and gave her a shy wave. He had on the same *Nietzsche Is My Homeboy* shirt that he'd worn the day she met him. It was exactly as it should be.

"Matty!" She called his name louder this time, wondering if he could hear the relief she felt at seeing him. She ran down the steps, needing him more than she could ever have imagined. It had been a long summer of heartache, but at least she finally knew whom her heart had been aching for.

She couldn't reach him fast enough.

Matt rushed forward and caught her as she flew into his arms. She wrapped her legs around his waist and her arms around his neck, hugging him tightly. It had been so long since she had been close to him. Too long.

"Julie." There was nothing more wonderful than the way he said her name. How had she never noticed that? "What's wrong? Are you OK?" She heard his confusion and concern.

She laughed as she hung on to Matt. "I am now."

She sniffed, aware that she'd become a blubbering mess in an instant. But that's what love does to you. Gut-wrenching, overpowering, crushing, fulfilling, complex, bring-you-to-your-knees love.

"I missed you," she whispered into his ear. And she had. His voice, his touch, the way he moved…everything about him.

"Yeah?" he asked softly.

"Yes. So much."

He held her close while she rested her head on his shoulder and ran her hands over his back, neither of them willing to let the other go. And with the way they were glued to each other, she knew that this was not like the last time they had been this close. This was not good-bye.

"I'm so sorry. It was always you," she said.

"What?" he murmured.

She lifted her head and pressed her cheek against his. "It was always you. I thought it was somebody else, but it was you. You were the person I felt."

Julie heard him catch his breath, and she dropped her feet to the ground, keeping her body against his. Matt put his hands on her hips, pulling her in more. God, he felt so perfect. Then his lips were on hers, kissing her hard, passionately. Differently than before. No more pretending, no more denying, no more sadness. His fingers moved just under the bottom of her shirt, lightly brushing her lower back, and then her waist was in his hands. His grip was firm, solid, comforting. God, the feel of his hands against her skin...He kissed her neck, his lips soft, his tongue hot, and his breathing picking up. She whimpered quietly. He was such a guy, totally picking the worst time ever to get them all riled up. *Later*, she told herself. *Later they could be alone.*

Julie forced herself to back away ever so slightly. "Come on. We're going to have an audience soon." She grabbed his hand and pulled him behind her, determined not to let go of him again. "And we're leaving in an hour."

"I could make a lot of things happen in an hour," Matt offered.

Julie spun around and raised an eyebrow as she walked backward. "I bet you could." He was making it tempting to take off with him, but this day was important. "I promise you'll have that chance. But for now, we have to go eat. You, Celeste, Flat Finn, and I are leaving together. We have someplace to be."

"We do?"

"Yes." She couldn't stop smiling.

"I thought Flat Finn was being assigned attic duty for the rest of his existence?"

"Plans change."

"So we don't get to sneak off somewhere and fool around?" Matt groaned.

"Not yet."

"These better be some damn good plans."

***

"Look, this blindfold thing is really starting to creep me out. I don't know when you became a dominatrix, Julie, but my sister is in the car, so it hardly seems appropriate to be demonstrating your specialized skills in front of her." Matt reached to pull off the blindfold that Julie had tied over his eyes.

"Don't you dare!" Celeste leaned into the front seat of the Volvo and smacked Matt's hand. "Behave yourself. This is a good surprise."

"Are we almost there yet? I'm hungry," Matt said. "I need to pee. I'm bored. How much longer? Let's play *I Spy*. Oh, wait. I can't. I'm blindfolded. This is the worst trip ever!"

"Matt, shut up!" Julie pulled into the far right lane on the highway, keeping her hand in Matt's. "Only one more exit, and then we'll be there. This will be worth the two-hour drive. Trust us."

"When you say *worth*, do you mean there will be cash incentives involved? Apple is having a press conference in a few days, and I'm sure they'll be releasing some wildly unnecessary gadget that I need."

"Celeste, make your brother behave," Julie said.

"The fact that you are still holding his hand after he has been persistently annoying during this whole drive indicates to me that he is now equally *your* problem. I am going to enjoy this scenic drive and let you manage Matty's irritating outbursts."

"Great." Julie sighed dramatically. "Lengthy bouts of obtuse chatter interspersed with moments of mind-numbingly boring trivia about the history of the Internet. It's a tradeoff for the occasional bits of charm, I suppose," Julie admitted. "But one that I'll just have to live with."

"I'm still here!" Matt hollered. "I can hear you talking about me. I have feelings, you know!" He faked a sob and sniffed loudly.

"I'll make a note of that," Julie said.

"Oh, Julie, there's the sign," Celeste said. "We're here! This is the perfect send-off for Flat Finn. The real Finn would approve. You will too, Matty."

Julie pulled the car into the parking lot. "Guess where we are?"

"Yosemite? The Grand Canyon?" Matt said. "Vegas? Oh my God, we're in Vegas, aren't we? Is Celine Dion here? Cher? Are we going backstage? No, it's the Liberace Museum. I can feel it. It's a dream come true! I've waited my whole life for this."

"That is ridiculous, Matt," Celeste scolded. "We are not in Las Vegas. Try harder."

"Disney World? The Mall of America? Pike Place Fish Market? Graceland?"

"It's flattering that he thinks we're lame enough to subject him to a tourist trap, isn't it? Celeste, he'll never figure it out," Julie said. "Let's show him." She slid the blindfold off his eyes and watched him. He adjusted to the light and read the sign in front of the car.

Matt was serious now. "I never would have guessed this was where you two were taking me." He paused and bit his lip, a soft smile forming. "The last time I was here was with Finn."

Julie clapped her hands together. "We're going skydiving."

He looked at her. "What do you mean *we're* going?"

She nodded. "You're not very bright, are you? I mean that you and I are going to jump out of a plane, and then a life-saving parachute thingy will pop out, and we will land on the ground in one piece. "

"Both of us are going?"

"Yes," she said. "I want to jump with you, Matt. For real this time."

She loved when he was speechless.

"And Flat Finn too," Celeste said. "We called the skydiving center this week. They remember you and Finn, and they said that you could take Flat Finn when you jump. I think it's a fitting way to celebrate. The real Finn would genuinely like this idea."

"Of course I'll take him," Matt said. "Of course. Julie, are you sure about this?"

"Yes," she said. And she meant it. She trusted him completely. "I want to do this with you."

Matt leaned over and put a hand on the back of her neck. He pulled her in gently, kissing her softly and perfectly.

"I knew it!" Celeste squealed. "I told you, Julie, didn't I? I said this would work out, and it has. Does this mean that there will not be any more unpleasant spats between you two? I found those squabbles to be incredibly disquieting."

Julie sat back and laughed. "I don't know about *that*." She looked into Matt's eyes. "Even so, I love you."

Matt smiled at her and winked. "I know."

Celeste and Julie both smacked him.

"This would be an appropriate time not to be a dork or a smartass," Julie said.

Celeste popped her head into the front seat. "Be the hero, Matty. Come on. You're supposed to be the hero now. The romantic lead."

"I know that too," he said. Matt did not hesitate a moment longer. "Julie, I love you. I absolutely love you."

"Good," Celeste said, satisfied. "Now it's time to jump."

ACKNOWLEDGMENTS

Tremendous thanks to my entire family for putting up with my obsessive demeanor (and occasional lack of showering) while writing this book. A special thanks to my dad, who put on his psychotherapist hat while reading my manuscript and took copious and helpful notes. I love you, Daddy.

A gazillion hugs to Jessica Whitney, who always calls me "sweet girl" when I need it the most. Everyone should have such a delightful coconspirator.

Lori Gondelman has obtained goddess status. She proofread chapters, offered endless encouragement, yelled at me to write faster, told me what should stay and what should go, and mailed me bags of Dunkin' Donuts coffee so I that could throw myself into a caffeine high and write until midnight. I suspect that she would have held my hand as I wrote would it not have interfered with typing. No one could have done more, and I am impossibly grateful for her unfailing belief in this book and in me.

Christy Poser shared her skydiving experiences with me via telephone and even sent DVD copies of her jumps. Although she is obviously a freakish daredevil, Julie owes her one. As do I.

Authors Karen MacInerney and Heather Webber are simply brilliant. Both pointed me in the right direction and managed not to be obnoxious about how right they were. They are total smarties, talented writers, and fabulous friends.

Thank you to Meg Travis, Shelly Toler Franz, Caitlyn Henderson, Carrie Spellman, and Pixie Poe for reading various versions of the outline and manuscript and showering me with support. I've known Meg since junior high, and she is as unforgettable now as she was then. Shelly and Caitlyn are both an author's dream and proof that Facebook friends are, in fact, real friends. Carrie is a trusted reader and reviewer, and her glowing words were the boost I needed to finish the book. Not only is Pixie a book fiend, but she has a cool name and owns a pink Christmas tree. What more can a girl ask for in a friend?

The obscenely brilliant Adam Conner-Sax deciphered MIT speak and put up with my babbling as I figured out my characters. As he has his entire life, he showed himself to be warm, adorable, and frighteningly well rounded.

A captain's nod to Jonathan Slavin, who enjoys every *Jaws* movie as much as I do.

The incomparable and devastatingly funny David Pacheco was generous enough to provide the large majority of the status updates for the book. (Dave, pay attention; this is where you are getting credit for your genius.) He patiently tolerated my many questions and answered them all with more attention and humor than they deserved. As a thank you, I will be sending him a zombie, a time travel machine, a ledger for the Procrastinator's Club, and a spray-cheese sandwich. Follow him on Twitter @whatdoIknow if you think you can keep up. But don't worry, most of us can't.

Carmen Comeaux and Jim Thomsen were both kind enough to do fantastic editing work on a very rough manuscript.

Carmen bravely forged ahead, even when my grammatical errors caused her to write "Horrors!" in the margins. And Jim will hereby be known as "The Hyphen King." You two are impeccable, tough, and outrageously skilled.

Brian Yagel did everything from giving me real life technical support to spouting off geeky terminology that I still don't totally understand. But it made sense to him. And he managed to remain charming even when saying things like "third-party app" and "console logs." Enjoy your two minutes for those FB updates, kiddo.

Amazon has changed my life, and without them I might not be writing anymore. I'm not a fan of playing by the rules, and self-publishing through KDP gave me the ability to write *Flat-Out Love* with total abandon. I got to write the story that I wanted to—the one I believed in—instead of the one that I thought legacy publishers wanted me to write. Deciding to self-publish this book was the smartest thing I've ever done.

Now that I've signed with Amazon Children's Publishing, I not only get to hold on to so many of the benefits that I've had in the past, but now I have the added support of a dynamic team. Amazon Children's Publishing not only supports writing outside of the box—they embrace it. Signing over *Flat-Out Love*, and my next book, to such a stupendous team is pure joy. Associate Publisher Tim Ditlow and the entire publishing team at Amazon are outstanding; their belief in me and in my career is deeply humbling, and I am deeply grateful. I have true partners now, and there is no better feeling than that. Amazon may be a massive company, but I know without a doubt that my team has heart, dedication, and a drive to try new things. They run to unchartered territory, and those are my kind of people.

My agent, Deborah Schneider, has been devoted to this book from the beginning—and took the repeated this-book-will-never-sell rejections from traditional publishers as hard as I did. When I decided to self-publish, she cheered me on. "Give 'em hell!" she said. And I did. *We* did. Finally. Deborah, thank you for everything that you have done for me and, most of all, thank you for letting me yell, "Congratulations! You're still my agent!" without hanging up on me.

ABOUT THE AUTHOR

Hailed by *The Huffington Post* for blazing a path in the uncharted terrain of independent publishing, (http://www.huffingtonpost.com/2012/06/06/how-amazon-saved-my-life_n_1575777.html?ref=books) Jessica Park has proven herself as a visionary who is fearless in creating stories that traverse the occasionally treacherous roadmap of becoming one's self. In addition to a prodigious imagination, *Flat-Out Love*'s antecedents and inspirations include the Snow White fairy tale, an odd little video seen almost by chance of a couple with a flat, life-size rendition of Rick Springfield, and the voice of the story's fragile thirteen-year-old Celeste—which flowed through Jessica onto her screen and pages with a force and clarity akin to a channeling experience.

The only child of her devoted parents, Jessica grew up in Newton, Massachusetts. Despite being a somewhat shy kid, she enjoyed a childhood replete with friends and an adolescence in which she was neither A-list nor outcast. While she "loved" high school, the reverb of its pain, rawness, and fulsome awkwardness continues to provide emotional fuel and grist for her novels and stories. She saw the precipice of leaving home and beginning college as a similar transitional milestone, which is why she set her story around the character of eighteen-year-old Julie Seagle, despite the objection of traditional young adult publishers to *Flat-Out Love* featuring a post-high-school-age protagonist.

Married to a professional chef and mother to their son, Nicholas, Jessica now lives in New Hampshire where she writes full-time—mostly while sitting with her laptop on her bed, often in her pajamas, and occasionally to the neglect of her personal hygiene during the genesis of a story's more taxing passages. And though she admits that her efforts have drawn mixed results, Jessica has also plunged into forays in knitting, gardening, bird watching, and an eclectic assortment of transitory hobbies. A more constant and abiding interest is music, which she cites as part of her daily arsenal of writing tools. She is encircled by, and gives support to, friends who write, critique, and contribute to her own and others' writing efforts.

Jessica describes her next novel as being more "R-rated," as a plunge into which she credits *Flat-Out Love* for helping her to go unflinching into life's darker tunnels and pathways. She hopes that her story will illuminate those areas and provide connection and comfort to those who have found themselves stuck or passing through these challenging sojourns, and who hope to find the light of some not-too-distant horizon.

Please visit Jessica on the web, Twitter, and Facebook at these locations:

jessicapark.me

@JessicaPark24 https://twitter.com/JessicaPark24

https://www.facebook.com/authorjessicapark